Calvinistic Controversy

Calvinistic Controversy

by Wilbur Fisk

Copyright © 4/1/2015

ISBN-: 978-1511556705

Printed in the United States of America

All rights reserved. No part of this book may be reprinted or reproduced or utilized in any form or by any electronic, mechanical, or other means, now known or hereafter invented, including photocopying and recording, or in any form of storage or retrieval system, without prior permission in writing from the publisher.'

Contents

A DISCOURSE 4
NUMBER I. 23
NUMBER II. 29
NUMBER III. 32
NUMBER IV. 35
NUMBER V. 38
NUMBER VI. 42
NUMBER VII. 46
NUMBER VIII. 53
NUMBER IX. 58
NUMBER X. 65
NUMBER XI. 72
NUMBER XII. 80
NUMBER XIII. 88
NUMBER XIV. 95
NUMBER XV. 102
Footnotes 110

A DISCOURSE

ON

PREDESTINATION AND ELECTION.

According as he hath chosen us in him before the foundation of the world, that we should be holy and without blame before him in love.

Having predestinated us unto the adoption of children, by Jesus Christ, to himself, according to the good pleasure of his will, Ephesians i, 4, 5.

In this passage, the kindred doctrines of predestination and election are brought into view. To discuss them, to notice some errors respecting them, and to exhibit what is believed to be the Scriptural and rational view of these doctrines, is the proposed object of the present discourse. In doing this, much that is new cannot be expected. The whole ground of this controversy has been examined and re-examined; and the various arguments, on both sides, have been urged and opposed, by the most able polemics in philosophy and theology. The most, therefore, that can now be expected, is to give a concise view of the subject, in a form and manner suited to the present state of the controversy, and to the circumstances of the present congregation.

It is hoped, at least, that the subject may be investigated in the spirit of Christianity; and that there will be no loss of brotherly and Christian candour, if there be no gain, on the side of truth. Yet, in a desire to give no offence, I must not suppress the truth, nor neglect to point out, as I am able, the absurdity of error, and its unprofitable influences on the minds of those who propagate or receive it. The truth should be spoken, but it should be spoken in love. Neither the subject, nor the age, nor the occasion, will admit of temporizing. With these views, we come to our subject, by examining,

I. Predestination in general;

II. Predestination, in its particular relation to the doctrine of election.

I. By predestination, we understand an efficient predetermination to bring about or accomplish any future event. But as God alone has knowledge to comprehend futurity, and power to direct and control future events; predestination, in a *proper* and *strict* sense, can only be used in reference to him. And with respect to God, predestination is that efficient determination which he has maintained from eternity, respecting the control, direction, and destiny of the laws, events, and creatures of the universe.—That God hath a predetermination of this kind, there can be no doubt; and therefore, on this fact, there can be no dispute. But the ground of controversy is, the unlimited extent to which some have carried this idea of predestination. Calvin, on this subject, says, "Every action and motion of every creature is governed by the hidden counsel of God, so that nothing can come to pass, but was ordained by him." The Assembly's Catechism is similar:—"God did, from all eternity, unchangeably ordain whatever comes to pass." And Mr. Buck defines predestination to mean, "The decree of God, whereby he hath, for his own glory, foreordained whatever comes to pass." With these definitions, which, it is seen, are the same in substance, agree all the Calvinistic divines in Europe and America.—To this view of predestination, others, and we confess ourselves of that number, have objected. We believe that the character and acts of intelligent beings, so far at least as their moral accountability is concerned, are not definitely fixed, and efficiently produced, by the unalterable purpose and efficient decree of God. Here therefore we are at issue. We believe, with the rigid predestinarians, that God hath fixed the laws of the physical and moral world, and that he hath a general plan, suited to all the various circumstances and contingencies of his government; but that it is no part of this plan, efficiently to control and actuate the human will. So far, therefore, as these ultra-predestinarians go beyond us, they affirm what we deny; and of course the burden of proof falls upon them. We shall first, then, hear and answer the arguments in defence of their system, and then bring up our arguments against it.[1]

The supporters of this system endeavour to establish their views by a threefold argument—the foreknowledge of God—the necessity of a plan—and Scripture testimony.

1. The first argument is founded on foreknowledge. It is sometimes contended that predestination and foreknowledge are the same. This, however, by the more judicious, is not now insisted on. For it is self-evident, that *to know*, and *to decree*, are distinct operations; and to every one acquainted with the common definition of the terms, they must convey distinct and different ideas. And if these are distinct operations in the *human* mind, they must be also in the *Divine* mind, unless it can be shown that these terms, when applied to God, have an entirely different meaning from that by which they are understood among men. And as this cannot be pretended, the more common and plausible argument is, that the foreknowledge of God necessarily *implies* predestination. "For how," they ask, "can an action that is really to come to pass, be foreseen, if it be not determined? God foreknew every thing from the beginning; but this he could not have known, if he had not so determined it." "God," says Piscator, "foresees nothing but what he has decreed, and his decree precedes his knowledge." And Calvin says, "God therefore foreknows all things that will come to pass, because he has decreed they shall come to pass." But to this idea there are insuperable objections. Prescience is an essential attribute of the Divine nature. But a determination to do this or that, is not essential to the Divine nature. For aught we can see, God might determine to make a particular planet or not to make it, and in either case the perfection of his nature is not affected. But *to know*, is so essential to him, that the moment he ceases to know all that is, or will be, or might be, under any possible contingency, he ceases to be God. Is it not absurd, then, to say the least, to make an essential attribute of Deity depend upon the *exercise* of his attributes?—the Divine prescience depend upon his decrees and determinations? It would seem, by this argument, that, if not in the order of time, at least, in the order of thought, and in the order of cause and effect, the exercise of an attribute preceded the attribute itself; and, in short, the attribute must be exercised, as a cause, to bring it into existence! To this monstrous conclusion we are led by following out this argument. And connected with it is another, equally monstrous and absurd. If God must predetermine events in order to

know them, then, as the cause is in no case dependent on the effect, the decrees of God must be passed and his plan contrived, independently of his knowledge, which only had an existence as the effect of these decrees. What must be the character of that plan, and of those decrees, which were formed and matured without knowledge, we will not stop to examine, for the idea borders too closely upon the ludicrous to be dwelt upon in a serious discourse. And yet I cannot see how this conclusion can be avoided, reasoning from such premises. It seems to us, therefore, altogether more consistent to consider that, in the order of cause and effect, the exercise of the Divine attributes is consequent upon their existence; and that the plan of the Almighty is the result of his infinite knowledge; and that the decrees of his throne flow forth from the eternal fountain of his wisdom. This idea, moreover, accords with the Scriptures:—"For whom he did foreknow, he also did predestinate to be conformed to the image of his Son." "Elect according to the foreknowledge of God the Father." In these passages predestination and the decree of election are most clearly founded on foreknowledge. This, therefore, must settle the question: God foreknows in order to predestinate; but he does not predestinate in order to foreknow.[2]

But foreknowledge is pressed into this argument in another form. "The foreknowledge of God," it is said, "is tantamount to a decree; because, inasmuch as God cannot be in a mistake, whatever he foreknows must take place—his knowledge makes it certain." This is indeed shifting the argument; for if God's knowledge makes an event certain, of course it is not his predetermination. But, according to this notion, every thing contained in the idea of predestination is implied in foreknowledge, which is only throwing the subject back on the ground first glanced at, that knowledge and decree are both one, which is obviously absurd. Beside, such an idea would make the scriptures that represent God's foreknowledge as distinct from his decree and antecedent to it, worse than unmeaning: "Whom he did foreknow, them he did predestinate," would mean, "whom he did predestinate, them he did predestinate"—and, "Elect according to the foreknowledge of God," would only mean, "that the decree of election was *according* to the decree of election!" the absurdity of which is too apparent to need comment. And it may be urged, farther, in reply to this argument, that knowledge or foreknowledge cannot, in the nature of things, have the least possible influence in making an event certain. It is not at all difficult to conceive how the certainty of an event can beget knowledge; but if any one thinks that knowledge is the cause of certainty, let him show it—to me such a connection is inconceivable. Whatever God foreknows or foresees, will undoubtedly come to pass. But the simple question is, Does the event take place because it is foreknown, or is it foreknown because it will take place? Or, in other words, Does God know an event to be certain because it is certain, or does his knowing it to be certain make it certain? The question thus stated, at once suggests the true answer; for he would be considered a fool or a madman who should seriously assert that a knowledge of a certainty produced that certainty. According to that, a certainty must exist in order to be foreknown; and it must be foreknown in order to exist! From all which it appears that foreknowledge can have no influence in making a future event certain. Since, therefore, foreknowledge is not predestination; and does not, according to Scripture or reason, follow predestination as a consequence, and has no possible influence in making an event certain, no proof can be drawn from the Divine prescience in favour of the doctrine that *God hath foreordained whatsoever comes to pass.*

2. But predestination is argued from the necessity of a Divine plan. "It cannot be conceived," it is said, "that God would leave things at random, and have no plan. But no alteration of his plan can take place upon condition that his creatures act in this or that way." But this argument is easily answered, at least for the present. For it assumes what ought to be proved; and what has not, to my knowledge, ever been proved, viz. that to

deny Calvinian predestination, is to deny that God has a perfect plan. We acknowledge and maintain that God has a plan, one part of which is, to govern his responsible subjects, without controlling their will, by a fixed decree—to punish the incorrigible, and save those who repent and believe. Does such a plan imply the necessity of a change, "on condition that his creatures act in this or that way?" If, indeed, it was necessary for God to decree an event, in order to foreknow it, this inference might be just. But as this is seen to be false, it follows that a perfect God, whose eye surveys immensity and eternity at a glance, and who necessarily knows all possibilities and contingencies; all that is, or will be, can perfectly arrange his plan, and preclude the possibility of a disappointment, although he does not, by a decree of predestination, fix all the volitions and acts of his subjects. Even in human governments, where the rulers can have no knowledge of the individuals who will transgress, or of the nature and extent of the transgressions, the principles and plan of government undergo no change to accommodate themselves to the contingent acts of the subjects. How absurd, then, to suppose that the all-wise Ruler of the universe will be subject to disappointment, unless he predestinate the transgressions of sinners, and the obedience of his saints! The truth is, in my view, this idea detracts from the wisdom of God; for the perfection of his plan, as they maintain it, is predicated on the imperfection of his attributes. But our view of the Divine plan accords well with our idea of his infinite nature. Over the universe, and through eternity, he throws his all-pervading knowledge—as he is in every point of wide immensity, so he is in every moment of long eternity—and can such a God be disappointed?

3. "But," say the advocates of this system, "supposing there are difficulties in this subject, the Scriptures abound with passages which at once prove the doctrine." If this is true, then indeed we must submit. But the question is, where are these passages? After such a strong assertion, it would probably appear surprising to one unacquainted with this subject, to learn that there is not a single passage which teaches directly that God hath foreordained whatsoever comes to pass. Yet this is the fact. If this doctrine is taught in Scripture, it is in an indirect manner. Nor will it follow, because God hath predestinated some things, that he hath, therefore, decreed all things. All those passages then which have been so frequently quoted as proof of this doctrine, which only go to prove, that God hath predetermined certain events, are not proof in point. Where are the passages that say he hath decreed all things? We know of many which say of certain events that have come to pass, that God did not *command* them, nor *will* them; so that the abundant Scripture proof seems altogether on the other side of the question. It is argued, however, that certain acts of moral agents, even those acts for which they are held responsible, are, according to the Scriptures, the results of God's predetermination, and therefore it is reasonable to infer that all are. This general conclusion, however, is not contained in the premises; nevertheless, if the premises are true, if it can be proved from Scripture that God holds his creatures responsible for the results of his own decrees, such Scripture proofs would be strong arguments to ward off the objections that are brought against this system. For if it is consistent with a righteous God to make a moral agent responsible for one event which was the result of a Divine decree, upon the same principle, perhaps, he might make him responsible for all, though all were decreed. Let us then look at those scriptures, "As for you," says Joseph to his brethren, speaking of their injustice to him, "ye thought evil against me, but God meant it for good." Now without stopping here to inquire whether Joseph was inspired to utter this sentiment, we are ready to acknowledge, that there are a number of similar scriptures which teach that, in the results of the wicked acts of wicked men, God had a design and a controlling influence, and thereby made them subservient to his own purposes. He hath wisdom and power "to make the wrath of man praise him, and to restrain the remainder of wrath." But does he therefore decree the wrath itself? And is this wrath necessary to the accomplishment of his purposes? As well

might it be said, that because a government, in quelling a rebellion, replenished its exchequer from the confiscated estates of the rebels, therefore that government decreed the rebellion, and was dependent upon it for the prosperity of the nation. Let it be distinctly understood then, that to overrule and control the *results* of an act is altogether different from making the act itself the result of an overruling and controlling power.

Again it is said, "The Lord hath made all things for himself, yea, even the wicked for the day of evil." That the Lord hath made all things for his own glory, is a proposition easily understood, and doubted, I trust, by none; and this is evidently the meaning of the former member of this passage. The latter clause, if it helps the cause for which it is quoted at all, must mean, that the Lord has predestinated men to be wicked, that he might make them miserable. But it is not necessary to make the text speak this shocking sentiment. We should do the text no violence to explain it thus—The Lord hath destined the wicked for the day of evil, and this shall be for his glory.

But there is another class of passages like the following:—"He doeth according to his will in the army of heaven, and among the inhabitants of the earth." "He worketh all things after the counsel of his will." "I will do all my pleasure." But these passages establish nothing, in opposition to our views, unless it should first be proved, by other passages, or in some other way, that it is God's will and pleasure to work *all things*, even wickedness, in the wicked. These scriptures prove that all *God's works* are in accordance with his own will and pleasure; and that he will accomplish them in spite of the opposition of sinners. If it pleases him to form his moral government, so as to leave the responsible acts of his subjects unnecessitated by his decree, this he will do, for "he will do all his pleasure."

But there is still another class of texts, which are supposed to favour the doctrine we are opposing, more than any others, viz. those passages which seem to represent God as bringing about and procuring the wickedness of the wicked. Like the following:—"And I will harden Pharaoh's heart, that he should not let the people go." "Now therefore the Lord hath put a lying spirit in the mouth of all these thy prophets." "He hath blinded their eyes and hardened their hearts." "Him, being delivered by the determinate counsel and foreknowledge of God, ye have taken, and by wicked hands ye have crucified and slain." On these and similar passages it may be remarked, that God blinds men and hardens their hearts judicially, as a just punishment for their abuse of their agency. And for this act of his, in blinding and hardening them, he does not make them responsible. But he holds them responsible for that degree of wickedness which made it just and necessary to give them over to this hardness of heart and blindness of mind. And since there are wicked men and lying spirits, they become fit instruments in deceiving and tormenting each other; and therefore God gives them power and liberty to go abroad, "deceiving and being deceived." But how does this prove that God hath decreed sin? The idea that God hath made sin and wicked spirits the instruments of hardening and tormenting the incorrigible sinner, and finally of shutting the door of hope against him, has no kind of affinity to the idea, that he decreed the sin which occasioned this hardness, or ordained the wickedness of this lying spirit.

As to the passage from the Acts, none of us deny but that Jesus Christ was delivered up to suffer and die, by the determinate counsel and foreknowledge of God; but it is most emphatically denied, that this or any other scripture proves, that the taking and slaying of Jesus Christ by wicked hands, was the result of the determinate counsel and foreknowledge of God. If any think otherwise, let them prove it.

Having stated and, as our time would permit, examined the arguments in favour of the sentiment we are opposing, we are prepared to urge against this doctrine, not only that its arguments are unsound and insufficient, but also that the system itself is liable to the most serious and formidable objections.

1. This doctrine of predestination makes God the author of sin. Some acknowledge this, and expressly assert, that God is the "*efficient* cause" of sin. Others affirm it in fact, while they deny it in word. Take for instance the words of Calvin. "I will not scruple to own," he says, "that the will of God lays a necessity on all things, and that every thing he wills, necessarily comes to pass." In accordance with this, Piscator, Dr. Twiss, Peter Martyr and others tell us, that "God procures adultery, cursings, and lyings"—"God is the author of that act, which is evil"—"God, by his working on the hearts of the wicked, binds them and stirs them to do evil." They deny, however, that God is the author of sin, because they say, "God necessitates them to the *act*, and not to the *depravity* of sin:" or, that "God does not sin when he makes men sin, because *he* is under no law, and therefore cannot sin." But these are miserable shifts. Has not the *deformity* of sin come to pass? Then God has decreed this deformity. To deny this, is to give up the doctrine. But to acknowledge it, is to own that God is as much the author of the deformity, as he is of the act. Again, God doubtless decreed that sin should be *sin*, and not *holiness;* and it came to pass as sin, because it was so decreed. Is he not then the direct procuring cause? A thousand turns of this kind, therefore, are nothing but evasions. The *fiat* of God brought forth sin as certainly as it made the world.

We are often told, when we quote Calvin and his contemporaries, that these are old authors; that modern Calvinists do not hold thus, and that they ought not to be accountable for these writers. But the fact is, we make them accountable only for the logical consequences of their own doctrine. The whole system turns on this hinge, "God foreordains whatsoever comes to pass." For he that, by his will and decree, produces and causes sin, that makes sin a necessary part of his plan, and is the author of the very elements and materials of his own plan, must be the proper and sole cause of sin, or we have yet to learn the definition of common words, and the meaning of plain propositions. The distinction therefore, of *ancient* and *modern*, of *rigid* and *moderate* Calvinists, is more in word, than in reality. And it would add much to the consistency of this system, if all its advocates would acknowledge, what is evidently deducible from the premises, that God is the efficient cause of sin.

2. This doctrine of predestination destroys the free agency, and of course the accountability of man. That it destroys free will was seen and acknowledged by many predestinarians of the old school. And the opposers of Mr. Wesley and Mr. Fletcher violently assailed them on this subject. Mr. Southey informs us, in his Life of Wesley, that the Calvinists called this doctrine of free will, "a cursed doctrine"—"the most God-dishonouring and soul-destroying doctrine of the day"—"one of the prominent features of the beast"—"the enemy of God"—"the offspring of the wicked one"—"the insolent brat of hell." Others, and the greater part of the Calvinists of the present day, endeavour to reconcile the ideas of *necessity* and *free agency*. Man, they say, sins voluntarily, because he chooses or wills to sin; therefore he is a free agent. Hence they exhort sinners to repent, and tell them they can repent if they will. By which they mean, the only impossibility of their repenting, is in their will—their *cannot* is their *will not*. This has led many to think that there is no difference, between their preachers and the Arminians. But let us look at this subject a little, and see if there is not some sophistry concealed in this dexterous coil of words. God, according to this doctrine, secures the end as well as the means, by his decree of predestination. And therefore, as Calvin says, "every action and motion of every creature is governed by the hidden counsel of God." The will, therefore, in all its operations, is governed and irresistibly controlled by some secret impulse, some fixed and all-controlling arrangement. It is altogether futile, then, to talk about free agency under such a constitution; the very spring of motion to the whole intellectual machinery is under the influence of a secret, invincible power. And it *must* move as that power directs, or it is the hand of Omnipotence that urges it on. He *can* act as he *wills*, it

is true, but the whole responsibility consists in the volition, and this is the result of God's propelling power. He wills as he is *made* to will—he chooses as he *must* choose, for the immutable decree of Jehovah is upon him. And can a man, upon the known and universally acknowledged principles of responsibility, be accountable for such a volition? It is argued, I know, that man is responsible, because he *feels* that he acts freely, and that he might have done otherwise. To this I reply, that this is a good argument, on our principles, to prove that men are free—but on the Calvinistic ground, it only proves that God hath deceived us. He has made us *feel* that we might do otherwise, but *he knows* we *cannot*—he has *determined* we *shall not*. So that, in fact, this argument makes the system more objectionable. While it does not change the fact in the case, it attributes deception to the Almighty. It is logically true, therefore, from this doctrine, that man is not a free agent, and therefore not responsible. A moral agent, to be free, must be possessed of a self-determining principle. Make the will any thing short of this, and you put all the volitions, and of course the whole moral man, under foreign and irresistible influences.

3. Another strong objection to the doctrine we oppose, is, it arrays God's secret decrees against his revealed word. God commands men not to sin, and yet ordains that they shall sin, In his word, he sets before them, in striking relief, motives of fear and of hope, for the express purpose, as he informs us, "that they sin not;" but by his predestination and secret counsel, he irresistibly impels them in an opposite course, for the express purpose, as this doctrine informs us, to secure their transgression. *His* rule of action is in direct opposition to *our* rule of duty. And yet he is the author of both! Is God at war with himself, or is he sporting and trifling with his creatures? Or is it not more probable than either, that the premises are false? When or where has God ever taught us, that he has two opposing wills? A character so suspicious, to say the least of it, ought not, without the most unequivocal evidence, to be attributed to the adorable Jehovah. In his word, we are taught, that he is "of *one* mind"—that his "ways are equal;" and who can doubt it? We are told, it is true, to relieve the difficulty, that this seeming contradiction is one of the mysteries of God's incomprehensible nature. But it is not a *seeming* contradiction, it is a *real* one; not an insolvable mystery, but a palpable absurdity. *God prohibits the sinful act—God ordains and procures the sinful act—God wills the salvation of the reprobate, whom he has from all eternity irreversibly ordained to eternal death!* When I can embrace such opposite propositions by calling them mysteries, I can believe that two and two are more than four, that all the parts are less than the whole, and that a thing may be made to exist and not exist at the same time and explain them by a reference to the mystery of God's incomprehensible nature.

4. In close connection with the foregoing objection, it may be added, that this system mars, if it does not destroy, the moral attributes of God. If he holds men responsible for what is unavoidable—if he makes laws and then impels men to break them, and finally punishes them for their transgressions—if he mourns over the evils of the world, and expostulates with sinners, saying, "How can I give thee up—my heart is melted within me, my repentings are kindled together,"—"O Jerusalem! Jerusalem! how oft would I have gathered you, and ye would not,"—and still he himself "impels the will of men," to all this wickedness—if I say God does all this, where is his veracity? Where is his mercy? Where is his justice? What more could be said of the most merciless tyrant? What, of the most arrant hypocrite? What, of Satan himself? What does this doctrine make of our heavenly Father? I shudder to follow it out into its legitimate bearings. It seems to me, a belief of it is enough to drive one to infidelity, to madness, and to death. If the supporters of this system *must* adhere to it, I rejoice that they can close their eyes against its logical consequences, otherwise it would make them wretched in the extreme, or drive them into other dangerous theoretical and practical errors. Indeed, in many instances it has done this—which leads to another objection to this doctrine.

5. It puts a plea into the mouth of sinners to justify themselves in their sins, and leads to Universalism and infidelity. They reason thus: Whatever God decrees is according to his will, and therefore right. And God will not punish his creatures for doing right. Whatever God decrees is unavoidable, and God will not punish his creatures for what is unavoidable. But "every action and motion of every creature is governed by the hidden counsel of God." Therefore God will not punish any of his creatures for any of their acts. Now, who can point out any fallacy in this reasoning? If therefore predestination be true, Universalism is true, according to the universally acknowledged principles of justice. And it is a notorious fact, that modern Universalism, which is prevailing so generally through the country, rests for its chief support on the doctrine of predestination. Others having seen, as they thought, that the Scriptures would not support the doctrine of Universalism, and that matter of fact seemed to contradict the above reasoning, inasmuch as men are made to suffer, even in this life, for their sins, have leaped over all Scriptural bounds into infidelity and philosophical necessity. I have personally known numbers who have been driven, by the doctrine we object to, into open infidelity. And it is well known, that the doctrine of fate, which is closely allied to Calvinian predestination, is the element in which infidelity "lives and moves and has its being." And can this be the doctrine of the Bible? How much is it to be regretted, that our worthy pilgrim fathers should have sowed this Geneva seed in our happy country! The evils done to the Church are incalculable.

These, candid hearers, are some of the objections we have to this doctrine—objections so serious, and, as we think, so obvious, that you may well ask, What has induced good men to advocate it so long? It is, doubtless, because it stands connected intimately with the doctrine of unconditional election, and what have been called by Calvinists "the doctrines of grace." But for unconditional election, predestination would not be desired, even by those who now hold to it; and but for predestination, unconditional election could not be maintained. Hence these have very properly been called "twin doctrines," and must stand or fall together. Let us pass then to the next proposition.

II. We come to examine predestination in its particular relation to election.

Several kinds of election are spoken of in the Scriptures. There is an election of individuals, to perform certain duties appointed by God:—thus Christ was God's elect, for the redemption of the world; and Cyrus was elected by him to rebuild the temple. There is an election of whole communities and nations to the enjoyment of certain peculiar privileges, political and ecclesiastical, relating of course to this life:—thus Jacob and his descendants were God's chosen people, to the enjoyment of religious and national privileges, from which Esau and his descendants, together with the whole Gentile world, were excluded; and thus, too, subsequently, the middle wall of partition, made by the former decree of election between Jew and Gentile, being broken down, the Gentiles became equal sharers with the Jews in the privileges of the new covenant, called the "election of grace." This election is unconditional, and is believed to be the one spoken of in our text, and many other passages of Scripture. Of these, however, I shall speak more particularly in another place.

There is a third election—an election unto eternal life, and this is the one which has given rise to the great controversy in the Church.—Those who contend for predestination, as objected to by us, maintain that, "By the decree of God, for the manifestation of his glory, some men and angels are predestinated unto everlasting life, and others foreordained to everlasting death. Those of mankind that are predestinated unto life, God, before the foundation of the world, hath chosen in Christ, unto everlasting glory, *without any foresight of faith or good works*." Others, and this also is our doctrine, hold that "God did decree from the beginning, to elect, or choose in Christ, all that should believe unto salvation, and this decree proceeds from his own goodness, and is not built on any goodness of the creature; and that God did from the beginning decree to reprobate all who should finally and obstinately continue in unbelief." Thus it is seen, from the statement of the two doctrines, that ours is an election of character, and so far as it relates to individuals, it relates to them only as they are foreseen to possess that character; whereas the other relates directly to individuals, without any reference to character. It is an absolute act of sovereignty—God elects them for no other reason or condition than because he chooses. He makes no account of man's agency or responsibility in this decree of election, but it precedes and is entirely independent of any knowledge of the character of the elect. Our views of election, on the contrary, make it conditionally dependent on the responsible agency of man. In the one case, the sinner is made to receive Christ, because he is elected; and in the other, he is elected, because he receives Christ. From this difference, too, proceed other differences. The Calvinistic election, to be consistent with itself, requires that, as the end is arbitrarily fixed, so the means must be also—hence the doctrines of irresistible grace, effectual calling, and infallible perseverance. Calvinian election, therefore, stands intimately allied to Calvinian predestination; and the whole forms a chain of doctrines differing materially from ours. And here we acknowledge we have a position to prove as well as our opponents. We assert that election to eternal life is conditional; they, that it is unconditional. We will first attempt to prove our position—then state and answer the arguments in favour of unconditional election—and finally, urge some objections against unconditional election and reprobation.

   1. Our first argument in favour of conditional election to eternal life, is drawn from the position already established, that the decrees of God are predicated on his foreknowledge. And especially, that the decree of election to salvation, according to the Scriptures, is founded on the Divine prescience. "Elect according to the foreknowledge of God, through sanctification of the Spirit unto obedience, and sprinkling of the blood of Jesus Christ." "Whom he did foreknow, he also did predestinate, to be conformed to the image of his Son." These scriptures seem to us decisive, that the decree of election rests on foreknowledge, and that this election is made, not according to the arbitrary act of God, but on the ground of sanctification and obedience. The doctrine, therefore, that men are predestinated to eternal life, "without any foresight of faith or good works," must be false.

   2. The rewardableness of obedience, or the demerit of disobedience, can only exist in connection with the unnecessitated volitions of a free moral agent. The Scriptures abundantly teach, that to be saved, man must believe and obey; and hence they command and exhort men to believe and obey, and promise them the reward of eternal life if they do this, and criminate them, if they neglect it. But, according to the doctrine of free agency already explained, man's obedience or disobedience, if it has any just relation to rewards and punishments, must rest, in its responsible character, upon the self-determining principle of the will. And if this view of the will be correct, there is an *utter impossibility* of an unconditional election. For the very act of God, imparting this self-determining principle to man, renders it impossible, in the nature of things, for the Almighty himself to elect a moral agent, unconditionally. The argument stands thus— The Scriptures make man a responsible moral agent; but this he cannot be, if his will be controlled by foreign and unavoidable influences, therefore it is not so controlled: that is, man has within himself a self-determining principle, in the exercise of which he becomes responsible. This being established, we argue again—The doctrine of unconditional election necessarily implies irresistible grace, absolutely impelling and controlling the will. But this would be to counteract God's own work, and to destroy man's accountability; therefore there is no such irresistible grace, and, of course, no such unconditional election. And since there is an election to eternal life, spoken of in the

Scriptures, it follows conclusively, if the foregoing reasoning be sound, that this election is conditional.—Hence we may bring forward, in one overwhelming argument, all the numerous and various Bible conditions of salvation, as so many Scripture proofs of a conditional election.

3. The cautions to the elect, and the intimations of their danger, and the possibility of their being lost, are so many Scripture proofs of a conditional election. Why should the saints be exhorted "to take heed lest they fall?" "lest there be in them an evil heart of unbelief, in departing from the living God?" "lest a promise being left of entering into rest, any should come short?" lest *they* should "also be cut off?" Why should St. Paul fear lest, after having preached to others, he should be a castaway? Either there is, or is not, danger of the elect's being lost. If not, then all these passages are not only without meaning, but savour very strongly of deception. They are false colours held out to the elect, for the purposes of alarm and fear, where no fear is. Will it be said, that possibly some of those addressed were not of the elect, and were therefore deceiving themselves, and needed to be cautioned and warned? I answer, they had then nothing to fall from, and no promise of which to come short. Besides, to warn such to *stand fast*, seems to imply, that the Holy Spirit cautioned the reprobates against the danger of becoming the elect, which idea, while it intimates a very ungracious work for the "Spirit of grace" to be engaged in, clearly indicates, that there was danger of breaking the decree of reprobation! We ask again, therefore, What do these scriptures mean? Will it be said, as some have argued, that these warnings and cautions are all consistent, because they are the very means by which the decree of election is made sure? But let it be understood, that the end is fixed, before the means; because Calvinism tells us, that this election is "independent of any faith or good works foreseen," and that "God's decree lays a necessity on all things, so that every thing he wills necessarily comes to pass," and is therefore sure, "because he has decreed it." The moment, therefore, God decrees an event, it becomes sure, and to talk of danger of a failure in that event, implies either a falsehood, or that God's decree can be *broken*. But Calvinists, I presume, will not allow that there is any danger of counteracting or frustrating the plan of the Almighty. Hence there is no danger of the elect's coming short of salvation. All the exhortations, cautions, and warnings therefore, recorded in the Scriptures, are false colours and deceptive motives. They are like the attempts of some weak parents, who undertake to frighten their children into obedience, by superstitious tales and groundless fears. God knows, when he is giving out these intimations of danger, that there is no such danger; his own eternal, unchangeable decree had secured their salvation before the means were planned—all this if election is unconditional. But far be this from a God of truth. If he exhorts his creatures to "make their election sure," *he* has not made it sure.—If he teaches them to fear, lest they fail of the grace of God, there is doubtless real danger. The conclusion therefore is irresistible, that Cod hath suspended his decree of election to eternal life, on conditions; "He that believeth: shall be saved."

4. This accords also with Christian experience. What is it that produces much fear and trembling in the mind of the awakened sinner? Why does he feel that there is but a step between him and destruction? Is it fancy, or is it fact? If it is imagination merely, then all his alarm is founded in deception, and he has either deceived himself, or the Spirit of God hath deceived him. In either case, this alarm seems necessary, in order to lead him to Christ. That is, it is necessary for the conversion of one of the elect that he be made to believe a lie. But if it be said, that it is no lie, for he is really in danger, then we reply again, the decree of God hath not made his election sure, and of course, therefore, it is conditional.

5. Express passages of Scripture teach a conditional election. We have time only to notice a few of them. Matt. xxii, 14, "For many are called, but few are chosen." This

passage, with the parable of the wedding that precedes it, teaches that the *choice* was made subsequently to the call, and was grounded on the fact, that those chosen had actually and fully complied with the invitation, and had come to the wedding duly prepared. John xv, 19, "If ye were of the world, the world would love you, but because ye are not of the world, but I have chosen you out of the world, therefore the world hateth you." This passage teaches that Christ's disciples were once of the world, and that he had chosen them out of the world, and this *choice* evidently refers to that time when they became of a different character from the world; for then it was, and in consequence of that election, that the world hated them.—2 Thess. ii, 13, "Because God hath from the beginning, *chosen* you to salvation, through sanctification of the Spirit and belief of the truth." Here is a condition plainly expressed. This is not an election *unto* sanctification, but an election *through* or *by* sanctification and faith unto salvation.

From the whole then it appears, that the Holy Scriptures, the Divine attributes and government, and the agency of man, stand opposed to an unconditional, and are in favour of a conditional election.

In opposition to these arguments, however, and in favour of unconditional election, our opponents urge various scriptures, which, as they think, are strong and incontrovertible arguments in favour of their system. And as these scriptures are their strong and only defence, it is proposed that they should be noticed. The limits of this discourse, however, will admit of but a short notice, and that not of individual texts, but of classes of texts.

1. The first class of passages that we will now examine, which are supposed to favour the idea of unconditional election, is those that speak of a predestination *unto* holiness. Our text is one of the strongest instances of this kind, "He hath chosen us from the foundation of the world, that we should be holy—having predestinated us unto the adoption of sons," &c. See also Rom. viii, 29, "For whom he did foreknow, he also did predestinate to be conformed to the image of his Son," and "whom he did predestinate — he called—justified—and sanctified." The argument upon these and similar passages is, that the decree of predestination could not be founded on their faith or holiness; because they were predestinated to *become* holy—the decree of predestination had their holiness for its object and end. But if these passages had an allusion to a personal election to eternal life, they would not prove unconditional election, "because," to use the language of another, "it would admit of being questioned, whether the choosing in Christ, before the foundation of the world here mentioned, was a choice of certain persons *as men merely*, or as *believing* men, which is certainly the most rational." This exposition must necessarily be given to the passage from the Romans, since those who were the subjects of predestination, were first *foreknown*: foreknown, not merely as existing, for in this sense *all* were foreknown, but foreknown, as possessing something which operated as a reason why *they* should be elected, rather than others: foreknown doubtless as believers in Christ, and as such, according to the plan and decree of God, they were to be made conformable to the image of Christ's holiness here, and glory hereafter. And according to the same Divine plan, the order of this work was, 1. The call; 2. Justification; 3. Glorification. And this interpretation, which so obviously upon the face of it is the meaning of the passage from Romans, would also be a good meaning to the passage in Ephesians, if that passage should be understood in reference to personal election. But I do not so understand it; and I think any unprejudiced reader, by looking at the context, and especially from the 9th to the 11th verses inclusive, in this chapter, and at most of the 2d chapter, will perceive that the apostle is here speaking of that general plan of God, which had been fixed from the beginning, of admitting the Gentiles as well as the Jews to the privileges of the covenant of grace, on equal terms and conditions. Thus the middle wall of partition was to be broken down between Jew and Gentile; and this was the mystery which was concealed for ages, not being understood even by the Jews themselves, but

then by the Gospel was brought to light. According to this plan, the Ephesians and all other Gentiles were chosen or elected to these Christian privileges, the very design and purpose of which were to make them holy; and in the improvement of which, according to the prescribed conditions of faith in Christ, and repentance toward God, they should become his adopted children.

This fore appointing of the Gentiles to the privileges of the gracious covenant, is the election most spoken of in the New Testament.—And the reason why it was so often introduced, especially in the writings of Paul, who was the chief apostle to the Gentiles, was, because the Jews so uniformly and earnestly opposed this feature of Christianity. They could not be reconciled to the idea, that the peculiar and distinctive character of their theocracy and ecclesiastical policy should be so changed, or that the dealings of God with the world should be explained in such a manner as to give *them* no superior claims, in the privileges of the Divine covenant, over the Gentiles. They considered themselves to be God's elect and favourite people, but the Gentiles were reprobates. The apostles felt themselves under the strongest obligations to oppose these notions, not only because, if allowed, they would operate as a barrier to the diffusion of the Gospel among the heathens, and thus the designs of Divine mercy to the world would be thwarted, but also because these Jewish sentiments were in direct opposition to the grace of God. They implied, that the original design of God in favouring the Jews, was founded, not upon his mere mercy and grace, but upon some goodness in them or their fathers. Hence they not only limited the blessings of the Gospel, but they also corrupted its gracious character, and thereby fed their own Pharisaic pride, and dishonoured God. This will open the way for explaining many other scriptures which the Calvinists press into their service.

2. Especially will it assist in explaining those passages which speak of election as depending solely on the sovereign will of God. The strongest of these are in the ninth chapter of the Epistle to the Romans. This portion of revelation is the strong hold, as is supposed, of Calvinism. Whereas, we humbly conceive that *there is not one word* in the whole chapter, of unconditional and personal election to eternal life. It is only necessary to read that epistle carefully, to see that the apostle is combatting that exclusive and Pharisaic doctrine of the Jews, already alluded to, and is proving in a forcible strain of argumentation, from reason and Scripture, that the foundation of the plan of salvation for sinners, was the goodness and unmerited love of God—that all, both Jews and Gentiles, were sinners, and therefore stood in the same relation to God—all equally eligible to salvation, and must, if saved at all, be saved on the same terms. To prove this, he argues strenuously, that God's favour to the Jews, as a nation, was not of any goodness in them, but of his own sovereign will and pleasure, so that his covenant of favour with the Hebrews, and his covenant of grace which embraced the Gentiles, was "not of works, lest any man should boast," "not of him that willeth, nor of him that runneth, but of God that showeth mercy." The apostle shows them, too, that the covenant made with Abraham was not for circumcision, nor for the works of the law, so far as it affected him or his posterity, because it was made while Abraham was in uncircumcision, and on the condition of faith. He argues farther, that this election of the Jews to the enjoyment of these national and ecclesiastical privileges, was not because they were children of Abraham, for Ishmael was a child of Abraham, and yet he and his posterity were rejected; nor yet because they were the children of Abraham through Isaac, because Esau and his posterity were reprobated from these national privileges, while Jacob and his posterity were the chosen seed—not chosen to eternal life, because many of them perished in sin and unbelief, but to the peculiar privileges of God's covenant people. And all this because it was the good pleasure of his will. And as a sovereign, he had the same right to elect the Gentiles to the enjoyment of the covenant of mercy, and upon the same conditions of faith. The apostle concludes this reasoning by an argument which cuts off

entirely the idea of unconditional personal election and reprobation. He informs us, that the reason why the unbelieving Jews did not attain to personal righteousness, was "because they sought it not by faith, but as it were by the works of the law;" and the Gentiles attained to personal righteousness, because they sought it by faith. Hence, those that were not his people, became his people, and those that were not beloved, became beloved—and these, "not of the Jews only, but also of the Gentiles." Whereas, if the doctrine we oppose be true, the elect were *always* his people, and *always* beloved, and that because he pleased to have it so. That portion of Scripture, therefore, on which Calvinism leans for its greatest support, not only affords it no aid, but actually teaches a different doctrine. There is indeed something of mystery hanging over the providence of God, in bestowing peculiar advantages on some, and withholding them from others. But on this subject much light is cast from various considerations which we have not time to enlarge upon; but especially from that wholesome and consistent Scripture doctrine, that "it is required of a man according to what he hath, and not according to what he hath not." This removes at once all complaint of Jew and Gentile, and authorizes the reply, so often misapplied, "Who art thou that repliest against God?" As a sovereign, God has a right to make his creatures differ in these things, so long as he requires only as he gives. But this differs as widely from the Calvinistic idea of sovereignty, as *justice* from *injustice*, as *equity* from *iniquity*. In fact, God no where in the Scripture, places the election of individuals to eternal life, solely on the ground of his sovereignty, but uniformly on the ground of their complying with the conditions of the covenant of grace. Hence his people are a *peculiar people*—his sheep *hear his voice and follow him*—they are *chosen out of the world*—they are *in Christ*, not by an eternal decree of election, but *by faith*—for "if any man be *in Christ*, he is a *new creature*"—and of course, he is not *in him*, until he is a "new creature"—then, and not before, they become his, and he seals them as such, "In whom, *after that ye believed*, ye were sealed with the Holy Spirit of promise." But if they were elected from eternity, they would be his when they did not *hear his voice*, and were not *new creatures*.

3. From what has been said, we can easily answer a third class of scriptures which the Calvinists dwell upon to support their system —viz, those which declare salvation to be of *grace* and not of *works*. Of these there is evidently a large catalogue of very express and unequivocal passages. Take two or three for an example of the whole, "Even so then, at the present time, there is a remnant, according to the election of grace, and if it be by grace then it is no more of works, otherwise grace is no more grace; but if it be of works, then it is no more grace, otherwise work is no more work." "By grace ye are saved." "Having predestinated us unto the adoption of his children, &c, to the praise of the glory of his grace." "Not by works of righteousness which we have done, but according to his mercy he saved us, by the washing of regeneration and renewing of the Holy Ghost." Now we profess to believe these scriptures as unqualifiedly and as cordially as the Calvinists; and we think them perfectly in accordance with our views of election. For we believe, as has been already stated, that God's plan for saving sinners originated entirely in his love to his undeserving creatures. There was nothing in all the character and circumstances of the fallen family, except their sin and deserved misery, that could claim the interposition of God's saving power. The way of executing his gracious plan, and rendering it available in any case, he of course, as a sovereign, reserved to himself. And if he saw that a conditional election was best suited to the principles of his government, and the responsibility of man, shall it be said, this cannot be, for it destroys the idea of grace? *Cannot* a conditional election be of grace? Let the intelligent and candid answer. Even many of the Calvinists acknowledge that *salvation* is conditional, and yet it is of grace; for "by grace ye are saved." Now if salvation is conditional and yet of grace, why not election? Let Calvinists answer this question.

But that our doctrine of election is of grace, will appear evident, I think, from the following considerations. 1. It was pure unmerited love that moved God to provide salvation for our world. 2. The Gospel plan, therefore, with all its *provisions* and *conditions*, is of grace. Not a step in that whole system, but rests in grace, is presented by grace, and is executed through grace. 3. Even the power of the will to choose life, and the conditions of life, is a *gracious power*. A fallen man, without grace, could no more choose to submit to God than a fallen angel. Herein we differ widely from the Calvinists. They tell us man has a *natural* power to choose life. If so, he has power to get to heaven without grace! We say, on the contrary, that man is utterly unable to choose the way to heaven, or to pursue it when chosen, without the grace of God. It is grace that enlightens and convinces the sinner, and strengthens him to seek after and obtain salvation, for "without Christ we *can do nothing*." Let the candid judge between us, then, and decide which system most robs our gracious Redeemer of his glory, that which gives man a *native* and *inherent* power to get to heaven of himself, or that which attributes all to grace. 4. Finally, when the sinner repents and believes, there is no merit in these acts to procure forgiveness and regeneration, and therefore, though he is *now*, and *on these conditions*, elected, and made an heir of salvation, yet it is for Christ's sake, and "not for works of righteousness which he has done." Thus we "bring forth the top stone with shouting, crying *grace, grace*, unto it." Having gone over and examined the arguments in favour of unconditional election, we come to the last part of our subject; which was to urge some objections against this doctrine.

1. The doctrine of the unconditional election of a part, necessarily implies the unconditional reprobation of the rest. I know some who hold to the former, seem to deny the latter; for they represent God as reprobating sinners, in view of their sins. When all were sinners, they say God passed by some, and elected others. Hence, they say the decree of damnation against the reprobates is just, because it is against *sinners*. But this explanation is virtually giving up the system, inasmuch as it gives up all the principal arguments by which it is supported. In the first place, it makes predestination dependent on foreknowledge; for God first foresees that they will be sinners, and then predestinates them to punishment. Here is one case then, in which the argument for Calvinian predestination is destroyed by its own supporters. But again if God must fix by his decree all parts of his plan, in order to prevent disappointment, then he must fix the destiny of the reprobates, and the means that lead to it. But if he did not do this, then the Calvinistic argument in favour of predestination, drawn from the Divine plan, falls to the ground. Once more: this explanation of the decree of reprobation destroys all the strongest Scripture arguments which the Calvinists urge in favour of unconditional election. The passages, for instance, in the ninth of Romans, which are so often quoted in favour of Calvinian election, are connected with others, equally strong, in favour of unconditional reprobation. When it is said, "He will have mercy on whom he will have mercy," it is said also, "Whom he will he hardeneth." He that "makes one vessel unto honour, maketh another unto dishonour." He that says, "Jacob have I loved," says also in the same manner, "Esau have I hated." Now if these relate to personal election to eternal life, they relate also to personal reprobation to eternal death. But if there is any explanation, by which these are showed not to prove unconditional reprobation to eternal death, the same principle of explanation will, and *must* show, that they do not prove Calvinistic election. From henceforth, therefore, let all those Calvinists who profess not to believe in unconditional reprobation, cease to urge, in favour of their system, any arguments drawn from the foreknowledge of God, or the necessity of a Divine plan, or from those scriptures that are most commonly quoted in favour of their doctrine. But when they do this, their system must necessarily fall; for all its main pillars will be removed. But I have not done with this objection yet. Whoever maintains that "God hath foreordained

whatsoever comes to pass," must also hold to unconditional reprobation. Does it come to pass, that some are lost? Then this was ordained. Was sin necessary, as a pretence to damn them? Then this was ordained. From these and other views of the subject, Calvin was led to say, that "election could not stand without reprobation," and that it was "quite silly and childish" to attempt to separate them. All, therefore, who hold to the unconditional election of a part of mankind to eternal life, *must*, to be consistent with themselves, take into their creed, the "horrible decree" of reprobation.—They must believe that in the ages of eternity God determined to create men and angels for the express purpose to damn them eternally! That he determined to introduce sin, and influence men to commit sin, and harden them in it, that they might be fit subjects of his wrath! That for doing as they were impelled to do, by the irresistible decree of Jehovah, they must lie down for ever, under the scalding phials of his vengeance in the pit of hell! To state this doctrine in its true character, is enough to chill one's blood—and we are drawn by all that is rational within us, to turn away from such a God with horror, as from the presence of an Almighty Tyrant.

2. This doctrine of election, while it professes to vindicate free grace and the mercy of God, destroys them altogether. To the reprobates, there is certainly no grace or mercy extended. Their very existence, connected as it necessarily is with eternal damnation, is an infinite curse. The temporal blessings which they enjoy, the insincere offers that are held out to them, and the Gospel privileges with which they are mocked, if they can be termed grace at all, must be called *damning grace*. For all this is only fattening them for the slaughter, and fitting them to suffer, to a more aggravated extent, the unavoidable pains and torments that await them. Hence Calvin's sentiment, that "God calls to the reprobates, that they may be more deaf—kindles a light, that they may be more blind—brings his doctrine to them, that they may be more ignorant—and applies the remedy to them, that they may not be healed," is an honest avowal of the legitimate principles of this system. Surely, then, no one will pretend, that, according to this doctrine, there is any grace for the reprobate. And perhaps a moment's attention will show, that there is little or none for the elect. It is said, that God, out of his mere sovereignty, without any thing in the creature to move him thereto, elects sinners to everlasting life. But if there is nothing in the creature to move him thereto, how can it be called *mercy* or *compassion?* He did not determine to elect them because they were miserable, but because he pleased to elect them. If misery had been the exciting cause, then as all were equally miserable, he would have elected them all. Is such a decree of election founded in love to the suffering object? No: *it is the result of the most absolute and omnipotent selfishness conceivable*. It is the exhibition of a character that sports most sovereignly and arbitrarily, with his Almighty power, *to create, to damn, and to save*.

Some indeed pretend that, at any rate, *salvation* is of grace, if election is not, because God saves *miserable, perishing* sinners. But who made them miserable perishing sinners? Was not this the effect of God's decree? And is there much mercy displayed in placing men under a constitution which necessarily and unavoidably involves them in sin and suffering, that God may afterward have the sovereign honour of saving them? Surely the *tenderest* mercies of this system are cruel—its brightest parts are dark—its boasted mercy hardly comes up to sheer justice, even to the elect; since they only receive back what God had deprived them of, and for the want of which they had suffered perhaps for years; and to obtain which, they could do nothing even as a condition, until God by his sovereign power bestowed it upon them. And as for the reprobates, the Gospel is unavoidably to them, a savour of death unto death. To them Christ came, that they might have death, and that they might have it more abundantly. Thus, turn this system as you will, it sweeps away the mercy and goodness of God, destroys the grace of the Gospel, and in most cases, transforms even the invitations and promises into scalding messages of aggravated wrath.

3. The doctrine we oppose makes God partial and a respecter of persons; contrary to express and repeated declarations of Scripture. For it represents God as determining to save some and damn others, without reference to their character, all being precisely in the same state. To deny this, is to acknowledge that the decree of election and reprobation had respect to character, which is to give up the doctrine. Some indeed pretend, that the decree of election was unconditional, but not the decree of reprobation. But this is impossible; for there could be no decree of election, only in view of the whole number from which the choice was to be made; and the very determination to select such a number, and those only, implied the exclusion of all the rest. If it be said, as the Sublapsarians contend, that the decree of election did not come in until all were fallen, or viewed in the mind of God as fallen; and therefore since all might have been justly damned, there was no injustice to those who were left, though some of the guilty were taken and saved; we reply, That even this would not wholly remove the objection of partiality. But we need not dwell here, because we have a shorter and more decisive way to dispose of this argument. The truth is, it does not cover the whole ground of our objection. Had God nothing to do with man until his prescient eye beheld the whole race in a ruined state? How came man in this state? He was plunged there by the sin of his federal head. But how came *he* to sin? "Adam sinned," says Calvin, "because God so ordained." And so every one must say, that believes God foreordained whatsoever comes to pass. Taking all the links together, they stand thus:—God decreed to create intelligent beings—he decreed that they should all become sinners and children of wrath—and it was so. He then decreed that part of those whom he had constituted heirs of wrath, should be taken, and washed, and saved, and the others left to perish; and then we are told there is no unjust partiality in God, since they all deserve to be damned! What a singular evasion is this! God wishes to damn a certain portion of his creatures, and save the rest; but he cannot do this without subjecting himself to the charge of partiality. To avoid this, he plunges them all into sin and ruin, and forthwith he declares them all children of wrath, and heirs of hell. But in the plenitude of his grace, he snatches some from the pit of ruin, and leaves the rest in remediless wo! Is such a supposition worthy of our righteous God?—Does it accord either with his justice or wisdom? Reason, with half an eye, can see through the flimsy veil, and discover the weakness of the device. I know an attempt has been often made to charge these consequences upon our system, as well as upon the Calvinistic doctrine. For if it is acknowledged that man is born depraved, and this depravity is damning in its nature, does it not follow, it is asked, that all deserve to perish? And therefore God may elect some and justly pass by the rest. I answer—Although all moral depravity, derived or contracted, is damning in its nature, still, by virtue of the atonement, the destructive effects of derived depravity are counteracted; and guilt is not imputed, until by a voluntary rejection of the Gospel remedy, man makes the depravity of his nature the object of his own choice.—Hence, although abstractly considered, this depravity is destructive to the possessors, yet through the grace of the Gospel, *all* are born free from condemnation. So the Apostle Paul, "As by the offence of one, judgment came upon all men to condemnation, so by the righteousness of one, the free gift came upon all men, unto justification of life." In accordance with these views also, the ground of condemnation, according to the Scriptures, is not our native depravity; but the sinner is condemned for *rejecting Christ*,—for *refusing* to occupy upon the *talents given*,—for *rejecting light*,—for *quenching the Spirit*,—for *unbelief*. Here then is the difference on this point between the Calvinists and us. They hold that God, by his decree, plunged Adam and all his race into the pit of sin, from which none of them had the means of escape; but by an omnipotent act of partial grace, he delivers a part, and the remainder

are left unavoidably to perish. We, on the contrary, believe that by Adam's unnecessitated sin he, and in him all his posterity, became obnoxious to the curse of the Divine law. As the first man sinned personally and actively, he was personally condemned; but as his posterity had no agency or personal existence, they could only have perished seminally in him. By the promise of a Saviour however, our federal head was restored to the possibility of obtaining salvation, through faith in the Redeemer. And in this restoration, *all* the seminal generations of men were included. Their possible and prospective existence was restored; and their personal and active existence secured. And with this also, the possibility of salvation was secured to all. To such as never come to a personally responsible age, this salvation was secured unconditionally by Christ; to *all* those who arrived to the age of accountability, salvation was made possible, on equal and impartial conditions. Thus, while on our principle, there is not the slightest ground for a charge of partiality; on the Calvinistic principle, the charge seems to lie with all its weight. It makes God, in the worst sense of the terms, *partial, and a respecter of persons.*

4. This doctrine is objectionable, because, contrary to express and repeated passages of Scripture, it necessarily limits the atonement. It will surely not be expected, that we should attempt to prove that Christ "tasted death for every man"—that he "gave himself a ransom for all"—that he "died for all"—that he became "a propitiation for the sins of the whole world"—because, these are so many express Scripture propositions, and rest directly on the authority of God. And while these stand, the doctrine of particular and unconditional election must fall, for the two doctrines are incompatible. That particular election and partial redemption must stand or fall together, has been acknowledged, and is still maintained by most Calvinists; and therefore they have endeavoured to explain away those passages, which so clearly declare that "Christ died for all." But in this work they have found so many difficulties, that others, and among them most of the Calvinistic clergy in New-England, have acknowledged a general redemption, and have undertaken to reconcile with it the doctrine of particular election and reprobation. But this reconciliation is as difficult as the other. To say nothing now of the utter uselessness of making an atonement for the reprobates, unless for the purpose of making their unavoidable damnation more aggravated, we would ask, What is the object of the atonement? Let these very Calvinists themselves answer. They tell us, that its object was, to open the way, by which it might be possible for sinners to be saved. But has the atonement made it possible for the reprobates to be saved? If so, then perhaps they will be saved, and therefore the idea of unconditional election and reprobation is false. But if the atonement has only made it possible for the elect to be saved, then it was made only for the elect. Let the supporters of this system choose which horn of this dilemma they please; either will destroy their doctrine. For as it is absurd to talk about redeeming grace and Gospel provisions, *sufficient* to save those who are eternally and effectually excluded from these blessings, so it is idle to talk about a redemption for *all*, which includes provisions sufficient only to save the *elect*. Not even the fiction of a *natural ability* in all men to serve God and get to heaven, will help this difficulty. For allowing, in the argument, that the reprobates have ability to serve God and gain heaven, without grace, and in spite of God's decree, still, as this is called a *natural* ability, it is plain it is not the fruit of the atonement. It is equally irrelevant to argue that the atonement may be said to be universal, because it contains enough to save the whole world, if they would or could embrace it, and it is only their excessive depravity which renders it impossible for them to receive the atonement. For this is the same as to say, that a physician has an efficient remedy to heal his patient, only he is so sick he cannot take it. This excessive weakness is that for which the physician should prescribe, and to which the medicine should be applied. And if it does not come to this it is no medicine for this case. So the atonement, if it is not a remedy for man's extreme depravity, it is no provision for him. If it does not

give a gracious power to all sinners to embrace salvation, it has accomplished nothing for the depraved reprobate. Since, therefore, according to Calvinism, the atonement provides for the reprobate neither natural nor moral ability to serve God, nor makes it possible for him to be saved, it follows, that the atonement is made only for the elect. But as this is contrary to the word of God, the doctrine that leads to this conclusion must be false.

5. If time would permit, I might here notice at some length several objections to this doctrine:—Such as that it takes away all motives to repentance, by giving the sinner just cause to say, "If I am to be saved, I shall be, do what I may; and if I am to be damned, I must be, do what I can;"—it leads to the idea of infant damnation —it weakens the zeal and paralyzes The efforts of devotion and benevolence—it destroys the end of punishment, the original design of which was to prevent sin, but which, according to this doctrine, was designed merely for the glory of God; and sin was ordained for the purpose of giving God an opportunity of glorifying himself in punishing it. These and others might be dwelt upon with effect; but passing them all, I hasten to the conclusion of my arguments, by urging only one more objection to the system I am opposing.

6. We are suspicious of this doctrine, because its advocates themselves seem studious to cover up and keep out of sight many of its features, and are constantly changing their manner of stating and defending their system. A little attention to the history of the controversy between predestinarians and their opposers, will show the truth and force of this objection. The charge that Calvinism covers up and keeps out of sight some of its most offensive features, does not lie so much against its advocates of the old school, as those of the modern. With the exception of some logical consequences, which we think chargeable upon the system, and which they were unwilling to allow, these early defenders of unconditional election came out boldly and fearlessly with their doctrine. If modern Calvinists would do the same, we should need no other refutation of the system. But even the early supporters of Calvinism, when pressed by their opponents, resorted to various forms of explanation and modes of proof, and also to various modifications of the system itself. Goodwin, in his work entitled, "Agreement of Brethren," &c, says:—"The question, as to the object of the decrees, has gone out among our Calvinistic brethren into endless digladiations and irreconcilable divisions," and then goes on to mention nine of these "irreconcilable divisions" that prevailed at his day. At the present day these school subtleties are not so prevalent, but numerous changes of a more popular cast, and such as are suited to cover up the offensive features of the system, are now introduced. The modern defence of this doctrine consists chiefly in the dexterous use of certain ambiguous technicalities which, in this theology, mean one thing, and in common language another. And this is carried to such an extent, that it is now a common thing to hear parishioners contend strenuously that their pastors do not hold to predestination, when it is well known to some, at least, that they do; and that they are exerting themselves to spread the sentiment.

This is a subject, permit me here to say, on which I touch with more reluctance than upon any other point involved in this controversy. To represent the thing as it is, seems so much like accusing our brethren of insincerity and duplicity, that nothing but a regard to truth would induce me to allude to it. Whether this arises from an excessive but honest zeal for their system, or whether it is supposed the cause is so important, and at the same time so difficult to be sustained, that the end will justify what, in other cases, would be judged questionable policy, and hardly reconcilable with the spirit of a guileless Christianity, is certainly not for me to decide. With respect to their motives, they will stand or fall by the judgment of Him that trieth the reins. But the course, at any rate, seems very reprehensible. Take one instance:—All sinners, we are told, may come to Christ *if they will;* and therefore they are criminal if they do not.—Now this mode of speech corresponds very well with Scripture and reason. And who, that had not been specially instructed in the dialect of this theology, would understand that this mode of speech, according to Hopkinsian technics, implied an inability and an impossibility of obtaining salvation? And yet this is the fact: for though, according to this system, if we have a will to come to Christ, we *may*, yet by a *Divine constitution* it is as much impossible to have this will as it is to break the decree of Jehovah,—Hence all such modes of speech are worse than unmeaning; they have a deceptive meaning. They mean one thing in this creed, and another thing in popular language. It never occurs to the generality of mankind, when they are told they may do thus and thus, *if they will*, that there is a secret omnipotent influence impelling and controlling the will. They suppose these expressions, therefore, mean that, independent of all irresistible foreign influences, they have, within themselves, the power to choose or not to choose: and yet the real meaning of the speaker differs as much from this, as a negative differs from an affirmative.

In perfect accordance with the foregoing, is the common explanation that is given to the doctrine of election and reprobation. Reprobation is kept out of sight; and yet it is as heartily believed by modern Calvinists, as it was by John Calvin himself. It is taught too; but it is taught covertly. And yet when we quote old-fashioned Calvinism, in its primitive plain dress, we are told *these are old authors;* we do not believe with them: "if we had lived in the days of our fathers, we would not have been partakers with them in *their errors*," and yet "they are witnesses unto themselves, that they *are the children* of them" who taught these errors. They recommend their writings, they garnish their sepulchres, they teach their catechisms to the rising generation; they say, even in their Church articles of faith, "We believe in the doctrines of grace, as held and taught by the *fathers* and *reformers* in the Church,"—and especially do they hold to that root and foundation of the whole system, "God hath, from all eternity, foreordained whatsoever comes to pass."

Since I have alluded to Church articles, it will be in support of this objection to say that the written creeds of Churches partake of this same ambiguous character. They are either expressed in texts of Scripture, or in doubtful and obscure terms; so that different constructions can be put upon them, according to the faith of the subscriber. And instances have been known, in which articles of faith have been altered, again and again, to accommodate scrupulous candidates. And yet their candidates for holy orders, and for professorships, in their theological institutions, are required to subscribe to a rigid Calvinistic creed. In this way it is expected, doubtless, that the doctrine will be maintained and perpetuated, though in other respects public opinion should be accommodated. How would honest John Calvin, if he could be introduced among us, with the same sentiments he had when on earth, frown upon the Churches that bear his name! He would not only call them "silly and childish," but he would, doubtless, in his bold, blunt manner, charge them with disingenuousness and cowardice, if not with downright duplicity, for thus shunning and smoothing over and covering up the more repulsive features of their system. How would he chide them for shifting their ground, and changing their system, while they nevertheless pretend to build on the same foundation of predestination! He would, we believe, sternly inquire of them what they meant by saying, all sinners, not excepting reprobates, may come to Christ and be saved?—why they pretended to hold to election, and not to reprobation?—how they could reconcile general redemption with particular election?—and especially would he frown indignantly upon that new doctrine, lately preached and defended, in what has been supposed to be the head quarters of orthodoxy in New-England, by which we are taught that derived depravity is not any taint or sinful corruption of our moral constitution, but consists, exclusively and entirely, in *moral exercise!* But probably he would get little satisfaction from those who profess his creed and bear his name. They would tell him that the old forms of this system were so repulsive, the people would not receive them; and that, being hard pressed by their antagonists, they had thrown up these new redoubts, and assumed these new positions, not only to conceal their doctrine, but if possible to defend it. And as he could get little satisfaction of *them*, he would get less from us.—Could we meet the venerable reformer, we would thank him for his successful zeal and labour in the Protestant cause; but we would expostulate with him for giving sanction and currency to his "horrible decree." We would tell him he had committed to his followers a system so abhorrent to reason, and so difficult to be supported by Scripture, that they had been *driven* into all these changes in hope of finding some new and safe ground of defence; and that, while we considered this as a striking and convincing argument against the doctrine itself, we viewed it as auspicious of its final overthrow; that these changes, refinements, and concealments, were symptoms that the doctrine was waxing old, and was ready to vanish away.

But I must conclude this discourse. To your serious consideration, Christian brethren, I commend the sentiments contained in it. Whatever you may think of the discourse itself, I cannot fail, I think, of escaping censure. Those who accord with the sentiments here defended, will of course approve; and those who believe in predestination will of course be reconciled to the preaching because God hath decreed it. It hath come to pass that I have preached as I have, and therefore it is a part of the Divine plan. It hath come pass that Arminianism exists, and therefore this is a part of the Divine plan. We beg our brethren who differ from us, not to fight against God's plan if they say it is right for us to fight against it, because this also is decreed—I answer, This only confirms our objections against the system, for it arrays the Deity against himself. From all such inconsistencies, *may the God of truth deliver us*. Amen.

NUMBER I.
REPLY TO THE CHRISTIAN SPECTATOR.[3]

This sermon had been before the public almost two years before it received any notice, so far as the author is informed, from any of the advocates of predestination. After the third edition was announced, there were several passing acrimonious censures in some of the Calvinistic periodicals, which did not affect the merits of the question at issue between us and the predestinarians. At length the Rev. Mr. Tyler, of this city, (Middletown, Conn.) published a sermon which was evidently written in reference to the sermon on predestination. This sermon of Mr. T. might have been noticed; but its general positions were so indefinite, and its modes of illustration so vague, it seemed hardly calculated to narrow the field of controversy or hasten a decision of the question at issue. For example: Mr. T. defines election to be "the eternal purpose of God to renew, sanctify, and save every man whom he wisely can, and no others." With such a proposition there certainly can be no controversy, for it leaves the subject more vague, and the point in dispute more confused than before a definition was attempted. There are two errors, the antipodes of each other, which, in all controversy, and especially religious controversy, ought to be carefully guarded against. The one is an attempt to make the subjects of difference more numerous and consequential than they are in truth; and the other is an attempt to cover up real differences under indefinite propositions and ambiguous terms. Both these errors may be the result of honest motives: the former may arise from a jealous regard to the truth, and the latter from a love of peace. Both, however, are injurious; for neither does the one promote the cause of truth, nor does the other secure a permanent peace. Indeed, bringing antagonist principles into contact gives an additional impulse to their repellent forces, so that a transient union produces, in the end, greater discord. Though the controversy in the Church, between Calvinists and Arminians, has been long and injurious; yet, as an individual, I never can sign a *union creed* of doubtful terms and ambiguous articles. Nor can I deem it worth my while to contend about such terms and articles. I should fear the searching interrogatory of Him who questioned Job:

"Who is this that darkeneth counsel by words without knowledge?" In the present controversy there is danger of this ambiguity also from a less commendable principle than a love of peace, viz. an adherence to old symbols of faith to avoid the imputation of a change; while, at the same time, to escape the force of unanswerable argument, vague propositions, ambiguous definitions, and equivocal terms are made the bulwark of defence. This principle was alluded to in the sermon on predestination; and although it has given great offence to some of the Calvinists, and is represented by the author of the review which we are about to notice as being "utterly unworthy of the attention of a person who is honestly inquiring after truth;" yet it seems to me he knows little of his own heart who thinks himself incapable of such a course. Nor does it seem *utterly unworthy* of an honest inquirer after truth to mark the effects of arguments upon systems, since the changes effected in those systems, by the arguments urged against them, show the strength of the one and the weakness of the other. If, therefore, I should undertake to answer Mr. Tyler's sermon, my strictures would consist chiefly in pointing out its indefiniteness and incongruity. But this, without convincing, might give offence. And although I see no way of continuing the controversy, as the Calvinists now manage it, without alluding to this course of the advocates of predestination, yet I am happy to say there is less of it in the "review" before us than is common in modern treatises on that subject. Though it is a laboured article of about forty-three pages, yet it is generally in a manly style, and sustained by a train of close and skilful argumentation. It would afford me great pleasure to be able to equal the reviewer's ingenuity, and still more to throw into my reply the serenity of his spirit. I have little occasion, however, in the present case, to dread his talents or lose my temper; for if I understand the reviewer, though his essay bears upon it, if not the "rugged," at least the decided "aspect of controversy" with my sermon, he is nevertheless in principle an Arminian. I allude now more especially to his views of predestination. On election there is evidently a greater difference between us; and yet it strikes me when a man discards Calvinian predestination, consistency would require that the peculiarities of Calvinian election should be discarded also. At any rate, as the settling of the former question will have a very strong bearing upon the other, I shall confine myself in this article to predestination. I am not certain that I understand the reviewer; but his candour authorizes me to believe that he will explain himself frankly, and correct me if I misunderstand him. If we are agreed on this point we ought to know it, and give over the controversy. If we are not, let us know the precise ground of difference. And in either case we shall be the better prepared to pursue the question of election.

The question in dispute is simply this: What relation is there between the decrees or purposes of God and the responsible acts of man? The Arminian views on this question, as I understand them, are these: God, as a Sovereign, in deciding upon his works, had a right to determine on such a system as pleased him; but, being infinitely wise and good, he would of course choose, in the contemplation of all possible systems, to create such a one as, all things considered, would bring the most glory to himself, and the greatest good to the universe. In infinite wisdom he decided that such a system would be a *moral government*, consisting of himself, as the supreme and rightful Governor, and of intelligent subjects, having full and unrestrained power to obey or disobey the mandates of their Sovereign. He foresaw that one of the unavoidable incidents of such a government would be the possible existence of moral evil; and, in glancing through the proposed system, he foresaw that moral evil would *certainly* exist, involving innumerable multitudes in its ruinous consequences. He did not approve of the evil; he did not decree that it should exist: but still evil was a remote result of a decree of his: for although he foresaw that *if* he made such free agents, and governed them in the manner proposed, they would certainly sin, yet he determined, notwithstanding this *certainty*, to make these agents and govern them as proposed. He determined, however, that they should be under no necessity of sinning, either by his decree, or by the circumstances in which they should be placed; but if they sinned, it should be their own free choice. As he foresaw they would sin, he also determined upon the plan he would pursue in reference to them as sinners, and arranged, in the counsels of his own infinite mind, the extended concatenation of causes and effects, so as to make the "wrath of man praise him," and deduce the greatest possible good from the best possible system. Such, it is believed, is Arminianism—such is Methodism—such is the doctrine of the sermon—and such are the dictates of the Bible and of sound philosophy.

The next question is, What is the doctrine of the reviewer? He shall speak for himself. On page 612, of the review, he asks the question, "But in what sense are we to understand the position that he (God) purposes the existence of sin?" He proceeds to answer: "Not necessarily, in the sense of his preferring its existence in his kingdom to its non-existence, &c. In affirming the doctrine of predestination we affirm no more necessarily than that God, with the knowledge that these beings would sin in despite of the best measures of providence and government he could take, purposed to create them and pursue those measures, not for the sake of their sin, but for the good which he nevertheless saw it was possible to secure in his moral kingdom. This would be a purpose with respect to the existence of sin, a purpose to permit its existence, rather than to have no moral system."—Again, page 613: "Nothing more (touching free agency) is implied in the purpose spoken of than a certainty *foreseen* of God, that if he creates and upholds that being, and pursues wise and good measures of providence, he (the being) will at a given time, fully choose in a given way." In page 612 he says, "God confers on them (mankind) in their creation the powers of free agency, and he uses *no influence* in his providence or government to procure their sin." Page 614, "He (God) most obviously has no will opposed to his law, though with a foresight of their conduct he should purpose to permit their sin, rather than dispense with the existence of a moral kingdom." But it is useless to multiply quotations. Suffice it to say that the reviewer's whole ground of defence against the arguments of the sermon, on the question of predestination, is solely this Arminian explanation of the doctrine of predestination. He acknowledges, nay boldly asserts, in a strain "of rugged controversy" with his brethren who may differ from this view of the subject, that there is no other explanation by which the arguments of the sermon can be avoided—that is, as I understand it, the only way to avoid the arguments against the doctrine of Calvinian predestination is to give it up, and assume the Arminian sentiment on this subject. If the reviewer does not mean this, he will of course explain himself fully, and point out the precise difference between his views and those of the Arminians. If, on this subject, the reviewer is an Arminian, he has too much candor, I trust, not to acknowledge it frankly, and too much moral courage to be afraid of the name. If he is not, the cause of truth and his own consistency of character imperiously demand an explanation. Until this point, therefore, is decided, farther arguments on the merits of the question in which we are supposed to be at issue, are useless.

I am not, however, quite ready to dismiss the review. I stated at the commencement it was difficult to pursue this controversy without alluding to the manner in which it had been conducted on the part of our Calvinistic brethren; but that there was less ground for objection in this article in the Spectator than in most others. There are some things in this article, however, that I cannot justify. I will state them frankly, though I trust in Christian friendship. I cannot approve of the reviewer's use of terms: though, to my understanding, he has evidently given the doctrine of predestination not merely a new *dress*, but a new *character*, yet he more than intimates that it is the old doctrine with only a new method of explanation; and seriously and repeatedly complains of the author of the sermon for "confounding the *fact* of God's foreordaining the voluntary actions of men with this or any other *solution* of that fact or theory as to the *mode* in which it comes to pass." And so confident is the reviewer that he still believes in the *fact* of predestination, in the old Calvinistic sense, that in stating his sentiments on this subject he uses the same forms of expression which Calvinists have used, when their meaning was as distant from his as the two poles from each other. He tells us, for instance, that "God determined that the events which take place should take place in the very manner in which they do, and for the very ends." Now if the writer mean what the words naturally imply, then he believes that, in the case of a finally impenitent sinner, God predetermined that all his sins *should* take place in the manner they did, and for the very end that he might be damned! Again he tells us, "God, in his eternal purpose, has predetermined all events." And, quoting from the Assembly's Catechism, "God, from all eternity, did freely and unchangeably ordain whatsoever comes to pass," he tells us that this expresses essentially the views entertained by the orthodox Congregationalists of New-England, among whom, I suppose of course, he would include himself. Now, after what I have said of the reviewer's Arminianism, I doubt not but some of my readers will be startled at these quotations, and be ready to accuse me of great credulity in the judgment I have formed of the writer's sentiments. I shall exculpate myself, however, by saying, in the first place, that if there is any contradiction in the writer's sentiments or language, it is not my fault, but his; and if I should attempt to reconcile them, perhaps the reviewer would not thank me for my officiousness. Beside, after what has been said, I feel safer in understanding the reviewer in an *Arminian sense*, because he and some others take it very ill of me that I have represented them as Calvinists. But, in fairness to the reviewer, it is presumed that he will not consider himself justly chargeable with contradiction. He has used these old terms, it is true, and thus has *subscribed* to the Calvinistic creed as positively as the staunchest Calvinist; but then, let it be understood, he has *explained* that creed, and defined the terms, and protests against being held responsible for any other construction than his own. Hence by God's predetermining that sin *should* take place, in the very manner, and for the very ends it does—by God's foreordaining whatsoever comes to pass—he only means that God foresaw that sin would certainly take place, and predetermined that he would not hinder it, either by refraining from creating moral agents, or by throwing a restraint upon them that would destroy their free agency. In short, that he would submit to it as an evil unavoidably incident to the best possible system, after doing all that he wisely could to prevent it! This is *foreordaining sin!!* This is *predetermining* that it *should be!!!* I cannot but express my *deepest regret* that a gentleman of the reviewer's standing and learning should lend his aid and give his sanction to such a perversion of language—to such a confusion of tongues. We do not complain of the doctrine contained in the *explanation;* but we protest, in the name of all that is pure in language, in the name of all that is important in the sentiments conveyed by language, against such an abuse of terms. Alas for us! When will the watchmen see eye to eye! when will the Church be at peace! while our spiritual guides, our doctors in divinity, pursue this course? By what authority will the reviewer support this definition? Do the words *predestinate,* or *foreordain,* or *decree* mean, in common language, or even in their radical and critical definition, nothing more than *to permit—not absolutely to hinder—to submit to as an unavoidable but offensive evil?* The reviewer certainly will not pretend this. Much less do they mean this when used in a magisterial or authoritative sense, to express the mind and will of a superior or governor toward an inferior or a subject.—What is the *decree* of a king? What is the *ordinance* of a senate? What is the official determination of a legislative body? Let common sense and common usage answer the question. Not a man probably can be found, from the philosopher to the peasant, who would say these words would bear the explanation of the reviewer. Yet it is in this official and authoritative sense that theologians, and our reviewer among them, use these terms. The Assembly's Catechism, as quoted by himself, says, "God, from all eternity, *did, by the most wise and holy counsel of his own will, freely and unchangeably ordain,*" &c. Now it would be a gross insult to common sense to say of such language as this, in the mouth of an earthly potentate, that the sovereign meant by this nothing more than that he permitted the existence of certain unavoidable, and in themselves, highly offensive evils in his kingdom, because he could not remove them without embarrassing the essential operations of his government. There is not, probably, a clearer case in the whole range of philology.

But the use of these terms by those who believe as I understand the reviewer to believe, is the more unjustifiable, because they are used by most Calvinistic authors in a different sense.—Why, then, should the reviewer, believing as he does, continue to use them in the symbols of his faith? Different persons might give different answers to such a question. For one, I would prefer he should answer it himself.

I cannot approve of the reviewer's censures upon my manner of treating the doctrine of predestination. He accuses me of confounding the *doctrine* itself, with *modes* of explanation. He says they are perfectly distinct; and though some may have been unfortunate in their modes of explanation, and though he acknowledges my arguments bear against such, yet the *fact* of the doctrine itself is not thereby affected. His mode of explanation, for example, he thinks untouched by the arguments of the sermon. But his mode of explanation, as we have seen, turns the doctrine into *Arminianism*. And it would, perhaps, be no difficult matter to show, that any explanation of the doctrine, short of doing it away, would be exposed to all the weight of the arguments urged in the sermon. But the sermon was never written to oppose those who hold to the decrees of God in an Arminian sense. Why then does the reviewer complain of the sermon? Why does he so "deeply regret" that the author of the sermon "should come before the public with an attack on the faith of a *large part* of the Christian community, conducted in a way so obviously erroneous and unjust?" The sermon was against Calvinism, not Arminianism. It is true, the reviewer may say, the sermon alludes, in some parts, to the Calvinism of New-England, and therefore he felt himself implicated. But he certainly was not unless he is a New-England *Calvinist*—unless he believes that "God foreordains whatsoever comes to pass," in the proper sense of those terms. Indeed, it seems that Calvinism, in its proper character, is as obnoxious to the reviewer, as to the author of the sermon; and the former seems to have taken this opportunity to show the *nakedness* of the system, and bring into notice a better doctrine. If so, is it safe that the reviewer should still accord to them their old symbols of faith? And is it just, that the author of the sermon should be held the defendant on the record, when the execution is issued against Calvinism itself? In answer to the former question, I would say, it is utterly *unsafe*, and never will be approved of, I believe, by Arminians. With respect to the latter question, if it is *safer* to attack Calvinism in this indirect way, I will not object, though it may seem at present to my disadvantage. But I cannot see that it would be safer—an open bold front always ends best. What if it should subject the reviewer, and the theological doctors in New-Haven generally, to the charge of heresy? Still they ought not to shrink from their responsibilities—they occupy a commanding influence among the Churches and over the candidates of their theological school, and that influence should be openly and decidedly directed to discountenance error. They should remove it, root and branch. Especially should they discard those old symbols of faith, which are not only in themselves, in *their true and proper meaning*, a reflection upon the clerical character, and a *black spot* upon an otherwise orthodox creed, but are also especially obnoxious, because they are the very articles which the great body of the Calvinists have maintained, in a sense widely different from that of the reviewer. At the head of these stands Calvin, the author of the system, in the Protestant Church. Calvin, who says, "I will not scruple to own that the will of God lays a necessity on all things, and that every thing he wills necessarily comes to pass." "Adam fell, not only by the *permission*, but also by the *appointment* of God. He not only *foresaw* that Adam would fall, but also *ordained* that he should." "The devil and wicked men are so held in on every side, with the hand of God, that they cannot conceive or contrive or execute any mischief, any farther than God himself doth not *permit* only, but *command*—nor are they held in fetters, but compelled also, as with a bridle, to perform obedience to those commands." Calvin, it seems, was far from thinking that *appointment* only meant *permission*, or that to *ordain* only meant certainty *foreseen*. In this he was correct: in this he has been followed by a host of writers down to the present day, and copied in numerous ecclesiastical symbols, in different parts of Christendom; and does not the reviewer know that these terms are understood by Hopkins and Emmons, and all the Calvinists of that school, in a sense widely different from his explanation, and in a sense, too, much more in accordance with the *proper meaning* of the terms? Does he not know that a great majority of the Calvinists of the United States, and perhaps in New-England, even understand these terms, as indeed they ought to be understood, when used in reference to sin, as expressing a preference of sin, in that part of the Divine plan where sin occurs, to holiness in its stead? Indeed, as I understand the reviewer, from the days of John Calvin down to the present hour, there is, on this point, between the great body of Calvinists and himself, almost no likeness, except in the use of words. Theirs is one doctrine—his another. Why, then, does he oppose the opposers of Calvinism, and thus keep error in countenance? Especially, why does he hail from that party, and hoist their signals, and then, after *seeming* to get the victory, by espousing the very cause of the assailed, encourage the *Calvinists* to triumph, as if *their* cause had been successful? Is this justice to the author of the sermon? Is it the best way to promote truth? But I forbear. The reviewer's subsequent explanations may remove these difficulties. At any rate, the cause of truth will doubtless advance. The appearance of this review has given additional strength to the sentiment, Calvinism "is waxing old, and is ready to vanish away." The dogma that "God has predetermined all events, and elected (in a Calvinistic sense) out of our guilty world all who shall be heirs of salvation," withers at the touch of advancing truth, and is fast losing credit in the Christian Church.

Since writing the above, I have seen an inquiry of a correspondent in one of the Calvinistic papers, in these words, "Why do our Calvinistic writers retain the words which seem so sadly to perplex our Arminian brethren, when it is certain that we do not attach the signification to them which they always pretend?" and then instances in the word "foreordain." The editor, in reply, gives as a reason for using these words, that they are Scriptural; and seems to deem it necessary that they should *persist* in this use until we submit. This reply of the editor reminded me of a remark of Mr. Tyler, in his sermon already alluded to: "The Calvinist contends that God resolved, from eternity, to permit all the sins and miseries which were to take place; and this he calls, in the language of the Bible, *foreordination*." Now, not to stop here, to show that no true Calvinist would ever call *foreordination* and *permission* the same thing, for Calvin has, as we have seen, clearly distinguished the two words from each other, I beg the privilege of adding a thought or two on this idea of Scripture authority for the use or these terms. For if it is only because the Scriptures use these words in this sense, that they *persist* in using them, I think we may easily settle this question. Let it be shown that the Scriptures use "foreordination," or "predestination," in the sense of mere *permission—not absolutely hindering*. Again: let *one passage* be shown in which it is said, God "predestinates" all things, or "foreordains" whatsoever comes to pass. If this cannot be done, how futile, how more than absurd is it, to talk about using these words, because the Scriptures use them! To use Scripture words out of the Scripture sense, and then appeal to Scripture to sanction this use, is as sad a perversion of the Scriptures as it is of logic. Indeed, to give such a meaning to the word predestinate, is at once to take away the principal scriptures quoted by the reviewer, and others, to prove Calvinistic election. See Eph. i, 5; ii, 10;

Rom. viii, 29. Does predestination in these passages mean merely *to permit*, or not *to hinder?* and do these passages teach a personal election to eternal life? Is this all the Calvinists mean by the *election* of *sovereign grace*, not of man, nor of the will of mans but of God? Alas! for the elect! If man does not elect himself, and God *only predestinates*, that is, *permits—does not hinder* his election; who, we ask, will elect him? How does error destroy itself! These gentlemen may take which ground they please; they may either acknowledge that Bible predestination means an *efficient purpose of God* to accomplish an object, and then meet the sermon on the issue there proposed; or they may interpret these words as the reviewer has, and then give up those passages which they consider their strong hold, in favour of Calvinian election. In either case their system must suffer serious loss. Nothing could be more unfortunate, I think, than this appeal to the Bible to sanction such an abuse of terms. As to the word foreordain, I do not recollect that it occurs in our translation. Jude 4, has "before of old ordained," &c, but it is in the original very different from the word rendered predestinate. The allusion is to characters that were proscribed for their sins, and designated for deserved punishment. The original for predestinate, proorizo, is used in only one place, so far as I can find, with any direct reference to a sinful act, Acts iv, 28. This passage is quoted by the reviewer. But the determination here spoken of, he himself informs us, relates to "the purpose of God to make an atonement for the sin of the world, by means of the death of Jesus Christ." Hence the predetermination of God, in this instance, probably refers to the *work* of atonement, without including therein any special decree in respect to the means of the suffering. Christ *could* have suffered, even unto death, in the garden without any human means. But inasmuch as these men had the murderous purpose, God "chose to leave Christ to their power," &c, therefore *decreed* the atonement, but *permitted* the means. This seems to be the most rational construction. But whatever Calvinists may think of this passage, the Scriptural use of the word is clearly on the side of its *proper* meaning— an *authoritative ordinance* that the thing predestinated *shall be*.

I will avail myself of this opportunity to correct one or two errors of the reviewer, respecting the sentiment of the sermon, which had escaped my notice. He says, my "view of predestination is a determination of God to produce a given result by his *own immediate* and *efficient* energy." This is a mistake. I said nothing about *immediate energy;* this is an essential misrepresentation of the sermon. Again: "On Dr. Fisk's principle, it is impossible for God to use the voluntary agency of any creature, to accomplish any valuable end in his kingdom, and yet leave that creature accountable for his conduct." This is so manifestly incorrect and unjust, that I am sure I need only call the attention of the reviewer to it a second time, to secure a correction from himself.

NUMBER II.

A PROPOSITION TO CALVINISTS.

The communication below contains a proposition from Dr. W. Fisk, which, however much we dislike theological controversies, we believe is appropriate and interesting at this time. Such a discussion, under such arrangements, will give the merits of the controversy to both sides; and will, at least, convince all of one truth—that the Methodist Episcopal Church seeks not concealment from the world or her members, as charged by her adversaries. But it will develop a still more important truth, and that is, what are the settled and definite opinions of the old or the new school in the Calvinistic Churches. It is known to all the world, that there is great difficulty in ascertaining what are the theological opinions of those ancient Churches of the land. They seem to be as far apart from each other as they are from Arminianism; and their replies and rejoinders to each other are as severe as if directed against us. The discussion must be interesting and profitable, carried on by two such persons as Dr. Fisk and his opponent, and under the steady supervision, as to temper and manner, of third parties as proposed. —Eds.

I have just received a pamphlet of about forty-eight pages, containing a series of letters, in answer to my sermon on predestination and election. These letters are written by the Rev. David Metcalf, of Lebanon, Connecticut, and purport to be an answer, not only to the doctrinal part of the sermon, but to the "charges," as the writer is pleased to call them, contained in the sermon, and published afterward in a specific form, first in the Connecticut Observer, and then in the Christian Advocate and Journal.

It will be recollected by your readers, that I pledged myself to vindicate my statements against any responsible person, who, with his own proper signature, would come forward and deny them: or if I failed to support them, I would retract what I had written. This pledge Mr. Metcalf calls upon me to redeem; not indeed by bringing forward my proofs, or by making a reply; but, having thrown in his plea, he supposes that the cause is decided, and has himself made up the judgment, and issued the execution, and forthwith comes forward, and claims his damage. His words are—"Of the author of the sermon we claim a public acknowledgment of his errors, and make justice and equity the ground of our claim." Again, "If Dr. F. makes no public retraction from the ground taken in his sermon—if after he shall receive these letters, [!!] remembering also what is said in the Christian Spectator's review of his sermon, he shall allow another copy of it to be printed, I think he will find it difficult to convince any intelligent candid man, that he is not guilty of breaking the ninth commandment," &c. The intelligent reader, who has studied human nature, will know how to make suitable allowances for the dogmatical and premature decisions, and high claims contained in the foregoing extracts. It is not an uncommon thing, that a zealous advocate succeeds in *convincing himself* of the truth of his cause; but utterly fails with respect to all others. I do not say, that this writer will not gain his argument; but it requires more "foreknowledge" than I am disposed to accord to him, to affirm this as a "certainty." I demur against this hasty manner of making up the judgment. I wish to be heard in defence of my statements, and have objections also to bring against his statements, and supposed proofs and arguments.

In the first place, I object to him, that he has not come out and joined issue specifically and directly on any one of my "charges," but talks for most part in general terms, about the unfairness, injustice, and misrepresentations of the sermon. This circumstance would, of itself, free me from any obligation to notice these letters, on the ground of my pledge in the Observer. But yet, as I feel the most perfect readiness to discuss this subject, and as I hope the cause of righteousness may be served thereby, I will willingly proceed in this controversy, both as to doctrine and policy, provided we can secure some suitable public medium, through which to prosecute the discussion. And on this point Mr. M. complains bitterly of the former editors of the Advocate and Journal—for he had applied, it seems, for the privilege of having his letters inserted in that paper, and was refused, on the ground that "the sermon was not published in the Advocate, and therefore justice did not require that its answer should be." Now, since these letters are professedly an answer to the *whole sermon*, the editors, I think, were perfectly consistent with their former statements, in refusing to publish them. If Mr. M. had confined himself to the charges in the Observer, the editors would undoubtedly have given the subject a place in the columns of the Advocate: as it was, however, I think the charge of injustice and unfairness made against the editors by Mr. M. is entirely gratuitous and *unjustifiable*. If it was expected to produce an *effect* on the public, by such a complaint, I think such an expectation will be disappointed in all places where the subject is understood. And that this was the expectation appears evident from another charge against Methodist preachers, in the following words:—"It is supposed to be the common sentiment, if not 'the common talk in our land,' that the Methodist preachers have a strong aversion against their hearers reading our writings. The reason of this, in part, is supposed to be, that they choose to have their people receive all their knowledge of our creed from their statements of it, instead of ours; lest they should be convinced, by our arguments, of the truth of our belief." Now this charge we wholly and positively deny, and challenge the writer for the proofs of what we know to be, not only an ungenerous, but an unjust allegation. Nothing can be farther from the whole genius of Methodism than this. Does not the reverend gentleman know, that a great portion of our members in New England are those who were once members of Calvinistic congregations? Does he not know that they were trained up in these doctrines from their infancy, and have heard them explained and defended from their earliest recollections? Does he not know that Methodism has made its way against the impressions of the nursery, the catechetical instruction of the priest and the school master—the influence of the pulpit and the press, and in maturer age against the still stronger influence of academies and colleges? Does he not know, also, that all this has been done in this generation? And shall we now be told that Methodists examine but one side of the question? How astonishing such a charge, from a man who can make any pretension to a knowledge of ecclesiastical matters in our country! Does not this writer know, also, that the editors of the Advocate, and others, have called loudly, and almost continually, for information upon this subject, that we might know what the Calvinistic standards are, and ascertain what Calvinism is? and shall we now be told, that Methodists are ignorant of the Calvinistic faith, and, what is worse, the preachers strive to keep them in ignorance, and that with the base purpose of keeping them from a conviction of the truth! We say, if Calvinism is essentially what it was from five to thirty years ago, we know its character as well as we ever can know it. If we do not understand it now, it is either because we have not *natural ability* to understand it, (and therefore. Calvinism itself being judge, we are not criminal,) or it is because the teachers of Calvinism have not had *natural ability* to make it plain. But if Calvinism is not essentially what it was, we ask what it now is? If it is changed in the hands of its supporters, how much has it changed? Is it Calvinism still, or has it lost its identity? In what does the identity of Calvinism consist? Shall we take the Rev. Mr. Metcalf's answer to these questions? Shall we take the Christian Spectator's answers? Mr. M. appears fully to agree with the Spectator, for he makes frequent reference to it, with great apparent approbation. And yet two numbers of this periodical have been issued since my reply to the review of my sermon in that work, in which reply I stated my understanding of the reviewer's doctrine of predestination, and requested to be informed if I was incorrect; and neither my reply nor my request has been noticed. And yet, let it be understood, that in the last number there is a very laboured article, to show that Dr. Taylor does not differ essentially from the orthodox Calvinistic faith heretofore received.

It is also known, that though Drs. Woods, Griffin, Tyler, Green, and various others, come out and charge a portion of their brethren with a serious and dangerous dereliction from the Calvinistic faith, yet the accused, in their turn, strenuously maintain that they preserve the old landmarks unremoved, and the essential principles of Calvinism unimpaired; and that it is a calumnious charge to say they have departed from the faith of the party.

How shall we judge in this matter? If we think, from our understanding of their writings, that some of them have changed their views, and we ask them if they have, they are silent. If their brethren charge them with changing, they deny it; and, standing up before the world and before the Churches, and before their God, pronounce *deliberately* and *emphatically*, the old symbols of faith, as a test oath to prove their orthodoxy. Should we doubt their repeated asseverations? Mr. M., or somebody else, might write another pamphlet to screw us into repentance and confession, for bearing false witness against our neighbour. But if we hold them to the old doctrine, which we have had a good opportunity of learning, from our youth up, we are accused of misrepresentation, and of bearing false witness. None but the advocates of the New-Haven divinity have, to my knowledge, taken a public stand against my sermon; and *they* oppose it because *they* say it is a misrepresentation of their doctrine.

This, therefore, seems to us to be the state of the case with respect to these gentlemen— We make a representation of Calvinism as we have found it, and have heretofore understood it—they object, because this is not their belief, and therefore we break the ninth commandment! Their own brethren charge *them* with a departure from the old doctrines, and they deny it! and charge them in turn with bearing false witness! In the midst of our perplexity on this subject, while we are looking every way for light, up comes Mr. M. and tells us, we are unwilling our people should know what Calvinists believe!! Is this generous, or just? We repel the charge, and demand proof. And in the mean time, as a farther proof that the charge is unfounded, I will, Messrs. Editors, with your consent and approbation, make a proposition to Mr. Metcalf. It is certainly desirable, that both Calvinists and Methodists should hear *both sides*. Mr. M. seems very desirous to enlighten the Methodists. This is very well. But we also wish to enlighten the Calvinists. To accomplish this, the discussion on both sides should be put into the hands of the people on both sides. If, then, some reputable and extensively circulated Calvinistic periodical will publish my sermon, and the discussion which *has* arisen, or *may* arise out of it, on both sides, the Christian Advocate and Journal will publish Mr. M.'s letters and the discussions which shall follow; provided always, that it shall be submitted to the respective editors, whether the pieces are written in respectful and becoming style and language; and provided also, that the Calvinistic editor shall, by consenting to this arrangement, he considered as thereby acknowledging, that Mr. Metcalf is a suitable man to manage the controversy in behalf of the Calvinists, and that you, Messrs. Editors, by consenting to the arrangement, will thereby consent that you are willing to trust the controversy in my hands, to be managed in behalf of the Methodists. To give an opportunity for the Calvinistic periodical to be prepared, I shall wait a reasonable time, when, if the offer is not complied with, I shall want the privilege, perhaps, of occupying the columns of the Advocate, by the insertion of a few numbers touching the present Calvinistic controversy, both as relates to their own differences, and also as relates to the general question between them and us.

NUMBER III.

INDEFINITENESS OF CALVINISM.

The readers of the Christian Advocate and Journal will recollect the proposition, made to the Rev. David Metcalf, in the 8th No. of the present volume, on the subject of his review of my sermon. This proposition has not been complied with on the part of Mr. M., and according to the following extract from the New-York Evangelist, no compliance can be expected:—

"We have seen," says the editor of the Evangelist, "in the Advocate, since Mr. Metcalf's work was published, a letter from Dr. F., in which he shows his desire that the discussion shall still go forward. There is one condition he exacts, however, which we think impracticable. It is, that some person should be designated, by a sort of common suffrage, as the champion of Calvinism. Now the truth is, Calvinists, as a class, are rather remarkable for thinking for themselves; and of course, while there are great principles on which, as a class, they all agree, there are many things which will be held or stated differently, by different minds. Consequently, we can, each of us, defend ourselves, and defend Calvinists as a class; notwithstanding, each one may think his fellow holds some errors, and therefore, in his contest with Calvinism, Dr. F. must assume to himself the responsibility of selecting those doctrinal points and modes of statement which distinguish *Calvinists as a class*. And when he has found these principles, we hope he will either confute or embrace them."

I have copied the above for the farther notice of the public, not only as a remarkable paragraph in itself, but also as having an important bearing on the present controversy. There are several things in it worthy of special notice.

In the first place we see, if other editors think with this one, and that they do, we are left to infer from their not offering their periodicals for the controversy, there is no hope that my proposition will be accepted. We then have the reason—because there is one impracticable condition. But why impracticable? The editor tells us, "Dr. F. exacts that some person should be designated by a sort of common suffrage to be the champion of Calvinism." I cannot believe the editor means to misrepresent me; and yet he has done it. My words are, "Provided that the Calvinistic *editor* shall, by consenting to this arrangement, be considered as thereby acknowledging that Mr. Metcalf is a suitable man to manage the controversy on the part of the Calvinists." Here is nothing said about a "sort of common suffrage." In case of compliance by Mr. Leavitt, or any other editor, the only vote to be polled and counted would be his own. Not a very extensive suffrage this! And if Mr. L. thinks the condition impracticable, it must be owing to *moral inability* existing in his own mind, growing out of the belief that Mr. Metcalf *is not a suitable person* to manage this controversy. Hence it is well I took the precaution I did; for Mr. M. is a stranger to me; and I do not wish to engage in a controversy on this subject with any man who is not, by his class, considered responsible. Perhaps Mr. Leavitt knows of some one, who would be suitable, in his judgment, and who would accept of the offer; or perhaps he himself would be willing to engage in the discussion. I do not wish to confine it to Mr. M.; nor do I wish to be considered in the light of a general challenger who is seeking an adventure. The subject is an important one, and I am willing to discuss it with any candid responsible man. We were most unjustly, as I believed, accused of keeping our people in ignorance of Calvinism, and of preventing them from reading on the other side, for the base purpose of preventing them from being convinced of the truth. To render the subject fair and equal, therefore, and to wipe off this aspersion, I made the proposal; and if Mr. M. is not a suitable man, let some other be found.

But we are informed farther in this paragraph, that one great difficulty in complying with my condition is, that "Calvinists, as a class, are remarkable for thinking for themselves," &c. If the editor designs to say, as the natural construction would imply, that the whole class are remarkable, in their character as Calvinists, for thinking and believing differently and independently of each other, then his proposition is a contradiction. They, *as a class*, are remarkable *for not being a class at all*, having no properties or qualities in common! His argument also would require this construction, because he is showing why no one could be the proper champion of the class, for the reason that, as a class, they did not think alike. If *Calvinism* be a general term, it includes, in its extension, all those individuals or sub-classes of individuals, and only those, that hold certain doctrines in common, and it embraces all those doctrines, and only those that are held in common by the class. If, therefore, there is any such class, then most certainly they think alike in all those things that constitute them a class; and by consequence, any one of the number, otherwise competent, would be qualified to represent and defend the class as such, however much he might differ from many of "his fellows," in other things. If, therefore, there is any force in the argument, that it is impracticable for any one of the number bearing the name, to become the champion of *the class as such*, because they differ so among themselves, it must arise from the fact, that there are no "great principles" held in common among them, and, of course, there is *no class*. All the writer says afterward, therefore, about "great principles in which they all agree," is mere verbiage, signifying nothing. For if we give it any meaning, it would be a contradiction of what he had stated before, and a complete nullification of the only argument adduced as a reason for not complying with my proposal. There is another reason why I think the above a fair view of this subject. In the same paragraph it is said, "Therefore, in his contest with Calvinism, Dr. F. must assume to himself the responsibility of selecting those doctrinal facts and modes of statement which distinguish *Calvinists as a class.*" This is more unreasonable than the requisition of Nebuchadnezzar, when he commanded the wise men to *make known the dream,* as well as the interpretation. Would an intelligent and ingenuous man, such as we have a right to expect a religious editor to be, give such an answer, under such circumstances, if he could have told us what Calvinism is? We have been accused, not by Mr. Metcalf only, but by Calvinists of the old school, and the new school, and *all the schools,* that we misrepresent them, that our preachers make it their business to misrepresent them,—that my sermon was a most scandalous misrepresentation, and that we studied to keep our people ignorant of what Calvinism is. When this is replied to, by entreating and conjuring those who bear the name of Calvinism, to tell us what it is; and when we offer to discuss the subject, in their own periodicals, and give them an opportunity to discuss it in ours, and to inform our people, in their own way, on this doctrine —a death-like silence on the subject reigns throughout the whole *corps editorial;* until at length the Evangelist speaks,—We cannot comply; we each and all, as a class, are so remarkable for thinking for ourselves, it is impracticable for any one to state and defend those doctrinal facts which *distinguish us as a class,* and therefore Dr. F. must assume to himself the responsibility of selecting them!! If Calvinists cannot agree in their own system, and cannot trust any of their fraternity to state and defend it in behalf of the class, why do they accuse us of willful misrepresentations, in stating their system? Why, in short, do they not begin to doubt whether, *as a class,* they have any system? It is time for those who bear the name to know, and for the public to be distinctly informed, whether there is any thing *real* represented by the term Calvinism? If there is, then, whether the term is a common or a proper noun? If it is a common noun, or a general name, then, what are the qualities, the properties, or doctrines designated by it? If no one can tell,—if those who "write about it, and about it," week after week, think it *impracticable* to define or describe those doctrines for the class, because they think so differently, of course it follows, if the name is retained, it is not a general, but a *proper name,* and belongs only to individuals. And though it has been assumed by many individuals, yet it has in each case an individual definition, which by no means enters into the definition of the term, as assumed by any other individual. And therefore it is as inconsistent to talk about the *class of Calvinists,* as it is to talk about the class of Johns or Joshuas, and as absurd to infer that two men are in any of their real characteristics alike, because each is called *Calvinist,* as to argue that the editor of the Evangelist and Joshua, the son of Nun, belonged to the same class, because both are called Joshua. And this appears to me to be very nearly the true state of the case. Calvinism, as designating a class, has always been rather vague and unsettled in its definition, from the days of John Calvin himself. And this was one of the offensive objections brought against it in my sermon—an objection, however, that has been abundantly confirmed by recent events. As I wrote and published of another doctrine some years since, so I may say of Calvinism now. It is a proteus that changes its shape before one can describe it —an *ignis fatuus,* that changes its place before one can get his hand on it. And here I will stop to say, It will avail nothing for any one to take offence at this statement. It is not because I dislike men who are called Calvinists, that I thus speak. I know many of them personally, and esteem them highly, but of their doctrine, and their system, and their name, I must speak freely. And the best refutation they can give, is to come out if they can, and define and explain their system. I care not what shape it is presented in; I am willing to meet it. If it puts on an Arminian character and dress, like the review in the Christian Spectator, I will only ask the privilege of baptizing it anew, and giving it a legitimate name. But as there seems now little hope of being permitted to meet it in the manner proposed, it only remains that I proceed, according to promise, to "occupy the columns of the Advocate with a few numbers, touching the present Calvinistic controversy, both as relates to their own differences, and as relates to the general question between them and us."

I cannot but think this an important moment to look into this subject. The signs of the times indicate that the spirit of inquiry is abroad, and the old platforms are shaken. In this breaking up of erroneous systems, there is danger of extremes and extravagancies, more to be dreaded, perhaps, than the old errors themselves. Hence, the necessity for every man who *has* the truth to be on his guard against the currents, new and unprovided for, that may otherwise drive him from his safe moorings: and hence the necessity also, that he who has weighed anchor, and is afloat upon the unexplored sea of philosophic speculation should be aware of the rocks and the quicksands on the opposite shore. An abler hand than mine is certainly needed on this occasion; such a one I hope may be found. But in the mean time I will, as I am able, say a *few things*, with the sincere prayer that I and my readers may be led into all truth.

NUMBER IV.

SKETCH OF THE PAST CHANGES AND PRESENT STATE OF CALVINISM IN THIS COUNTRY.

In the former No. it was seen that the indefiniteness and mutability of the Calvinistic system had thrown a kind of irresponsibility around it; which renders this controversy, in many respects, extremely unsatisfactory. This might, at first, lead to the conclusion, that farther discussion would be useless. On farther thought, however, it *may* appear, that this very circumstance will render the controversy both easier and more promising. This diversity of opinions has produced serious discussion among the predestinarians themselves, and has thrown the system open to public view, and driven its advocates to a clearer statement of their respective opinions. The effervescence, in short, growing out of this excitement, has led to a more distinct analysis of the system, and of course to a clearer discovery of its constituent parts. Their arguments against each other, and the logical consequences which they urge against each other's views, are, in many cases, precisely the same that we should advance, and have often urged, in opposition to predestination. Much of the work, therefore, is prepared for us, and brought forward in a way to produce an effect among Calvinists themselves, where we could not be heard.

To understand this subject however fully, and to follow out this discussion advantageously, it will be necessary to glance at the different changes and modifications of the Calvinistic system; and to take a brief survey of the present state of the parties.

The religious faith of our puritanical fathers is too well known to need a delineation here. This faith was at an early day defined and formally recognized, in the Cambridge and Saybrook platforms. The first refinement (improvement it can hardly be called) upon this ancient faith, was the metaphysical theory of Dr. Hopkins. The leading dogmas of this theory were, that God was the *efficient cause* of all moral action, holy and unholy; and that holiness consisted in disinterested benevolence. Insomuch, that the answer to the question, "Are you willing to be damned?" was deemed a very good criterion by which to judge of a religious experience. While the doctrine of predestination was in this manner *going to seed*, and bearing its legitimate fruits, in one direction, it received a remarkably plausible modification in another. The atonement, which was formerly limited to the elect, was now extended to all; and the invitations of the Gospel, instead of being restrained, as before, to the world of the elect, were extended to the world of mankind.

But as it would be useless to hold out invitations to those who could not accept of them, another refinement was introduced, and man was found to possess a natural ability to receive salvation, although he laboured under an invincible moral *inability*, which would for ever keep him from Christ, until drawn by irresistible grace. This discovery led to other refinements in language, so that a kind of technical nomenclature was formed, out of words in popular use, which words, by an accompanying glossary, were so defined as to correspond with the Calvinistic system. Thus, "You can repent if you will," meaning, according to the technical definition, "You can repent when God *makes* you willing," and so of the rest.

This theory, sustained as it was by Dr. Hopkins, Dr. Emmons, and others, gained many proselytes, and seemed likely, at one time, to become the universal creed. Its metaphysical abstrusities and distinctions gave it an interest for the student; and its plausible and commonsense terms gave it popularity with the people. In the mean time, however, several causes conspired to introduce a great revolution in the religious sentiments of many, which, as it has had a very important influence in modifying Calvinism itself; I must here stop to notice; I allude to the introduction of Unitarianism and Universalism. The proximate causes of the introduction of these sentiments were, among others, probably the following. The Antinomian features of old Calvinism had introduced into the Churches a heartless Christianity and a very lax discipline. It was natural, therefore, when religion had come, in point of fact, to consist chiefly in external performances, for its votaries to seek a theory that would accord with their practice. Unitarianism was precisely such a theory. It is also to be noticed, that the state of formality and spiritual death that prevailed, was greatly increased by the withering alliance which then existed between the Church and civil government. This revolution was undoubtedly hastened also by the ultraism, on the one part, and the technical inconsistencies on the other, of the Hopkinsian theory. The elements had been long in motion, and at length they united in an array of numbers and influence that wrested the fairest portions of their ecclesiastical domain from the orthodox Churches of Mass., and turned them over, together with the richly endowed university of the state, into the hands of the Unitarians.

In Connecticut, Unitarianism, as that term is commonly understood among us, has not prevailed. There is, I believe, but one Unitarian pastor, properly so called, in the state. This sentiment, however, prevails very extensively in this and all the other New-England states, as well as in many other parts of the union, under the name of Universalism; a sentiment which differs but little from Socinianism, and had its origin doubtless from the same source. About half a century since, a Calvinistic clergyman, as he was supposed to be to the day of his death, left a posthumous work, which was published, entitled, "Calvinism Improved." It was merely an extension of the doctrines of unconditional election and irresistible grace to all instead of a part. From the premises, the reasoning seemed fair, and the conclusions legitimate. This made many converts. And this idea of universal salvation, when once it is embraced, can easily be moulded into any shape, provided its *main feature* is retained.—It has finally pretty generally run into the semi infidel sentiments, of *no atonement—no Divine Saviour—no Holy Ghost*, and *no supernatural change of heart;* as well as "no hell—no devil—no angry God." It may be a matter of some surprise, perhaps, to a superficial observer, or to one not personally acquainted with the circumstances of the case, why, in leaving Calvinism, these men should go so far beyond the line of truth. But in this we see the known tendency of the human mind to run into extremes. The repulsive features of the old system drove them far the other way. It ought to be remembered, also, that there were few, if any, who were stationed on the medium line, to arrest and delay the public mind in its fearful recoil from the "horrible decree." Had Methodism been as well known in New-England fifty years ago, as it now is, it is doubtful whether Universalism or Unitarianism would have gained much influence in this country. Late as it was introduced, and much as it was opposed, it is believed to have done much toward checking the progress of those sentiments. And perhaps it is in part owing to the earlier introduction, and more extensive spread of Methodism, in Connecticut, that Unitarianism has not gained more influence in the state. This is undoubtedly the fact in the states of Vermont, New-Hampshire, and Maine, where Methodism was introduced nearly as early as those other sentiments. The result has shown that the foregoing supposition is corroborated by facts in those cases where the experiment has been tried. These remarks may not now be credited, but the time will come, when the prejudices of the day are worn out, that the candid historian will do the subject justice. But to return—though Unitarianism and Universalism are believed to be dangerous errors, yet, as is often the case, they have contributed much, doubtless, to detect the errors and modify the features of the opposite system. Simultaneously with them, the Methodists have engaged in opposing the Calvinistic dogmas. This close examination and thorough opposition, with such other causes as may have cooperated in the work, have driven some of the peculiarities of the Hopkinsian theory into disrepute, more suddenly even than they rose into credit. The sublimated doctrine of disinterested benevolence was so like "an airy nothing," that even the speculative minds of the shrewdest metaphysicians could not find for it "a local habitation," in heaven or on earth; and the almost blasphemous dogma, that God was the efficient cause of sin, was more abhorrent, if possible, than even the horrible decree of reprobation. Both, therefore, with the exceptions hereafter mentioned, disappeared. The former, being of an ethereal character, silently evaporated into "thin air;" but the other, being of a grosser nature, and withal more essential to the system itself, *settled to the bottom*, and is now rarely visible, except when the hand of controversy shakes up the sediment. The doctrine of universal atonement, however, was retained, and the theological vocabulary was not only retained, but enlarged and improved. So that from that day to this, we hear but little of the doctrine of reprobation, or of the decrees of God, but much is said of God's "electing love," his "Divine sovereignty," and "gracious purposes." By which is meant, according to the glossary, the doctrine of unconditional election and reprobation, and of absolute predestination. The scriptures, also, which used to be quoted to prove the direct efficiency of God, in producing sin and securing the condemnation of the reprobate, receive a different explanation, varying but little, if any, from the Arminian interpretation of those passages. It cannot be doubted, I think, but there has been quite a change in the views of the great body of the Calvinists—and yet not so great and so thorough a change as appearances and terms might at first view seem to indicate. It is not easy to *eradicate* old prejudices. And it is often found that the mind will cling to the first principles of a favourite system, even after the other parts are so modified as that the new principles would supplant the old, if suffered to be carried out into a consistent whole. In every such case, much labour and argument will be spent in trying to unite the old with the new; but in every instance the rent becomes worse. This leads to a kind of vacillating policy, and an ambiguous course of argument, accompanied with reiterated complaints, that the opposers of the system misunderstand and misrepresent it. And it would be no wonder if the constant friction in the incongruous machinery should chafe the mind, and lead to a dogmatic and an impatient spirit. How far this corresponds with the existing facts, in the Calvinistic controversy, others can judge. In my own view, the peculiar circumstances of the case, connected with the known character of the human mind, fully account for the *apparent* tergiversation and changing of argument, in this controversy, without criminating the *motives* of our predestinarian brethren, as some have unjustly accused me of doing. The different parts of the system have lost, in a measure, their original affinities, and yet they have some partial and irregular attractions, which lead them to unite in unnatural and grotesque forms. And as there is no common consent and settled mode of operating among the many who are experimenting upon the materials, there are various sectional and individual formations, which are inconsistent with each other. And their incongruity is the more apparent from the unanimous effort (which I believe is the only work of union in "the class") to amalgamate each and every variety with the old substratum of the system,—"God foreordains whatsoever comes to pass."

The completion of this historical sketch, together with a view of the present state of the Calvinistic parties, may be expected in the next number. After which it is proposed to proceed to an examination of the doctrines in dispute.

NUMBER V.

SAME SUBJECT CONTINUED.

One modification of Calvinism remains to be mentioned. It is known by the name of the "New Divinity." The theological doctors connected with Yale college are the reputed authors of this system. It is evident, however, that the tendency of the Calvinistic theory has been in this direction for a number of years. The "New Divinity," so alarming to some of the Calvinists, is only the ripe fruits of the very plants which they have long cultivated with assiduous care. And why should they start back at results which they have long laboured to produce? This theory, in the first place, is an attempt to make the doctrine, and the technical terms alluded to, coincide. In the second place, it is designed, by a new philosophy of predestination, to get rid of the "logical consequences" that have always pressed heavily upon the old system. Finally, it is a device to reconcile the doctrine of depravity with the former current sentiment, that man has *natural ability* to convert himself and get to heaven without grace. The two pillars of the new system are, 1. "Sin is not a propagated property of the human soul, but consists wholly in *moral exercise*." 2. "Sin is not the necessary means of the greatest good;" or, in other words, "Sin is not preferable to holiness in its stead." The Calvinistic opposers of this theory tell us that these sentiments have been held and taught to some extent for the last ten years. They were more fully and more openly announced, however, by Dr. Taylor, of the theological school belonging to Yale College, in a concio ad clerum preached Sept. 10th, 1828. From the time of the publication of this sermon the alarm has been sounded, and the controversy has been carried on. The opposers of the new doctrine call it heresy; and in a late publication they seem to intimate that Dr. T. and his associates are nearly if not quite as heretical as the author of the sermon on predestination and election. The doctor and his friends, on the other hand, strenuously maintain that they are orthodox; and to prove it, they repeat, again and again, "We believe that God did, for his own glory, foreordain whatsoever comes to pass." The Christian Spectator, an ably conducted quarterly journal, is devoted chiefly to the defence of this theory, aided by the New-York Evangelist, and several other minor periodicals, and by a very respectable body of the clergy. What proportion, however, have embraced this system is not known; but many, both in and out of Connecticut, have espoused the cause with great zeal. The contest waxes warmer each year. Against the theory, Dr. Woods, of the Andover theological seminary, Dr. Griffin, of Williams college, Dr. Tyler, of Portland, the Rev. Mr. Hervey, of Connecticut, and several others have entered the lists of controversy; and last of all, a pamphlet, supposed to be the joint labour of a number of clergymen, has been published, in which the New Divinity is denounced as heresy, a formal separation of the Churches is predicted, and a withdrawal of patronage from Yale college is threatened on the ground that "Yale will become in Connecticut what Harvard is in Massachusetts." It is uncertain, however, whether those ultra measures will be responded to by the great body of the clergy in New-England. There is a party which still adheres to the old—I may say, perhaps, to the *oldest* modification of Calvinism in this country. This party are for maintaining the old landmarks at all hazards, rightly judging that these palliations and explanations of the system will ultimate in its destruction. They are not numerous, but still respectable as to numbers and talents. They are sustained in Boston by the Boston Telegraph, so called, a weekly periodical, which does not hesitate to go the whole length—*logical consequences and all*. Witness the following quotation from a review of my sermon, in the number for Jan. 23d. Speaking of the charge in the sermon, that Calvinism makes God the author of sin, the writer says:—"The word author is sometimes used to mean *efficient cause*. Now I am willing to admit that those scriptures which teach that God has decreed the sinful conduct of men, do imply that he is the efficient cause of moral evil. For his own glory and the greatest good he said, *Let there be sin, and there was sin!!!*" The following is another specimen of Calvinism from the same periodical. If any man "affirms that man really chooses, and that his acts of will are caused by his own free, voluntary, and efficient mind, then he is *no Calvinist*." In this last quotation, as well as in the preceding, there is the most direct opposition to Dr. Taylor, since he maintains, if I understand him, that man's is an independent agency—that the human mind is the originator of thought and volition. Thus are these two branches of the Calvinistic family directly at variance with each other. And, in fact, the Telegraph and its supporters are not only at variance with the newest divinity, but with all the different degrees of *new, newer, newest*, and denounce them all as heresy.

The present advocates of predestination and particular election may be divided into four classes:—1. The old school Calvinists. 2. Hopkinsians. 3. Reformed Hopkinsians. 4. Advocates of the New Divinity. By the reformed Hopkinsians I mean those who have left out of their creed Dr. Hopkins' doctrine of disinterested benevolence, Divine efficiency in producing sin, &c, and yet hold to a general atonement, natural ability, &c. These constitute, doubtless, the largest division in the "class" in New-England. Next, as to numbers, probably, are the new school, then Hopkinsians, and last, the old school. These subdivisions doubtless run into each other in various combinations; but the outlines of these four sub-classes are, I think, distinctly marked.

The preceding sketch has been confined mostly to the theological changes in New-England; but it will apply, to a considerable extent, to other parts of the nation. The Presbyterian Church, by reason of its ecclesiastical government, is more consolidated, and of course less liable to change than the independent Congregational Churches of the eastern states. But the Presbyterian Church has felt the changes of the east, and is coming more and more under their influence. It is now a number of years since the "triangle," as it was called, was published in New-York. This was a most severe and witty allegory, against the dogmas and bigotry of old Calvinism. From this work this old theory has obtained the epithet of "triangular." Whenever a man advocates the doctrine of limited atonement, imputed sin, and imputed righteousness, he is said to be "triangular." These old triangular notions are giving place very rapidly to modern improvements. And although the most strenuous opposition has been made in the General Assembly, in different publications, and elsewhere, yet the votes in the last General Assembly show, I think, that the whole Church is yielding herself up to the resistless march of innovation. It may be doubted whether the state of New-York is not emphatically the strong hold of the New Divinity, so far as popular sentiment is concerned; and whether, indeed, with the exception of New-Haven, there is not the greatest moral influence enlisted there, for the propagation of the new theory.

Thus have I endeavoured to glance over the various modifications and present characteristics of that mode of Christian doctrines called Calvinism. Here a few suggestions present themselves, which, from their relation to the present controversy, I will now set down.

It seems singular that, differing as they profess to, so materially, on many points, each individual of each sub-class should feel himself injured whenever Calvinism, under this common name, is opposed in any of its features. The sermon on predestination was against *Calvinism*, and lo! all parties rise up against the sermon. And yet, whether it object to Calvinistic policy or to Calvinistic doctrine, the different parties accuse their opponents of being guilty of the charge, but they themselves are clear. I cannot think of a single important position assumed by the sermon against predestination and election, which is not sustained by Calvinists themselves in opposition to some of their brethren; nor yet of a single charge against their policy, for their changes and ambiguous methods of stating and defending their doctrines, which has not been reiterated by professed Calvinists themselves against their brethren. Thus the sermon is sustained by the Calvinists themselves, and yet they all condemn it! If *some* Calvinists think that the objections of the sermon lie against some modifications of their system, is it not possible that these objections have a more *general* application than any of them seem willing to acknowledge? For example: it is objected to predestination that it "makes God the author of sin, destroys free agency, arrays God's decrees against his revealed word, mars his moral attributes, puts an excuse into the mouth of the impenitent sinner, implies unconditional reprobation, makes God partial and a respecter of persons, necessarily limits the atonement," &c. These charges, say the Calvinists, are very unjust, ungenerous—in fact, they bear false witness against our neighbours. This is said by Mr. Metcalf, and by others of the New-Haven school. And yet what says the Spectator, the organ and oracle of that school? It says of Dr. Tyler, and of others who oppose the peculiar views of Dr. Taylor, comprising, as we have seen, the great majority of Calvinists, that their views "limit God in power and goodness"—"make the worst kind of moral action the best"—"if carried out in their legitimate consequences, would lead to universalism, to infidelity, to atheism"—"they confound right and wrong, and subvert all moral distinctions"—"according to these views, mankind are bound to believe that they shall please and glorify God more by sin than by obedience, and therefore to act accordingly"—"nothing worse can be imputed to the worst of men than this theory imputes to God"!!![4] Has the author of the sermon said more than this, and worse than this, of Calvinism? And shall he be accused by these very men of bearing false witness against his brethren? And let it be observed farther, in justification of the sermon, that these charges in the Spectator are made by men who have been brought up at the feet of the Calvinistic doctors, and have themselves grown up to the character and rank of doctors in theology. They know the system thoroughly; they have made it the study of their lives, and have they testified to the truth respecting this theory? *So then has the author of the sermon*. Such is the testimony on the one side; and on the other we have decided predestinarians acknowledging, as an article of their creed, what in the sermon was urged as only a logical consequence. According to this system, says the sermon, "the *fiat* of God brought forth sin as certainly as it made the world." Hear the Boston Telegraph: —"God, for his own glory and for the good of the world, said, *Let there be sin, and there was sin!*" Now I beg the reader to look at this subject for a moment. For brevity's sake we will call the Boston Telegraph and its supporters No. 1; the Andover theological seminary and its supporters, which constitute by far the larger body of predestinarians in New-England, No. 2; and the New-Haven divines and their supporters No. 3. The sermon charges predestination with making God the author of sin. No. 2 says this is false: I neither believe it, nor is it to be inferred from my premises. *It is true*, says No. 1: I am willing to admit that God is the efficient cause of sin. He said, Let there be sin, and there was sin. *It is true*, responds No 3, that all who hold and explain predestination as Nos. 1 and 2 explain it, are exposed to the full force of the objections in the sermon—against such views "the arguments of the sermon are unanswerable." No. 2, in vindication, says that No. 1 is on the old plan—very few hold with him in these days. And as for No. 3, he is already a rank Arminian; and if he would be consistent, he must give up unconditional election, and embrace the whole Arminian theory. Thus do they destroy each other, and confirm the doctrine of the sermon. And shall we still be told that we do not understand this doctrine? Have anti-predestinarians misunderstood this from John Calvin's day to the present? Does honest No. 1 misunderstand it? Does well instructed No. 3 misunderstand it? What then is Calvinism, that cannot, through the lapse of centuries, make itself understood either by friend or foe? Is not this, of itself, a suspicious trait in its character? Let us quote a Calvinistic writer, whose sentiments are much in point, though aimed at the New Divinity:—"It is a serious ground of suspicion," says this writer, "that Dr. Taylor has failed, according to his own repeated declarations, to render his speculations intelligible to others. It must be granted that a man of sense, who is acquainted with the power of language, can, if he is disposed, make himself understood." "Some of the most intelligent men in the country have utterly failed to compass Dr. T.'s meaning in argument: so that he declares again and again, I am not understood—I am misrepresented. Who under such circumstances can refrain from suspicion?" "Another suspicious circumstance in the case is, that Dr. Taylor expresses himself in ambiguous terms and phrases, which, though they are designed to influence the mind of a reader, afford him the opportunity to avoid responsibility." See pamphlet by Edwardian, pp. 28 and 29. If this is justly said of Dr. Taylor's *recent* theory, what shall we say of a system the advocates of which, "according to their repeated declarations, have not been able to render their speculations intelligible," after the theory has had exhausted upon it the highly cultivated intellects of hosts of expositors through successive generations? "Who, under such circumstances, can refrain from suspicion?" especially since these advocates have learned "to express themselves in ambiguous terms and phrases which, though they are designed to influence the mind of a reader, afford them an opportunity to avoid responsibility." To Calvinism it may truly be said, "Out of thine own mouth will I judge thee." Let not the author of the sermon then be accused of bearing false witness, when his testimony is predicated on principles which Calvinists have laid down, and is also corroborated by men of their "own class."

Will it be said, All this is not argument. I answer, The sermon, it is supposed, contains arguments—arguments which professed predestinarians themselves tell us are unanswerable against the prevailing modes of stating and explaining the doctrine. Now let them be answered, if they can be. Let them be answered, not by giving up predestination, in the Calvinistic sense, and still professing to hold it—not by attempting to avoid the logical consequences, by giving the system the thousandth explanation, when the nine hundred and ninety-nine already given have made it no plainer, nor evaded at all the just consequences, so often charged upon it; and when these are answered, it will then be time enough to call for new arguments.

Having prepared the way, as I hope, by the preceding numbers, for the proper understanding of the controversy; and having, by the remarks just made, attempted (with what success the reader must judge) to repel the charges of misrepresentation and bearing false witness, made against me, as the author of the sermon which gave rise to the controversy, I am now prepared, in my next number to commence an examination of some of the questions of doctrine, connected with this discussion. In doing which, my object will be, to let "Greek with Greek contend" so far as to show, if possible, the inconsistency of both, and then present the doctrine which we believe to be the true system, and show how it stands untouched by the conflicting elements around it as the immovable foundation of the Church of God. I shall begin with the Divine purposes including foreknowledge; then take up human agency and responsibility; and last, regeneration, connected with the doctrine of human depravity, Divine and human agency, &c. May He that said, "Let light be, and light was," "shine in our hearts, to give the light of the knowledge of the glory of God, in the face of Jesus Christ."

NUMBER VI.

PREDESTINATION.

Definitions are the foundations of reasoning. Hence in any reply to my sermon on predestination and election it was natural and fair that the first inquiry should be, Are the definitions correct? The definition of predestination assumed in the sermon was, that unalterable purpose and efficient decree of God, by which the moral character and responsible acts of man were definitely fixed and efficiently produced. On this point the sermon joined issue. To this definition most of the notices and reviews, to the number of six or seven, which I have seen, have taken exceptions. The review in the Boston Telegraph, however, is not of this number.—That, as has already been noticed, agrees with the charge in the sermon, that "the *fiat* of God brought forth sin as directly as it made the world." We have only to leave those Calvinists, who accord to that sentiment, to struggle, as they can, against the arguments of the sermon—against the common sense of the world—against their own convictions of right and wrong—and, I may add, against their own brethren of "the class," some of whom have already publicly denounced the sentiment as "horrid blasphemy." At this day of light, in which *naked Calvinism* is abhorred by most of those who bear the name of Calvinists, it is hardly necessary to give a formal answer to such a review. We approve of the *logical consistency* of these men—we admire the moral courage that, from assumed premises, pushes out a theory to its legitimate results without flinching; but we are astonished at the *moral nerve* that can contemplate such results with complacency. For myself I confess when I see this naked system of Calvinism fulminating the curse of reprobation in the teeth of the miserable wretch whose only crime is, that his God has made him a sinner, my heart recoils with indescribable horror! Let him contemplate this picture who can. I covet not his head or his heart.

Of others who have expressed their views of the sermon there are two classes: 1. The conductors of the Christian Spectator and those who favour their views; and 2. Those who in a former number were called Reformed Hopkinsians. The latter comprehend the larger portion of Calvinists in New-England, and probably in the United States. Their views on predestination shall be noticed in another number. At present I shall direct my remarks to the letters of Mr. Metcalf and to the first and second notices of the sermon in the Christian Spectator. And here let me say, once for all, that I do not consider either of these gentlemen, or any who think with them, responsible for the doctrine of predestination as stated and opposed in the sermon. This I hope will be satisfactory. If these gentlemen should ask me why I published my sermon in terms that included Calvinists generally, without making the exception in their favour, I answer, 1. The views of Dr. Taylor and "those who believe with him," on this particular point, were unknown to me at the time. Nor is this strange, for it is but lately that those views have been fully developed—never so fully before, probably, as in Dr. Fitch's review of my sermon, already alluded to. 2. It never occurred to me that any man or any set of men holding, in respect to predestination, the doctrine of James Arminius, John Wesley, and the whole body of Methodists, would call themselves Calvinists!! This is all the apology I have, and whether or not it is sufficient, the public must judge. By acknowledging the views of these gentlemen to be Methodistical on the subject of predestination, I by no means would be understood to say this of their system as a whole—the objectionable parts will be noticed in their place. But whatever is true is none the less so for being mixed with error. There are some things, however, to be regretted and exposed in the manner in which these reviewers have expressed their doctrine of predestination, and also in the manner in which they have opposed the sermon and Arminianism generally. They complain of my definition of predestination. Mr. M. thinks it is bearing false witness. The reviewer thinks it is obviously erroneous and unjust. And yet they themselves acknowledge that the sermon is an unanswerable refutation of predestination as held by Dr. Tyler and others who oppose their views. But what is a matter of the greatest surprise is the determination with which these gentlemen persist in holding up the idea that their views essentially differ from ours. Dr. Fitch, in his answer to my reply, says:—

"There are three views, and only three, which can be taken of the Divine purposes in relation to a moral kingdom:—

1. That God, foreseeing the certainty of the conduct of his creatures, purposes merely to *treat them in a corresponding manner.*

2. That he, first of all, resolves *what the conduct of his creatures shall be,* and next resolves on such measures as *shall bring* them to that conduct.

3. That, foreseeing the conduct which will certainly ensue on the different measures it is possible for him to take, he purposes to *pursue those measures which will certainly lead to the best possible results.*"

"The first view is that which we understood to be advocated by Dr. Fisk, in the sermon we reviewed." The writer goes on farther to say that his objection to this is, "that it is utterly deficient"—"that it passes over in silence all those acts of God in creation and government by which he determines character." Of course he means to say that the *sermon* advocated a theory which left out of the question all the Divine influence in determining character. How strangely he has misunderstood the sermon, let those judge who have read it. It teaches that God hath fixed the laws of the physical and moral world: that he has a general plan, suited to all the various circumstances and contingencies of government; that God gives the sinner power to choose life; that his grace enlightens and strengthens the sinner to seek after and obtain salvation. In short, it must be obvious that no man who believes in the Divine government and in Gospel provisions can leave this influence out of his system. I will therefore venture upon the following declaration, which it is presumed Dr. Fitch cannot gainsay, namely, Dr. F. *never saw a man and never heard of a man* that was a believer in revelation, who left out of his creed all that conduct in God which determines character. That such was not the character of my creed, the reviewer might have learned in my reply to his first review, if he could not from the sermon. In the reply it is said, "As God foresaw men would sin, he also determined upon the plan he would pursue in reference to them as sinners, and arranged in the counsels of his own infinite mind the extended concatenation of causes and effects so as to 'make the wrath of man praise him,' and *deduce the greatest possible good from the best possible system.*"—And yet, strange to tell, in his answer to my reply, the reviewer says as decidedly as if it were an undisputed truth, "Dr. Fisk advocates the first," (meaning the first view of the Divine purposes given above.) "We brought forward the third," (meaning the third view.) "Now since the third upholds the fact of foreordination, free from the objections of Dr. F., we have succeeded in upholding the fact which Dr. F., as an Arminian, denies, and which Calvinists maintain." Whereas he ought to have said, for he had my statement for it directly before him, "Dr. Fisk advocates the third," and then he might have added, "Now since the third destroys the Calvinistic doctrine of foreordination, therefore in assisting Dr. Fisk to sustain the third we have succeeded in disproving the doctrine of foreordination, which Arminians deny, and Calvinists have attempted to maintain." In fact, as the reviewer says, there can be but those three views taken of the Divine purposes; and since neither I nor any other Arminian ever believed in the first, and as Dr. Fitch himself acknowledges we are directly opposed to the second, it follows that we must believe the third. But the third is the reviewer's creed: therefore on this point he is an Arminian, or we are Calvinists.

That the reviewer's theory on predestination is about the same with the Methodists' appears evident from the following quotations from Mr. Wesley, in which it will be seen that not only does Mr. Wesley's creed include all the Divine influence that goes "to determine character," but also that God "pursues measures which will certainly lead to the best possible results;" nay, that he does all that he *wisely can* to exclude sin from the moral universe. These are points for which the advocates of the New-Haven theory strongly contend. Let them see, then, how in this matter they have identified themselves with Arminians.

"To God," says Mr. Wesley, in his sermon on Divine providence, "all things are possible; and we cannot doubt of his exerting all his power, as in sustaining so in governing all that he has made. Only he that can do all things else cannot deny himself—he cannot counteract himself or oppose his own work. Were it not for this, he would destroy all sin, with its attendant pain, in a moment. But in so doing he would counteract himself, and undo all that he has been doing since he created man upon the earth. For he created man in his own image—a spirit endued with understanding, with will or affections, and liberty, without which he would have been incapable of either virtue or vice. He could not be a moral agent, any more than a tree or a stone. Therefore (with reverence be it spoken) the Almighty himself cannot do this thing. He cannot thus contradict himself or undo what he has done. But were he to do this, it would imply no wisdom at all, but barely a stroke of omnipotence. Whereas all the manifold wisdom of God (as well as all his power and goodness) is displayed in governing man as man—as an intelligent and free spirit, capable of choosing either good or evil."

Again. In the sermon entitled, The Wisdom of God's Counsels: "In the moral world evil men and evil spirits continually oppose the Divine will, and create numberless irregularities. Here therefore is full scope for the exercise of all the riches both of the wisdom and knowledge of God in counteracting all the wickedness and folly of men and all the subtlety of Satan, to carry on his glorious design, the salvation of lost mankind." Now let me ask the reviewer, is this leaving out all the Divine influence that determines character? Is not this maintaining that, "in view of the measures that it was possible for God to take, he purposes to pursue those measures that will certainly lead to the best possible result?" Is Dr. Fitch ignorant of what Methodists hold to? or is he unwilling to identify himself with us? Ignorant of *my* views he could not be, I think, after reading my reply.—Why, then, does he persist in talking of a difference where there is none?

Mr. Metcalf has taken a more correct view of the subject. After reading my reply, he says, "if you will preach this doctrine to your Methodist brethren thoroughly and forcibly, and sustain it with the strong arguments on which the doctrine rests, if they do not call it Calvinism, I will acknowledge they do not understand the term as I do. And if you will preach in the same way to Calvinists, if they too do not call it Calvinism, I will grant that even *they* too sometimes differ about terms. If you will take this course, I think when you shall see what the doctrine will be called, the astonishment you express that it should be regarded as Calvinism will wear away." Now how surprised Mr. M. will be when he learns that we have always preached this doctrine as thoroughly and forcibly as we could, and neither Methodists nor Calvinists ever suspected it was Calvinism until he and those who believe with him incorporated it into their creed, and *for some reason* unknown to us, called it Calvinism! And how surprised we all are to find that he who was so anxious to be heard in the Christian Advocate and Journal, for the purpose of informing Methodists what Calvinism was, and of disabusing their minds of erroneous conceptions on this subject, himself understands neither Methodism nor Calvinism!! Yet so it is, Calvinists themselves being judges. Dr. Tyler, Dr. Griffin, Dr. Woods, the author of "Views in Theology," the author or authors of the pamphlet by an Edwardian, all condemn the New-Haven theory of predestination as anti-Calvinistic, and as being essentially Arminian.

Dr. Fitch acknowledges that we agree in some of the first principles. In reply to my answer he says, "It was certainly our intention to place this contested doctrine on grounds which our Wesleyan brethren *could not* dispute, and it gives us pleasure to find that in this we have had complete success!" There are two things a little remarkable connected with this sentiment. One is, that the writer should so express himself as to convey the idea that *he* has traced up the subject to first principles with much care, and, to his *great satisfaction, has succeeded in convincing us* of the correctness of his premises. Whereas it is evident from the passages already given from Mr. Wesley, and from the universal sentiments of the Wesleyan Methodists, that the New-Haven doctors have *at length* come on to our ground; and it gives *us great pleasure* to find that, from *some source*, arguments in favour of our system have with them met with *complete success*. The other thing that strikes me as remarkable is, that after the reviewer had acknowledged that we were agreed in these first principles, he should immediately go on to say, as has already been mentioned, that I and the Arminians hold to the first view he has given of the three possible views that might be taken of predestination, and deny the third; when at the same time the third contains *those very first principles* in which he says we are agreed. This looks so much like a contradiction, almost in the same breath, that I really know not what other name to give it. If these gentlemen are disposed to come into the fortress of truth, and assist us in manning our guns and working our artillery against error, we certainly can have no objection. We are fond of help. But they must pardon us if we revolt a little at the idea of their taking the lead in this business, and accounting us as mere novices who have only learned, and that too from themselves, some of the *elementary principles*. Nay, they must not wonder if we refuse outright to be crowded from our present commanding position in the fortress of truth, and to be placed in front of our own batteries, merely to give our *new allies* an opportunity to blow us up *with our own ordnance!*

In reply to my objection to the reviewer that "it was an abuse of terms to call the *permission of sin, not hindering it*, &c, a foreordination or purpose that it shall be," &c, he has said, "If an evil, unavoidable and hateful, is allowed by the Creator to come into his kingdom, in one place and time rather than any other, and is thus *particularly disposed of* by his providence, because it is a disposition of it the best possible, is there no purpose of God in relation to the thing? In doing his own pleasure, in this case, does he not decide on the fact of the entrance of sin into his kingdom just when and where it does?" Now I beg the reader to go over this last paragraph once more, and then say if he does not agree with me in the following sentiment, namely, there rarely occurs in any writer an instance of so complete an evasion of a contested question as is here exhibited. Is there no difference between a "purpose in relation to a thing," and the foreordaining or decreeing that the thing shall be? And pray what is meant by God's "deciding on the fact of the entrance of sin into his kingdom?" You can make it mean almost any thing. But taking the whole of Dr. Fitch's theory on the subject, he means to say, doubtless, that since the entrance of sin was unavoidable, God determined to restrain and control it so as to suffer it to do the least harm possible—preferring holiness in its stead in every place where it occurs. And this is foreordaining sin!! This is predestination!! Let us illustrate this by a case in point. Cicero, a Roman consul, knew that Cataline was plotting treason against the commonwealth. Cicero perceived that this *hated treason*, though unavoidable, was not wholly unmanageable. He determined therefore to "make a disposition of it the best possible." He took his measures accordingly. By these Cataline and the principal conspirators were driven out of the city, and compelled, before their plans were matured, to resort to open hostilities. Thus the citizens were aroused and united, and the state saved. In this way the evils of the conspiracy were suffered to come upon the commonwealth "in one place and time rather than any other," and "were thus *particularly disposed of*" by Cicero. In this case the consul had a special "purpose about the thing." He determined to drive the conspirators into open war, rather than suffer them privately to corrupt all they could, and then fill the city with fire and slaughter. The question now is, and it is put not to the reviewer, for he still persists in the use of his terms, but it is put to the common understanding of community, Did the Roman consul ordain or foreordain, or predestinate the treason of Cataline? If by common consent all answer, No, such a statement is a libel upon the consul; and if, in addition to this common understanding of the term, the theological use of the term will not bear such a construction; if the great body of the Calvinists of the present day, and of New-England even, use the term in a different sense, it remains to be seen how the New-Haven divines can stand up before the world and say, "We believe God hath foreordained whatsoever comes to pass."

Before closing this number I ought, perhaps, to say a few things, if not in the defence, at least explanatory of that course of reasoning in the sermon in which I undertook to show that foreknowledge is antecedent to foreordination. To this Mr. Metcalf and others have objected because, say they, God must first have determined to make moral agents before he could know they would sin: therefore his knowledge or his foreknowledge in this case must depend upon his determination. This objection, at least so far as the New-Haven theology is concerned, is founded in error. What says Dr. Fitch? "That God, *foreseeing* the conduct which will certainly ensue on the different measures it is possible for him to take, *purposes*," &c. The sermon says, "God knows all that is, or will be, or might be, under any possible contingency," and that "his plan is the result of his infinite knowledge—the decrees of his throne flow forth from the eternal fountain of his wisdom." Where is the discrepancy here? God saw this general plan, as a whole, before he resolved upon its adoption; (I speak now of the order of thought;) he saw, if he made free moral agents, and governed them as such, sin would ensue. And he also saw what he might do in that case to counteract and overrule it to his own glory and the good of the universe.—And he judged, in his infinite wisdom, that such a moral universe, notwithstanding the sin that would certainly result from it, would, on the whole, be the best; and therefore upon this *foreknowledge* of the whole, God *founded* his determination to create the universe, and govern it as proposed. God's foreknowledge of the *certainty* of any event in this universe, it must be acknowledged, depended upon his determination to create and govern the universe. And in *this sense* his purpose was *causa sine qua non*, a cause without which any given event would not have happened, and therefore could not have been foreseen as *certain*. But then it should be remembered that there was a foreknowledge anterior to all this, and which was, in fact, the foundation of all subsequent instances of knowing or decreeing. It is therefore true in the sense in which the sentiment is advanced and sustained in the sermon, that "God foreknows in order to predestinate, but he does not (primarily) predestinate in order to foreknow."

To conclude: from the view taken in this number it appears that one class of Calvinists acknowledge that predestination is chargeable with all that was included in my definition of it. Another, and a rapidly increasing class, have given up Calvinian predestination, and, in all but the name, have in that point come on to the Methodist ground. There is still another class, who are evidently not Arminians, but still deny the correctness of my definition of their doctrine. They say they are not chargeable with such a doctrine, either directly or by inference. In the next number, therefore, an attempt will be made to sustain from their own positions this definition.

NUMBER VII.

PREDESTINATION, CONTINUED.

From my last number the reader will perceive that there are two classes of Calvinists, so-called, with whom we have no need to contend; with one there is no cause of controversy, because they have given up the doctrine; and with the other there is no *need* of controversy, because their plain manner of avowing the doctrine, *logical consequences and all*, renders any arguments against it unnecessary. Its character is too monstrous and abhorrent to gain much credit. There is yet another and a larger portion, who, while they reject the views both of the New-Haven divines and of the old school and Hopkinsian Calvinists, are nevertheless strongly opposed to the issue proposed in the sermon. They deny, as appears from some public intimations and many private statements, that I have given a fair representation of the doctrine. They appear to manifest as much horror as an Arminian would to the idea, that "the responsible acts of moral agents are definitely fixed and efficiently produced by the purpose and decree of God,"—that these acts "are the result of an overruling and controlling power,"—"that the will, in all its operations, is governed and irresistibly controlled by some secret impulse, some fixed and all-controlling arrangement." Hence, I suppose, if it can be proved that these are the genuine characteristics of Calvinism, the system itself will, by many at least, be given up. At any rate, since the exception is taken to the definition of the doctrine, it may be presumed, by sustaining this, we sustain our own cause and refute the opposite. The present inquiry then is, are these, in very deed, the characteristics of absolute predestination? I shall endeavour to maintain that they are. Let the intelligent and the candid judge.

1. It may be urged as a consideration of no small weight in this question, that all but predestinarians, as well as many predestinarians themselves, have entertained these views of the doctrine. With respect to anti-predestinarians, I know of no exception; all unite, in charging these things, directly or by consequence, upon the Calvinistic system. And will Calvinists say, this is owing to prejudice and to a want of understanding the subject? With what kind of modesty will they assume that they are free from blinding prejudice in *favour* of their own doctrine, and all the world beside are prejudiced against it? It may be asserted, as it often has been, that these doctrines are humbling to the pride of the natural heart, and this is the ground of the universal opposition to them! But this is a gratuitous assumption of what ought first to be proved, viz. that these doctrines are true; and it also exhibits a most reprehensible spirit of pride and Pharisaism—a spirit that says to a brother, "Stand by, for I am holier than thou!" There have doubtless been as many eminently pious Arminians as Calvinists, and how is it, that these men have never had this doctrine so explained to them as to be able to see it free from these charges?

But not only anti-predestinarians have universally entertained these opinions of this doctrine; even the advocates themselves have, in a great variety of instances, acknowledged the same. Mention has before been made, (in the sermon,) of the opposition raised against free will, by the Calvinists of Mr. Wesley's day—and quotations have also been given from the early Calvinistic authors, showing how decidedly they held that God moved the will to sin, by a direct positive influence. To these we may add all the Hopkinsians of modern days, who openly acknowledge "that those scriptures which teach that God has decreed the sinful acts of men, do imply that he is the efficient cause of moral evil." (See review of my sermon in the Boston Telegraph.) It should not be forgotten, moreover, that the New-Haven divines, who have studied Calvinism all their lives, with the best opportunities for understanding it, inform us that the view of Calvinism which makes sin preferable to holiness in its stead, is unanswerably exposed to all the objections brought against it in the sermon. It is known too, that most of the Methodists in New-England, and many elsewhere, were educated predestinarians; but have revolted from the traditions of their fathers for the very reason that Calvinism is what we have described it to be. The Universalists are almost all predestinarians, and they understand that this doctrine necessarily implies the *Divine efficiency* in producing sin; and hence they very consistently infer that God is not angry with them, and will not punish them for being controlled by his decrees.

Suppose now an intelligent person, who knew nothing of the arguments on either side, should be informed of what is true in this case, viz. that a great portion, probably on the whole by far the greatest portion of predestinarians, and *all* anti-predestinarians, understood the doctrine of absolute predestination, as involving directly, or by consequence, certain specified principles; but that a portion of predestinarians persisted in denying that these principles were involved in the doctrine; and suppose this intelligent person should be informed of the additional facts, that these predestinarians had tried all their skill at explanation and argument, generation after generation, but had never succeeded in the view of the other party in freeing their doctrine from these charges, nay, that they had so far failed of it, that many, very many were leaving them, and adopting the anti-predestinarian system, for the *very reason* that they could not rid the system, in which they had been educated, from those principles which were charged upon it—and that even among those who had adhered to the old doctrine there were new modes of explaining and stating the theory, constantly springing up, until finally numbers of them *had explained themselves entirely out of the doctrine*, and into the opposite sentiment; and that very many others, by adhering to the doctrine, and following out the principles involved in it, had come to the conclusion that there was "no hell"—no judgment, and "no angry God." Suppose, I say, this intelligent man should be informed of all these facts, and then be requested to *presume* whether or not these contested principles were involved in the doctrine—what would be his judgment? I need not answer this question. There is *strong* presumptive evidence that the views in the sermon are correct.

2. Another reason for believing that this doctrine is what we have defined it to be, and involves in it the principles we have charged upon it, is drawn from the terms in which it is expressed, and the manner and circumstances in which these terms are used. The more common terms are *decree, predestination, foreordination, predetermination, purpose*, &c.—These are all authoritative terms, and carry with them the idea of absolute sovereignty. But lest they should not be sufficiently strong and imperious, they are, in this theory, generally accompanied by some strong qualifying terms, such as *sovereign decree, eternal and immutable purposes;* and without any reference to other bearings, the whole is placed on the ground of God's absolute and sovereign will. These sovereign decrees, however, are not proposed to his subjects in the light of a law enforced by suitable sanctions, and liable to be broken. They are the *secret counsels* of his own will; and so far from being law, that often, perhaps oftener than otherwise, in the moral world, they are in direct opposition to the precepts of the law. When these decrees come in contact with the law they supersede it. Laws may sometimes be broken, the decrees, never. God commits his law to subordinate moral agents, who may break or keep them; but his decrees he executes himself. It should also be understood that the advocates of this theory, in their late controversy with Dr. Taylor, strenuously maintain that sin, wherever it occurs, is preferable to holiness in its stead, and is the *necessary means* of the *greatest good.* The idea that God, foreseeing what moral agents would do, under all possible circumstances, *so ordered his works* as to take up and incorporate into his plan the foreseen volitions of moral agents, and thus constitute a grand whole, as perfect as any system which involves a moral government could be, they discard as rank Arminianism. Now is it possible that decrees like these, concealed in the eternal mind of him that conceived them—dependent solely on Almighty power to execute them, not modified by subordinate agencies, but made to control these agencies with absolute and arbitrary sway; can it be *possible*, I say, that such decrees do not efficiently control and actuate the human will. Must not he who, in this manner, forms and executes the general plan, also form and execute all its parts? Must not he who gives the first impulse to this concatenation of events, linked together by his eternal purposes, follow up the whole with his continued and direct agency, and carry on this work in every mind and through every

emotion? Most assuredly he must. His is, undoubtedly, according to this doctrine, that operative, controlling and propelling energy that

"Lives through all life, extends through all extent,

Acts undivided, operates unspent."

And that we may be sure not to misrepresent the Calvinists on this subject, let them speak for themselves. Dr. Hill, who is a modern, and is reputed a moderate Calvinist, says:—"The Divine decree is the determination to *produce* the universe, that is, the *whole series* of *beings* and *events* that was then future." Dr. Chalmers, who has been esteemed so moderate a Calvinist, that some had doubted whether he had not given up absolute predestination altogether, comes out in his sermon on predestination in the following language:—"Every step of every individual character, receives as determinate a character from the hand, of God, as every mile of a planet's orbit, or every gust of wind, or every wave of the sea, or every particle of flying dust, or every rivulet of flowing water. This power of God knows no exceptions: it is absolute and unlimited. And while it embraces the vast, it carries its resistless influence to all the minute and unnoticed diversities of existence. It *reigns* and operates through all the secrecies of the inner man. It gives birth to every purpose, it gives impulse to every desire, it gives shape and colour to every conception. It wields an entire ascendancy over every attribute of the mind; and the will, and the fancy, and the understanding, with all the countless variety of their hidden and fugitive operations, are submitted to it. It gives movement and direction through every one point of our pilgrimage. At no moment of time does it abandon us. It follows us to the hour of death, and it carries us to our place, and to our everlasting destiny in the region beyond it!!!" These quotations need no comment; if they do not come up to all we have ever charged upon this doctrine, there is no definite meaning in words.

But we have another authority on this subject, which bears more directly on the Calvinists of this country, the Assembly's Catechism. Dr. Fitch, who is certainly as well qualified to judge in this matter as another man, informs us, through the medium of the Christian Spectator, that "the articles of faith prepared by that body, (the assembly of English and Scotch divines at Westminster,) are considered as expressing essentially the views not only of the Presbyterian Church in this country, but also of the orthodox Congregational Churches of New-England." It is known, also, that the Shorter Catechism has been almost universally used by them in their families, and in the religious instruction of their children. Here then we have a standard of faith, which all the *classes*, I suppose, will acknowledge,—and what saith it? After stating that the decrees of God are his eternal purpose, according to the counsel of his own will, whereby, for his own glory, he hath foreordained whatsoever cometh to pass, it goes on to say, "God *executeth* his decrees in the works of creation and providence," and then for farther explanation adds—"God's works of providence are his most holy, wise, and powerful, preserving and governing all his creatures and all their actions." This is certainly an awkward sentence, if I may be allowed to say this of the productions of an assembly which has been characterised as a paragon of excellency in erudition and theology. Its meaning, however, according to grammar and logic, must be, that by his acts of providence God, in a most holy, wise, and powerful manner, preserves and governs both all his creatures, and all their actions. But as it seems to be a solecism to talk about *preserving actions*, we will understand *preserving* to belong to *creatures*, and *governing* to *actions*, and then it will be thus: God powerfully preserves all his creatures, and powerfully governs all their actions: and it is in this way he *executes* his decrees. There are evidently two methods of governing. That control which is made up of legal precepts, and sanctions, and retributions, is called a government; not that all the subjects of such a government always obey its ordinances, but if they violate them, they are subjected to punishment. *This* is evidently not the kind of government that the assembly contemplated. It was a government by which God *executed his decrees;* but, as we have seen, his decrees are not his laws, for they are frequently in direct opposition to his laws. Decree and law are not only frequently opposed, in respect to the moral action demanded by each, but even where those demands are coincident they differ greatly in the *manner* and *certainty* of their fulfilment. Of course government, by *executing decrees*, is another thing altogether from government by *executing laws*. But there is another kind of government. It is that *efficient control* of a superior, by which a being or an act is *made to be what it is*, in opposition to *non-existence*, or a *different existence*. Now this appears to be precisely the kind of government alluded to when it said, "God *executes his decrees* by powerfully *governing* all the actions of his creatures." That is, he efficiently produces and controls all the responsible volitions, good and bad, of the moral universe. And what is this, but affirming all that the sermon has affirmed on this subject? If any one is disposed to deny that this is a fair exposition of the Catechism, let him reflect that as he cannot pretend that *government* here means a *legal administration*, it will be incumbent on him to show what other fair construction can be put upon it than the one given above; to show how God can execute a secret decree, by his own powerful act, in any other way than in the one already explained.

In corroboration of the foregoing views it should also be borne in mind, that the Calvinists uniformly use these very same terms, *decree, predestination*, &c. in the *same sense*, in reference to *all events*. They say, God's decrees extend to all events, physical and moral, good and evil, by which they must mean, if they mean any thing intelligible, that his predestination bears the same relation to all events. If then his decree of election embraces the means to the accomplishment of the end, so also must his decree of reprobation. If his decree of election requires for its accomplishment an *efficient* operation, so also does his decree of reprobation. If Divine agency is directly and efficiently, requisite to produce a good volition, it must follow that it is in the same sense requisite to produce a sinful volition.

To tell us a thousand times, without any distinction or discrimination, that all things are *equally* the result of the Divine decree, and then tell us that the relation between God's decree and sin is essentially different from the relation existing between his decree and holiness, would certainly be a very singular and unwarrantable use of language. How then, I inquire, does God produce holy volitions?—Why, say the Calvinists, by a direct, positive, and efficient influence upon the will, and in proof quote —"Thy people *shall* be willing in the day of thy power." Well, how, I ask again, does God execute his decrees respecting unholy volitions? Consistency requires the same reply. But, says the Calvinist, he need not exert the same influence to produce unholy volitions, because it is in accordance with the nature of sinful men to sin. Indeed! and is not this *nature* the result of a decree? It would seem God approaches his work of executing his decree *respecting sin*, either more reluctantly or with greater difficulty, so that it requires two steps to execute this, and only one the other. It is in both cases, however, equally his work. This will be seen more clearly if we turn our attention to the first sin; for it is certainly as much against a perfectly holy nature to commit sin, as it is against an unholy nature to have a holy volition. Hence the one as much requires a direct and positive influence as the other, and therefore the passage in the 110th Psalm, if it applies at all to a positive Divine influence in changing the will, must have a much more extensive meaning, than has been generally supposed. It should be paraphrased thus:—Not only shall thy elect people, who are yet in their sins, and therefore not yet in a strict and proper sense thine, be made willing to become holy in the day that thou dost efficiently change their will, but also thy angels and thy first created human pair, who were before their fall more truly thine, as they were made perfectly holy, shall be made willing to become unholy in the day that thou dost efficiently change their wills from submission to rebellion. For if

Divine efficiency is necessary to make a naturally perverse will holy, it is also necessary to make a naturally holy will perverse.

I am aware that we may be met here by this reply, that although God does efficiently control the will, still it is in a way suited to the nature of mind, and consistent with free agency, because he operates upon the mind through the influence of moral suasion, or by the power of motives. To this it may be answered, that the Calvinists generally condemn Dr. Taylor's views of conversion, because they suspect him of holding that motives alone convert the sinner; whereas they deem it necessary that the Holy Spirit should act directly upon the will; if so, then, as I have shown above, it is also necessary that there should be a direct Divine influence upon the will of a holy being, to make him sinful. And this more especially, since both changes are decreed, and both stand in the same relation to the Divine purpose. But this doctrine of motives leads me to another argument, viz.

3. That the view I have taken of predestination is correct, appears evident from the Calvinistic doctrine of motives, especially when this doctrine is viewed in connection with the Calvinistic theory of depravity.

The doctrine of motives I understand to be this, that "the power of volition is never excited, nor *can be*, except in the presence and from the excitement of motives," (see "Views in Theology,") and that the mind must necessarily be swayed by the strongest motive, or by what appears to the mind to be the greatest good. Dr. Edwards, following Leibnitz, incorporated this doctrine of philosophical necessity with the Calvinistic theology. In this he has been followed by a great portion, I believe, of the Calvinistic clergy. Without stopping here to attempt a refutation of this theory, my present object is to show that it necessarily fastens upon Calvinism the charges brought against it, and sustains the definition that has been given to predestination. For since God creates both the mind and the motives, and brings them together for the *express purpose* that the former should be swayed by the latter, it follows conclusively that God *efficiently* controls the will, and produces all its volitions. And this is according to express Calvinistic teaching:—"God," says the author of "Views in Theology," already quoted, "God is the determiner of perceptions, and perceptions are the determiners of choices." The inference therefore is plain and unavoidable, *God is the determiner of choices*. The plea that God does not produce volitions, by a direct influence, but indirectly, through second causes, avails nothing. Although there should be ten, or ten thousand intermediate links, if they are all arranged by our Creator in such order as to produce the intellectual vibration intended, whenever he pleases to give the impulse, what is the difference? In point of efficient agency, none at all. Nor yet will it alter the case to say, that "this effect is produced by God through such a medium as is suited to the nature of the mind, and therefore it cannot be said, that God does any violence to the will, or to man's free agency." God created the *mind*, and the *means* that were to influence it. He gave to mind its nature, and to motives their influence and arrangement, for *this very purpose*. Hence, unless man can unmake himself, he is *bound by the law of his nature* to act in all cases as he does. Why talk about a *free* agency when it is such an agency as *must*, by *the constitution* of *God*, lead inevitably to sin and ruin! That old, and in the premises, foolish reply, that man could do differently, *if he chose*, does not help the case. It is only saying, the nature of man is such that it is governed by his perceptions, and since "God is the determiner of perceptions, and perceptions the determiners of choices," whenever God pleases to alter the perceptions so as thereby to change the choice, *then*, and not before, man can do differently. According to this doctrine is it possible, according to the very nature of mind, for the choice to be different until the perceptions are changed? And can the perceptions be changed, until God changes them? To answer either or both of these questions in the affirmative, would be to give up the doctrine of motives. To answer them in the negative, would be to entail upon the doctrine all that I have charged upon it. The advocates of the theory may have their choice. Nor yet, again, will it destroy the force of this argument, to say "man has an *unholy nature;* and this is the reason why the motives presented influence him to sin; therefore the guilt is chargeable upon himself, and God is clear." For, in the first place, this would not account for the first unholy volitions of holy angels and the first human pair.

This argument presupposes that, but for the consideration of man's *unholy nature*, the charge against the Calvinistic theory would be valid. And inasmuch as here are cases in which the argument obviously affords no relief to the system, it follows that in these uses, at least, God is the efficient and procuring cause of unholy volitions—and therefore the charges against predestination are established. But by a little farther attention we shall see that this argument affords as little relief to the system in the case of man as he now is. For this first sin, which was itself the necessary result of the Divine arrangement and of positive Divine influence, threw, if possible, a stronger and a more dire necessity over all the coming generations of men. For this act entailed upon man a depraved heart. Hence this corrupt nature came upon man without his knowledge or agency. We trace it back then, thus:—Man's love of sin was produced by the unholy choice of the first pair—that choice was produced by perceptions—these perceptions were produced by motives—and these motives were brought by God to bear upon the minds which he had made for this very purpose—therefore God, by design, and because he purposed it, produced our corrupt nature; and then, for the express purpose of leading that unholy nature to put forth unholy volitions, he brings those motives to bear upon our minds, which, from the unavoidable nature of those minds, *must produce* the sin designed. It is thus that, according to his theory, our Creator binds the human mind by the strong cords of depravity with one hand, and with the other lashes it, by the maddening scourge of motives, into all the excitement of unholy delirium; and then, for his own glory, consigns the sinner over to the prison house of wo!! Turn this system, then, as you will, you find this doctrine of predestination binding the human mind, and efficiently producing all the volitions of the moral universe. The strong arm of Jehovah not more directly and irresistibly moves and binds the planets in their orbits, than it moves and controls, in the mysterious circle of his eternal decrees, "all the actions of all his creatures."

I know, as a closing argument, it is urged, whatever may be our inferences, we all know that we are free, and that we are responsible, because *we are conscious of it*. This is a most singular course of reasoning, and seems to have been adopted to reconcile contradictions. If this doctrine be true, I am not *sure* that I am free, and that I am responsible merely because I feel that I am. I am at least *quite* as conscious that I ought not to be held responsible for what is unavoidable, as I am that I am possessed of moral liberty. Break down my consciousness in one case, and you prepare the way for me to suspect it of fallacy in another. And if I must give up my consciousness, between two alternatives I will choose that which will not involve the government of God in injustice, and myriads of intelligent beings in unavoidable perdition. Hence, with Dr. Edwards' premises, which he holds in common with Lord Kaimes, I would come to his lordship's conclusion, viz. that God never intended to hold men responsible, and the universal feeling of responsibility is a kind of pious fraud—a salutary delusion, imposed as a check and restraint upon man here, but to be followed by no unpleasant consequences either here or hereafter. But this would be charging our Creator with both deception and folly—deception in the delusive consciousness of responsibility, and folly in suffering Lord Kaimes and others to disclose the secret, and frustrate the Divine purpose! This cannot be. The charge of deception and of fallacy, therefore, must be rolled back from consciousness and from the throne of God upon the doctrine of predestination. And if the reaction should crush the theory for ever, it would doubtless be a blessing to the Church and to the world.

To conclude. For the reasons given, I must still maintain that the charges contained in the sermon against that modification of Calvinism I am now opposing, are just; and the definition assumed, is correct. If the advocates of the system can clear themselves, or their doctrine, let it be done. If not, let one of two courses be pursued—either let the system be abandoned, or *let us have it as it is.*

I have dwelt the longer on this subject, because I am weary, and I believe we all are, of hearing the oft-repeated complaint, "You misrepresent us!" "You mistake our doctrine!"

In the next No., by the leave of Providence, the nature of human agency, and the ground of human responsibility, will be examined.

NUMBER VIII.
MORAL AGENCY AND ACCOUNTABILITY.

By what has been said on the theory of Calvinistic predestination, it will be seen, I think, that this system involves such necessity of moral action as is incompatible with free agency. It is possible, I grant, to give to the terms *will, liberty, free agency,* such a definition as will make these terms, *thus defined,* compatible with the other peculiarities of the Calvinistic system.—Both parties agree that man is a free moral agent; both maintain that he is responsible; but we maintain that what the Calvinists call free moral agency, is not such in fact as is commonly understood by the term, nor such as is requisite to make man accountable. Here, therefore, we are again thrown back upon our definitions, as the starting point of argument. What is that power, or property, or faculty of the mind, which constitutes man a free moral agent? It is the power of choice, connected with liberty to choose either good or evil. Both the *power* and *liberty* to choose either *good* or *evil* are requisite to constitute the free agency of a probationer. It has been contended that choice, though from the condition of the moral agent it must of necessity be exclusively *on one side,* is nevertheless free; since it implies a *voluntary* preference of the mind. Hence it is contended that the fallen and the holy angels, glorified and lost human spirits, though some of these are confined in an impeccable state, and the others have a perpetual and invincible enmity to good, are nevertheless free agents. With respect to the free agency of these beings, a question might be started, whether it is such as renders them responsible for their *present acts,* the decision of which might have some bearing on the subject under investigation; but not such bearing as would make it important to discuss it here. If they are responsible for their *present acts,* it must be on account of a former probation, which by sin they have judicially forfeited. Or if any one thinks otherwise, and is disposed to maintain that a being who is not, and *never was* so circumstanced as to render the choice of good possible to him, is nevertheless a free moral agent, in any such sense as renders him accountable, with such a sentiment at present I have no controversy. Indeed such an opinion is so violent an outrage upon all the acknowledged principles of justice, that to controvert it would be a work of little profit.

It is certain that the moral standing of those angels and men whose states are now unalterably fixed, differs materially from their probationary state; and this difference renders their moral agency unsuited to illustrate the agency of beings who are on probation. Man, in this life, is in a state of trial; good and evil are presented before him as objects of choice; and upon this choice are suspended eternal consequences of happiness or misery. Of a being thus circumstanced, it is not enough to say he is free to choose as he does, unless you can say, also, he is equally free to make an opposite choice.—Hence, in defining the free agency of man, as a probationer, we say, as above, that it implies a power of choice, with full liberty to choose either good or evil.

The foregoing definition, at first view, seems sufficient for all practical purposes, and so indeed it would have been, if a speculative philosophy had not thrown it into the alembic of metaphysics for decomposition and analysis. It is doubtful whether this process has subserved the cause of truth; nay, it is certain, I think, that it has produced many perplexing refinements and speculations that have greatly aided the cause of error. Into these abstrusities, therefore, it seems necessary to follow this question, to try, if possible, to draw out and combine the elements of truth.

Having defined free agency to mean *the power of choice*, &c, it is asked again, *What is this power of choice?* It is probable that the different answers given to this question constitute the fundamental differences between Calvinists and Arminians. To the above question some, like the reply of the Jews to Christ, have said, "We cannot tell." And they give this evasive reply perhaps for a reason similar to that which influenced the Jews; they fear that a definite answer will involve themselves or their theory in difficulty. This is a very convenient way to avoid responsibility, but not indicative of much fairness, or confidence in their cause. When men have involved their system in apparent contradictions, it will hardly satisfy the candid inquirer after truth to see them start aside from the very point that is to give character to their whole system. We are told by men who reason upon foreknowledge, &c, that "God hath decreed whatsoever comes to pass;" and then we are told that all men are free, and they enter into a great deal of metaphysical speculation about foreknowledge, the nature of voluntary action, &c, to prove these positions; but when they are pressed upon this point, "How can you reconcile with free agency that kind of Divine efficiency necessary to secure the execution of the decrees, and that kind of dependency of moral agents which this efficiency implies?" the reply is, "We cannot tell—the how in the case we cannot explain." This evasion might be allowable, perhaps, in either of the two following cases: 1. If the apparent discrepancy of the two positions grew out of what is *mysterious*, and not of what is *palpably contradictory;* or, 2. If both propositions were so *clearly proved*, that it would do greater violence to our reasons, and be a greater outrage upon all acknowledged principles of belief, to disbelieve either of them, than it would to believe them with all their apparent contradictions. With respect to the first alternative, it appears to me, and doubtless it would so appear to all whose prejudices did not mislead the mind, that the want of apparent agreement between the two is not for lack of light in the case, but from the natural incongruity of the things compared. When you say, "God executes his decrees by efficiently controlling the will of man," and say also, "The mind of man is free," both these propositions are clear; there is nothing mysterious about them. But you say, perhaps, "The mystery is in the want of light to see the *agreement* of the two; we cannot *see* their agreement, but we should not therefore infer that they do not agree." I answer, What is light, in this case, but a clear conception of the propositions? This we have, and we see that they are, *in their nature*, incompatible; and the more light you can pour upon this subject, the more clearly must this incompatibility appear. If you say that "perhaps neither you nor I fully understand the meaning of these propositions;" then I reply, *We have no business to use them.* "Who is this that darkens counsel by words without knowledge?" And this is what I have already complained of; men will reason themselves into propositions which they call doctrinal facts, but which seem to the eye of common sense to have all the characteristics of contradictions, and when we urge these contradictions in objection, the objection is not allowed to have any weight, because we do not fully understand the propositions. So then the propositions must be received, *though we do not understand them!* and though, as far as we do understand them, they are obviously incompatible!! Is this the way to gain knowledge, and to make truth triumphant? How much more consistent to say, Since it is evident the mind is free, and since the doctrine of predestination is apparently incompatible with that freedom, therefore this doctrine should be exploded!

Or will this second alternative be resorted to? Will it be said that both of these propositions are so clearly proved, that to deny them would do greater violence to our reasons, and the principles of belief, than to acknowledge them, notwithstanding their apparent incongruity? Let us examine them. Of one of them we cannot doubt, unless we doubt all primary truths, viz. That the human mind is free. It is presumed, if the question come to this, that they must either give up human liberty or the dogma of predestination, candid Calvinists themselves would not hesitate; they would say, the *former* must stand, whatever becomes of the *latter*. If I am correct here, it follows that, predestinarians themselves being judges, the doctrine of predestination is not so clear as some other moral truths. But is there any thing clearer than that man ought not to be held accountable for what is unavoidable? that he ought not to be held to answer for volitions that are efficiently controlled by a superior? To me this is as clear as consciousness itself can make it, and I think it must be to mankind in general. If I am correct, then we come to the conclusion at once, that to believe in the compatibility of predestination with human liberty and accountability does more violence to the laws of belief than it would to discard predestination. Whatever, therefore, may *seem* to be favourable to this doctrine, should be sacrificed to a stronger claim upon our belief in another direction. But, that the argument may be set in as strong light as possible, let the evidence of predestination be adduced. What is it? It is not consciousness certainly; and it is almost as clear that it is not moral demonstration by a course of reasoning. The most I believe that has ever been said, in the way of moral demonstration, has been in an argument founded on foreknowledge, which argument, it is supposed by the author, is fairly disposed of in the sermon on predestination, by reasoning which has not, to his knowledge, ever been refuted. A refutation has been attempted, I grant, by some of the reviewers of the sermon, but the only apparent success that attended those attempts was, as we have already seen, in consequence of their taking the very ground of the sermon, and building the decrees of God upon a prior view and knowledge of all possible contingencies. If consciousness and reasoning are taken away from this doctrine, it has nothing left to stand upon but testimony. And no testimony but Divine will here be of any authority; and does revelation prove this doctrine? In the sermon on predestination it was stated that "there was not a single passage in the Bible which teaches directly that God hath foreordained whatsoever comes to pass;" and it is not known to the writer, that among the different reviews of the sermon it has even been attempted to show that the statement was incorrect. But if a solitary passage could have been adduced, should we not have heard of it? The evidence from Scripture then, if there is any, is indirect, and merely by inference. And even this indirect testimony is far from being the best of its kind; so, at least, a great portion of believers in revelation think.

Now, candid reader, if you have carefully followed the chain of thought thus far, let me ask you to pause and propound for yourself, and honestly answer the following question—"Is there so much evidence in favour of predestination, that I should do more violence to my own reason, and the laws of belief, by rejecting it, than I should by believing that this doctrine is compatible with free agency and accountability?" Indeed, Calvinists themselves have so felt the force of these difficulties, when the terms predestination and free will have been understood in their common and obvious sense, that they have attempted a variety of explanations of these terms to do away, if possible, the apparent discrepancy. These attempts have been the principal cause of those changes and modifications in the Calvinistic system, alluded to in a former number. The various explanations and definitions that have been given to foreordination, have already been noticed. We have seen how every effort failed of affording any relief to the system, until we came down to the last; I mean that of the New-Haven divines. This new theory does indeed avoid the difficulty, but avoids it only by giving up the doctrine! Any thing short of this amounts to nothing; it stands forth still the "*absolute decree*," fixed as fate, and fixing, strong as fate, all the acts of subordinate intelligences. Any *real* modification of it is a virtual renunciation, and a substitution in its stead of the public and consistent decree of Heaven, "He that believeth shall be saved; he that believeth not shall be damned."

Not succeeding as was hoped in such a definition of predestination as would harmonize the opposing propositions, repeated trials have been made to define and explain *human liberty* and the *power of choice*, so as to *bend* these into a coincidence with the *inflexible decree*. This brings us back to the inquiry started above: "What is this power of choice?" Now as this is a point more metaphysical in its nature than the proposition embracing the decrees, so there is more ground for laboured argument and refined speculation. Only one theory, however, needs to be particularly noticed:—1. Because it is the most plausible of any other, so that if this will not bear the test, it is probable no other will; and 2. Because this is the theory which is now pretty generally, and perhaps almost universally adopted by the Calvinists; I mean the Calvinistic doctrine of motives. It is in substance this: the power of choice is that power which the mind has of acting in view of motives, and of deciding according to the strongest motive. The strength and direction of volition are always in accordance with the motive. And this relation between mind and motives is fixed by the very constitution of our natures, so that it may be said there is a constitutional necessity that the mind should be controlled by motives. These motives are multitudinous and various.—All conceptions and perceptions of the mind, from whatever cause, productive of pleasure or pain, exciting emotions of love or aversion, are motives; or, more properly, perhaps, the causes of these mental states are motives. Between these motives and the mind there is such a connection, that the *former* not only excite, but control the *latter*, in all its volitions. The nature of this relation is of course beyond the limits of human investigation: all we can say is, such is the nature of motives and of mind. Such is the theory. The arguments by which it is defended are in substance the following—experience and observation. We are conscious, it is said, of acting from motives, and it is universally understood that others also act from motives. It is on this principle that we govern ourselves in our intercourse with men; by this we calculate with moral certainty, in many instances, what will be the conduct of a man in a given case; and, upon such calculations, we form most of our maxims, and rules of conduct in social life: nay, it is said a man that will act without a reason must be insane—that, on this ground, whenever a man acts it is common to inquire what *induced* him. What motive had he? That even children, at a very early age so readily recognize this principle, that they are constantly inquiring why do you do this or that. Such are the strongest arguments by which this theory is sustained—arguments too strong it is supposed to be overthrown.

I object to the sovereign control of the mind by motives. But in offering my objections, it should first be observed that no man, in his senses, it is presumed, will deny that motives have an important influence in determining our volitions. Nor is it necessary, in order to oppose the doctrine of the controlling power of motives, to deny that the power of volition may have been waked up to action, in the first instance, by motive influence, or that the mind ever after may, in all its volitions, be more or less under this influence. As these are points which do not materially affect the question at issue between us and the Calvinists, they may be left out of the discussion for the present. The question is this—Has the mind a self-determining power, by which it can spontaneously decide, independent of the *control* of motives, or is the mind absolutely controlled by motives? We maintain the former—our opponents the latter. By establishing our position, we disprove theirs—by disproving theirs we establish ours—and it is believed that theirs can be directly disproved, and ours directly established; at least so far as we can hope to arrive at demonstration on these extremely difficult points.

1. My first objection to this doctrine of motive influence is, that most of the arguments by which it is defended, as directly and certainly prove that the Divine mind is subject to the absolute control of motives as that human minds are. It is argued, that to maintain the doctrine of spontaneous volition, independent of the *control* of motives, involves the absurdity, that "our volitions are excited without any intelligent reasons whatever, and as the effect, consequently, of nothing better than a mere brute or senseless mechanism." (*Views in Theology*, p. 163.)—Now if this has any bearing on the question, it relates not to human mind and human volition merely, but to *mind in general*, and must apply to the Divine mind. The same may be said, in fact, of most of the arguments that are brought in favour of this doctrine. Calvinists are convinced of this—and hence this also is a part of their creed. It was defended by Dr. Edwards, and is thus avowed by Professor Upham, in his System of Mental Philosophy. Speaking of the control of motives, he says, "Our condition, in this respect, seems to be essentially the same with that of the Supreme Being himself—he is *inevitably* governed in all his doings, by what, in the great range of events, is wisest and best." (Vol. ii, p. 381.) Thus the Divine Being is, according to this theory, and by the express showing of the leading advocates of the theory, "*inevitably*" made a subordinate to a superior. It is believed there is no avoiding this conclusion; and what then? Why then the doctrine makes God a necessary agent, and leads to atheism! It is nearly, if not exactly, the same as the old heathen doctrine of fate. The ancient heathens supposed that Jupiter himself, the omnipotent father of the gods and men, must yield to fate. Modern Christians teach that there is a certain fitness of things, certain constitutional relations, existing independent of the Divine will, which God himself cannot supersede, but to which he must yield. How does this sink, at once, both the natural and moral perfections of God! The exercises of his wisdom and goodness are nothing more than the result of certain fixed and irresistible influences. Fixed not by God himself, for that would be to give up the doctrine; for in that case, in the order of cause and effect, the Divine mind must have acted without control of motive, if this law of motive influence did not exist until the Divine volition willed it into being and if he could once act independent of this control, he might so act for ever; and the argument built on the absurdity of volition, without an intelligent reason, is contradicted. But if that argument has any weight, it fixes, in the order of cause and effect, a paramount influence eternally antecedent to the exercise of the Divine mind, and controlling that mind with irresistible sway. This is fate! This is atheism! Once set up an influence that controls the Divine mind, call that influence what you will, *fitness of things—fate—energy* of nature—or necessary relation, and that moment you make God a subordinate; you hurl him from his throne of sovereignty, and make him the instrument of a superior. Of what use is such a Deity? Might we not as well have none! Nay better, as it seems to me, if under the control of his own native influence he is led to create beings susceptible of suffering, and fix the relations of those beings to the motives around them such, that by a law of their nature they are "inevitably" led to sin and endless wo! Is it to be wondered at, that many Calvinists have become infidels? This doctrine of motives is the very essence of the system of Spinoza, whose deity was the *energy of nature!* The supreme controlling power of Dr. Edwards and his followers is the *energy of motives*, which exists in the nature of things, anterior to the will of God. Can any one point out any essential difference between the two systems?

Such are the objections to *any arguments* in favour of the doctrine that motives "inevitably" control the volitions of intelligent beings *in general*, involving of course the highest intelligence. But if any are disposed to give up this doctrine, as essential to intelligent volition in general, and choose to maintain it only in respect to the volitions of some particular intelligent beings; then they must give up all the strongest of their arguments. If God is free from this *control*, they must acknowledge also, or give some reason for their dissent, that he may, if he chooses, make and sustain subordinate intelligences, having the same freedom from this control; and if they acknowledge that there is nothing in the nature of the case that renders this an impossibility, then they must show, if they can, that though God *might* constitute beings otherwise, he has *so constituted man* as to render him incapable of choice, except *when* and *as* motives direct, by an inevitable influence. But in attempting this they must meet other difficulties in their course, which, it is believed, will greatly embarrass the system. These difficulties, however, together with the arguments which I design to advance directly in favour of the opposite view, must be reserved for another number.

NUMBER IX.
MORAL AGENCY AND ACCOUNTABILITY, CONTINUED.

Another argument against the Calvinistic doctrine of motives is, that it leads to materialism. The doctrine, it will be recollected, is this: When the mind is brought into connection with objects of choice, it is *inevitably* led, by a law of its nature, to the selection of one rather than of the other, unless there is a *perfect equality* between them; in which case I suppose, of course, the mind must remain in equilibrium; for if it moves only by the influence of motives, and to the same degree and in the same direction with motive influence, of course when it is equally attracted in opposite directions it must be at rest! It is on this ground that Leibnitz maintained that God could not make two particles of matter in all respects alike; because, in that case, being "inevitably" governed by motives in his decisions, he could not determine where to place them, both having the same influence on his mind for a location in the same place! The same writer represents this motive influence, also, as frequently imperceptible, but not the less effectual, and not the less voluntary! And to illustrate it makes the following comparison:—"It is as if a needle, touched with a loadstone, were sensible of and pleased with its turning to the north, for it would believe that it turned itself independent of any other cause, not perceiving the insensible motions of the magnetic power." This statement of Leibnitz, who had paid great attention to this philosophical theory, is important in several respects. It is, in the first place, an acknowledgment that consciousness is against the doctrine; and it is also a concession that the mind is *imposed upon*, in this matter, by the Creator. But with respect to the argument, that this doctrine leads to materialism, this quotation is important, because it shows that one of the most *philosophical*, if not one of the most *evangelical* of the defenders of this doctrine, considered the law of motive influence similar to the law of magnetic attraction, differing only in being accompanied by sensation and a deceptive consciousness. And what says its great evangelical champion in this country, Dr. Edwards? He compares our volitions to the vibrations of a scale beam, the different ends of which are respectively elevated or depressed as the opposite weights may chance to vary. What is this but teaching that motions of mind are governed by the same fixed laws as those of matter, and that volitions are perfectly mechanical states of mind? What the advocates of this doctrine charge on the opposite theory belongs, by their own showing, to their own system. —*They*, not we, make choices the result of animal instinct, or senseless mechanism. I know Professor Stuart, in his late exposition of the Romans, seems to reprobate these comparisons; and while he contends, as I should think, as strenuously as Dr. Edwards, for a complete and efficient control of the Divine Being over all our volitions, he appears to think that there is a great difference between the laws of intellectual and material action. So, indeed, do we think. But we think that difference consists in the mind's being free from that control for which the professor contends; and we believe when he contends for that control in the volitions of the mind, he contends for that which, from the nature of the case, entirely destroys the other part of his hypothesis, viz. that the operations of the mind are free, and essentially different from mechanical motion or the laws of attractive influence in the material world. If the attractive power of motives over the mind is any thing different from the law of gravitation or magnetic attraction, what is that difference? Should any one say, I cannot tell; I ask then, How does he know but it is *that very power* for which Arminians contend? Most probably it is that power. Or will it be said, the difference between motive influence and gravity is consciousness? I reply, Consciousness is no part of the relation between motives and the power of choice. I see not indeed how it affects that relation at all. And this the comparison of Leibnitz, already alluded to, clearly illustrates. Look at that flowing stream; it hastens on most freely, and by the law of its own nature down the gentle declivities or more precipitous slopes of its meandering channel. Suppose now that Omnipotence should impart consciousness to the particles of the continuous current, it would then wake up to perceive the action and feel the pleasure of its own delightful motions. It would roll on still by the law of its own nature, and would feel that it was free to move according to its own *inclination* and voluntary tendency, for its will would of course be in the direction of its *motive*, or in other phrase, its *gravitating* influence. But could it turn its course and roll back its waters to their fountains? It could if it was so *inclined*. But its present *inclination* is toward the bottom of the valley or the bosom of the ocean, and thither, by the relation that exists between its particles and the gravitating influence of the earth, it rolls on *with the utmost freedom*, though with the utter impossibility of changing its own course, without an inversion of the gravitating power. Let the hand of Omnipotence invert the slope of the mountain, and lo! with the same freedom these very waters roll back again to their original fountains! Thus it is with the human mind. It is conscious of being free to move in the direction of its inclinations, but require it to turn its course and move in the current of its volitions, in an opposite direction, and it would be utterly impossible, until Omnipotence himself should change the motive influence.—"God is the determiner of perceptions, and perceptions are the determiners of choices."

We see, therefore, that this doctrine of motive influence leads to materialism, for it makes the analogy between mental and material action so complete that it destroys all idea of *intellectual power*. Philosophically speaking, there is no *power* in the laws of nature. What we express by the *power* of attraction, or repulsion, or decomposition, is nothing more than the uniformity of the Divine agency. Does the earth attract elevated bodies to its surface?—This is not an energy inherent in nature; it is the God of nature acting by a uniform law. This is all that any intelligent man can mean by the power of nature. We, however, use the word *power* in an accommodated sense in these cases, but always I think in connection with that portion of matter that *appears* to act, and not *that* which is acted upon. The magnet, we say, has power to attract iron, because iron is attracted toward the magnet, and not the magnet toward the iron. The antecedent, or that which takes the lead in the motion, is more properly said to have the power, or is the efficient cause. If then we allow of the use of the term power at all, to express the relation of cause and effect, growing out of a philosophical constitution of things, the term should be applied to the antecedent, and not to the consequent. In the case before us, mental action is not the cause of the motive, but the motive is the cause of the mental action: therefore we should say motives have *power* to act upon the mind, and the mind has a *susceptibility* of being acted upon. Dr. Reid has well observed, that a power to be acted upon is no power, or "it is a *powerless power*," which is philosophically absurd. Therefore we come to the conclusion that the mind has no *power* of *choice*, but has a *susceptibility* of being drawn into a state called volition by the power of motives. It will avail nothing, as I conceive, to say that there is evidently a difference between the susceptibility of the mind in this case, and the susceptibility of matter in other cases, unless it be shown what that difference is: for when that difference is pointed out, it will doubtless be found to be what is in direct opposition to the motive theory. It is the misfortune of the Calvinistic system that it often has to assume positions to keep itself in countenance, which positions themselves are a virtual abandonment of the system. So the New-Haven divines have done to support predestination, and to this all Calvinists are driven in their attempts to reconcile free will, or the power of choice, with their doctrine of motives, dependence &c. We may be told in the case before us, that "when the mind is acted upon it is then excited to action." But how excited to action? Is the action any stronger than the motive influence?—Is it carried beyond this influence? or in a different direction? To answer any *one* of these questions in the affirmative is to give up the theory; but to answer them in the negative is to attribute to the mind nothing more than the inertia of matter. The *motives* are (under God) the *agent*, the *mind* is the *passive object*, and the *volition* is the *effect*. Can any one say then, on this theory, that the mind has the power of choice? It has no power in the first place, because its volitions are the result of philosophical necessity; and it has no power, secondly, because it is not the cause of its own volitions, but in these volitions it is the passive subject of foreign influences. Now, so far as moral action is concerned, how does this differ from materialism? It is true mental action differs from material action in some associated circumstances; it is accompanied by consciousness; but as consciousness of itself cannot give accountability, and as it gains nothing in this respect by being associated with such kind of mental action as results from philosophical necessity, it appears plain that man is not accountable; and if not accountable, it is more than probable that he has no future existence, and thus again we are driven to materialism and to deism, if not to atheism.

That man is not *accountable* upon the principle we are opposing, might have been made a distinct argument; but I have connected it with the argument that this doctrine leads to materialism because they imply each other. If materialism is true, we are not accountable, and if we are not accountable, materialism is probably true; and both are true, as I conceive, if the Calvinistic doctrine of motives is true.

It may, however, be urged by the advocates of this theory, that the mind is not wholly passive, because we are conscious of putting forth a mental energy and making a responsible volition; *that* I am ready to grant, but then our consciousness is a fallacy if this system be true; and on the contrary, if consciousness be true, this system is false. I believe no one who pays attention to his own mind will doubt of having this consciousness. But does that prove the truth of this theory? It is one thing to be conscious of having this energy of mind and responsible volition, and another to be conscious that the theory in question is true; indeed this consciousness destroys the theory.

Should it be urged in opposition to the alleged tendency of this system to materialism, that different minds are not uniformly influenced by the same motives, nor the same minds at different times, and therefore, in this respect, it is evident that the laws of mind and of matter differ; I reply, It is precisely so with matter; for *that* attracts or repels according to its different magnetic or electrical states; or should it be urged that mind differs from matter, and shows itself to be possessed of a peculiar energy, because it has power to suspend its decisions, to review the subject, to investigate, &c; I answer, this it cannot do without a motive; and this it *must* do if the motive preponderate in that direction, but not otherwise.

To have a proper view of this subject let us go back to the first perception. Could the mind, according to this doctrine, act otherwise than in coincidence with the motive influence of this perception; or could it even suspend the volition this influence was calculated to produce, until a second and more powerful motive was introduced? If it could, then this doctrine is false; if it could not, then the mind, like matter put in motion, must move on invariably in the same direction, and with the same velocity of thought for ever, or until a new motive should counteract the influence of the former! This is emphatically the *vis inertia* of matter. The bare statement of which seems sufficient to overthrow the theory.

Another objection to this doctrine of motives is, it leads to the notion of regeneration by *moral suasion* merely. There has been much said of late, by the various writers in the old and the *new* school, on this point. The new school are charged with holding that the *truth alone*, without any immediate agency of the Holy Spirit, converts the sinner. This is considered by the old school Calvinists as a fatal error. But why so? If motives *govern* the mind, with absolute sway, all you *need* to convert a sinner, is to bring a motive strong enough to induce him to choose God as his chief good, and he is converted. Until you do this there is no conversion, it is impossible for the Holy Ghost to convert a sinner in any other way than by motives, for choice of good we are told is conversion; there is no choice without a motive, and the strongest motive governs choice absolutely; therefore motive is the omnipotent power that changes the sinner's heart. This is the legitimate result of The Calvinistic premises. We have more than once had occasion to wonder that Calvinists should revolt at the result of their own doctrines; here we have another instance of it; here too we have the enigma of "*natural ability*" unriddled. The human mind, by the constitution of its nature, has the power of choosing according to the influence of the strongest motive; and therefore, so far as this can be called a power, it has the natural power to convert itself; and this is the reason why "*make you a new heart*" is the burden of almost every sermon and exhortation in modern preaching; all the sinner has to do is to choose, in view of motives, and he is converted. And here, too, is unravelled that other mystery which we have been so puzzled to understand, viz. that although all possess the natural power to convert themselves, yet no man ever did convert himself without the special interposition of the Divine agency; for, observe, God keeps the motives in his own hands; "God is the determiner of perceptions, and perceptions are the determiners of *choices;*" that is, of *conversions;* for to choose in a particular way, is to be converted. Whenever, therefore, he is disposed to let the sinner convert himself, according to his natural power; that is, when he is disposed to overpower the mind by an irresistible motive, he brings the motive and mind in contact, and *it is done*. Thus the sinner has as much power to convert himself as he has to resolve to eat when he is hungry; for all the power he has to do either, is a susceptibility of being operated upon, and controlled by the strongest motive; and thus you see, also, that *God* converts the sinner, because he supplies the motive that influences the choice; and here, too, is seen the occasion for misquoting so frequently and misapplying so universally, that passage in the Psalms: "[My] people shall be [made] willing in the day of [my] power." That is, when God applies the controlling motive to influence to a right choice, then shall the sinner, by a law of his nature, *become willing to be converted*. Such are the wonderful philosophical discoveries of modern theology! This is the way for man to convert *himself* by natural power, and this is the way for *God* to convert him, without the aid of *super* natural power! Well might a divine of this cast, whom I heard preach not long since, say of regeneration, "There is nothing supernatural or miraculous in it." For surely it is one of the most natural things in the world, according to this theory, to be converted. It is only to be operated upon by a motive, according to the law of his natural constitution, and the man is converted.

This *philosophy of Christian experience* has led modern orthodoxy to the very borders of natural religion. Another step, and we can do without a Holy Ghost or a Divine Saviour. We will sit down with the philosopher in his study, and *work out* a religious experience, as philosophically as a skilful casuist can solve a question of morals; we will show the *rationale* of the whole process, and demonstrate it so clearly, that infidels shall lose all their objections to the Gospel, and be induced to *"submit"* to God with scarcely a change of theory. Hereafter let no man say, that the work of regeneration is a mystery—that in this work we cannot tell whence the regenerating influence comes, or whither it goes; for it comes through the philosophical channel of motive influence by which it introduces a "governing purpose" into the mind, and the work is done. Let no man hereafter say that his "faith stands not in the wisdom of man, but in the power of God;" or "if any man would be wise let him become a fool that he may be wise;" or "the wisdom of man is foolishness with God;" for lo, the philosophy of regeneration is at length explained! and the whole secret is found to consist in the philosophical relation between motives and mind!! Can any one wonder, after this, that in Geneva, in Germany, and in New-England, Calvinism has finally resulted in Socinianism? And can any one help trembling for a large portion of the orthodox Churches among us at the present day? Grant that there is an increase of zeal, a greater stir among the people, more revivals, &c; all these, with a good foundation, would promise well for the Church; but we fear there is a worm at the root. By this it is not intended to insinuate that the work is always spurious and the professed conversions unsound. In many instances it is undoubtedly the reverse of this. It might be expected after the people had been lulled for a long time under the paralyzing opiates of old-fashioned Calvinism, that this new and *apparently* opposite theory should rouse many to action. "I had been taught," said a man not far from this, "that I must wait God's time to be converted, and I waited many years in vain; but more recently I have been instructed that I might convert myself; I set about the work, and I believe it is done!" Now this, which in the relation borders upon the ludicrous, might have been a genuine conversion. His new views might only have been sufficient to arouse him to a co-operation with the Holy Spirit in his conversion; and this may have been the case with thousands. In their practical effects two opposite errors may, in individual cases, neutralize each other.—But is either therefore safe? Will the general effect be salutary? Let the history of the Church speak; and in view of that record I confess I fear for our common Zion. But let not the old Calvinists lay this blame, and charge this danger upon the new school; the new school doctrine is a legitimate scion from that root which they have cultivated with such assiduity and care. It grows out of the doctrine of motives, it springs from the idea of the entire dependence of the human mind for each and all its volitions upon the directing influence of Omnipotence, whatever may be the theory by which that influence is explained.

Another argument in opposition to this doctrine is found in the consideration, that we are constantly liable to disappointment in most of our calculations respecting human agents.—Though we may judge something of what will be the conduct of men in given circumstances, yet our calculations are very far from coming up to mechanical exactness. Motives have some influence; but that influence is very variable and uncertain. Why is this? It is not so in matter; the same causes will produce the same effects to the end of time. But we see many choose, without being able to give what, *in their own estimation*, is a valid reason; they did thus because they chose to do so; they act in defiance of the strongest motives, drawn from whatever source. We see the greatest possible caprice in the volitions of men; we see their minds starting aside, and putting on the greatest possible and unaccountable mental states, in a way and form that baffles all human calculation, and will for ever baffle it. A man may spend all his life in trying to reduce to uniformity the phenomena of human volitions, and thereby to fix, in an unerring code, the laws that govern them, and he may hand his labours to his successor, and so on to the end of time, and after all, that living, spontaneous, thought-producing essence which we call the human soul, will slide from our grasp and elude all our calculations. If this consideration should have no direct weight in opposition to the theory I am opposing, it will at least show the absurdity of defending this system by what is called the *known regularity* and *uniform phenomena* of human volitions. To talk of *uniformity* here, is to talk of, to say the least, what does not exist.

In the examination of this subject, we find that the arguments in favour of the motive theory are generally of the negative kind; they are not so much direct proofs of the truth of the theory, as they are attempts to show the absurdity of denying it. But when statements of this kind are accompanied by no arguments, they need only be met by a denial. "We are conscious," say the theorists, "of being controlled by motives:" I reply, we are not conscious of this control, but we are conscious of the contrary fact. We know, indeed, that motives have their influence; but we know also that the mind has an influence over motives, and probably a greater influence than motives have over *it*. The mind is conscious too of having an influence over itself, and of possessing a self-directing energy, a spontaneous power, and its consciousness of responsibility is predicated on this power of spontaneity. Only let the mind become clearly conscious that motives beyond its power and influence have an irresistible power in controlling its decisions, and you would as certainly remove from man all sense of responsibility, as in those cases now, where the spasmodic motion of the muscle is not the result of the will.

It is said again, that to deny this control "involves the absurdity that our volitions are exerted without any intelligent reasons, and are the result of a brute or senseless mechanism." It appears to me, however, that a system which represents the will as mechanically governed by motives, as weights turn the scale beam, makes man a machine; while the theory that gives the mind a spontaneous power and energy of its own, makes him what he is, *an intelligent, responsible agent*.

Since, then, these negative arguments in favour of the theory that motives control the mind, are *assertions* and not *proofs;* and since the theory itself leads to *fate*, to *atheism*, to *materialism*, to *conversion* by mere *moral suasion*, to the subversion of *human liberty* and *moral responsibility*, we must believe the theory false. But against the theory of the spontaneous power of the mind, none of these objections lie. It accords too with consciousness; and is, in fact, the only theory on which the responsibility of a moral agent can be predicated. The opposite view claims our assent to two incongruous and apparently contradictory propositions, between which there is not only no agreement, but an evident repugnancy. This is the embarrassment in the one case, and it is fatal to the theory.

If there are embarrassments in the other case, and what theory of mind or matter has not its *inexplicables?*—these embarrassments are evidently of another kind; it is not the want of light to see how two antagonist principles can agree, the repugnancy of which must be the more apparent as light increases, but it is from the known limits to human knowledge. The principal embarrassment to the theory we defend is, we cannot understand the *manner* in which this faculty of the mind operates. But this is no more difficult than to understand the manner in which other faculties of the mind operate. To make this last statement clear, the reader is desired to recollect that the mind is not divided into parts and members like the body. When we talk of the *faculties* of the mind, we should understand the power that the entire mind has to act in this or that way. Thus we say, the mind has the faculties of will and of memory, that is, the mind, as a whole, has the powers of choosing, and of calling up its past impressions. Now if any one will tell me *how* the mind remembers, I will tell him how it wills; and I have the same right to ask him what causes the memory to remember, as he has to ask me what causes the will to will. In both cases it may be said, the mind *remembers* and *wills* because this is its nature —God *made it so*. When you analyze until you come to the original elements, or when you trace back effects until you come to first principles, you must stop.—And if you will not receive these first principles because you cannot explain them farther, then indeed you must turn universal skeptic. I frankly acknowledge I cannot tell *how* the mind acts in its volitions. And let it be understood that the motive theory, with all its other embarrassments, has this one in common with ours.—Can its advocates tell me *how* motives act upon the mind? True philosophy is an analysis of constituent principles, or of causes and effects, but the origin of these relations and combinations is resolvable only into the will of the Creator. *It is so, because God hath made it so.* And the nature of these relations is beyond the reach of the human mind. However impatient we may be at these restrictions, they are limits beyond which we *cannot* go; and our only duty in the case is, submission.

I am aware, however, that what I have now said may, without farther explanation, especially when taken in connection with a principle of philosophy already recognized, be considered as an important concession to my opponents. I have before stated, in substance, that in the material world there is, strictly speaking, no such thing as *power;* that the efficiency of the laws of nature is, in fact, the Divine energy operating in a uniform way. "Let it be granted," a Calvinist might say, "that what we call the operation of second causes is universally the supreme Intelligence operating in a uniform way, and it is all we ask to defend our system. Then it will be granted, that in each volition of the human mind the operation of the will is nothing more than the energy of the Divine mind operating in a uniform way."

To this I reply, Though matter, on account of its inertia, cannot in any proper sense be said to have power, yet the same is not true of mind. If any one thinks it is, then the supreme Mind itself has not power. In other words, as both matter and mind are inert, and cannot act only as acted upon, there is no such thing as *power* in the universe! and thus we again land in atheism. But if *mind* has power, as all theists must grant, then the *human* mind may have power. If any one can prove that it is impossible, in the nature of things, for the Supreme Being to create and sustain subordinate agents, with a spontaneous power of thought and moral action, to a limited extent, in that case we must give up our theory. But it is presumed no one can prove this, or will even attempt to prove it. We say, God has created such agents, and that they act, in their responsible volitions, uncontrolled by the Creator, either directly or by second causes. We are expressly told, indeed, that God made man "in his own image;" his *moral* image doubtless. Man, then, in his own subordinate sphere, has the power of originating thought, the power of spontaneous moral action: this, *this only*, is the ground of his responsibility. Will it be said that this puts man entirely out of the control of his Creator? I answer, By no means. It only puts him out of the control of such direct influences as would destroy his moral liberty. Does the power of moral action, independent of the magistracy and the laws, destroy all the control of the civil government over malefactors? How much less in the other case? God can prevent all the mischief that a vicious agent might attempt, without throwing any restraint upon his responsible volitions. It is thus that he "makes the wrath of man praise him, and the remainder of wrath he restrains."

Let it be understood, then, from this time forward, by all, as indeed it has been understood heretofore by those who have carefully examined the subject, that when the Calvinists talk about "free will," and "human liberty," they mean something *essentially different* from what we mean by these terms; and, as it is believed, something essentially different from the *popular* meaning of these terms. They believe in human liberty, they say, and the power of choice, and we are bound to believe them; but we are also bound not to suffer ourselves to be deceived by terms. *Theirs* is a liberty and power of a moral agent to will *as he does*, and *not otherwise*. *Ours* is an unrestricted liberty, and a spontaneous power in all responsible volitions, to *choose as we do*, or *otherwise*.

Thus far I have examined the mind in its power of choosing good or evil, according to its original constitution. How far this power has been affected by sin, on the one hand, or by grace, on the other, is a question that will claim attention in my next.

NUMBER X.

MORAL AGENCY AS AFFECTED BY THE FALL, AND THE SUBSEQUENT PROVISIONS OF GRACE.

My last number was an attempt to prove that God created man with a spontaneous power of moral action; and that this was the only ground of his moral responsibility. It is now proposed to inquire how far this power has been affected by the fall, and the subsequent provisions of grace. The doctrine of the Methodist Church on these points is very clearly expressed by the 7th and 8th articles of religion in her book of Discipline.

1. "Original sin standeth not in the *following* of Adam, (as the Pelagians vainly talk,) but it is the corruption of the nature of every man that naturally is engendered of the offspring of Adam, whereby man is very far gone from original righteousness, and of his own nature inclined to evil, and that continually."

2. "The condition of man after the fall of Adam is such, that he cannot turn and prepare himself, by his own natural strength and works, to faith and calling upon God: wherefore we have no power to do good works pleasant and acceptable to God, without the grace of God by Christ preventing us, (going before to assist us,) that we may have a good will, and working with us when we have that good will."

It is not pretended here that any intellectual faculties are lost by sin, or restored by grace; but that the faculties that are essential to mind have become corrupted, darkened, debilitated, so as to render man utterly incapable of a right choice without prevenient and cooperating grace. As muscular or nervous power in a limb, or an external sense, may be weakened or destroyed by physical disease, so the moral power of the mind or an inward sense may be weakened or destroyed by moral disease. And it is in perfect accordance with analogy, with universal language, and with the representations of Scripture, to consider the mind as susceptible, in its essential nature, of this moral deterioration. If any one should say he cannot understand what this moral defect is, I would answer by asking him if he can tell me what the essence of mind is? And if he chooses to object to this kind of depravity, because he cannot understand it, in its essence, he should turn materialist at once; and then, as he will find equal difficulty to tell what the essence of matter is, and in what its weakness and disorder essentially consist, he must turn universal skeptic.—The simple statement is, *the soul has become essentially disordered by sin;* and as no one can prove the assertion to be unphilosophical or contrary to experience, so I think it may be shown from Scripture that this is the real state of fallen human nature. And it may also be shown that this disorder is such as to mar man's free agency. There is a sense, indeed, in which all voluntary preference may be considered as implying free agency. But voluntary preference does not necessarily imply *such a free agency* as involves moral responsibility. The mind may be free to act in one direction, and yet it may so entirely have lost its moral equilibrium as to be utterly incapable, of its own nature, to act in an opposite direction, and therefore not, in the full and responsible sense, a free agent. It is not enough, therefore, to say, "Free agency (of a responsible kind) consists in the possession of understanding, conscience, and will;" (see Christian Spectator for September, 1830;) unless by *will* is meant the spontaneous power already alluded to. The understanding may be darkened, the conscience may be seared or polluted, the will, that is, the power of willing, may, to all good purposes, be inthralled; and this is what we affirm to be the true state and condition of unaided human nature.

It will be farther seen that the above account of human nature does not recognize the distinction of *natural* and *moral* ability. The fact is, man's inability is both natural and moral; it is natural, because it is constitutional; and it is moral, because it relates to the mind. To say a fallen man has natural power to make a right choice, because he has the faculties of his mind entire, is the same as to say that a paralytic man has the natural power to walk, because he has his limbs entire. It appears to me that the whole of this distinction, and the reasoning from it, proceed on the ground of a most unphilosophical analysis of mind and an unwarranted definition of terms. The simple question is, Has fallen man, *on the whole*, the power to make a right choice, or has he not? We say without grace he has not. And therefore fallen man is not, in the responsible sense of that term, a free agent without grace.

    This view of the subject is not novel in the Church. I readily acknowledge that a doctrine is not therefore true, because it has been held by many, and can be traced back to antiquity, unless it can be proved to be Scriptural. The fact, however, that a doctrine has been generally received in the Church, entitles it to respect and to a careful examination, before it is discarded. Hence to those who have only read modern Calvinistic authors on this subject, it may be a matter of surprise to learn that not only the more ancient fathers, but even St. Austin himself, the introducer of predestination into the Church, and Calvin, and the synod of Dort, were all supporters of sentiments substantially the same as are here vindicated—I say, those who have only read modern Calvinistic authors will be surprised to learn this, because these authors treat this doctrine as though it were so unreasonable and absurd as scarcely to be tolerated in the view of common sense. Though it may have an influence with some, in a paucity of better reasons, to scout a doctrine from the Church by calling it absurd, yet the candid will not readily give up an old doctrine for a new, without good reason.

    I had at first thought of quoting pretty freely from some of the fathers, and especially from the early Calvinists, to show their views on this point. But it may not be necessary, unless the statements here made should be denied. Let therefore one or two quotations from Calvin and from the synod of Dort, both of which I think Calvinists will acknowledge as good Calvinistic authority, suffice. Calvin denies all power to man, in his apostasy, to choose good, and says that, "surrounded on every side with the most miserable necessity, he (man) should nevertheless be instructed to aspire to the good of which he is destitute, and to *the liberty of which he is deprived*." The synod of Dort decided thus:—"We believe that God—formed man after his own image, &c, *capable in all things to will* agreeably to the will of God." They then speak of the fall, and say, "We reject all that is repugnant to this concerning the free will of man, since man is but a *slave to sin*, and has nothing of himself, unless it is given him from heaven." And speaking of the change by grace, they add, "The will thus renewed is not only actuated and influenced by God, but *in consequence of this influence becomes itself active*." And to show that Calvin did not consider the voluntary acts of a depraved sinner as proof of free will, he says, "Man *has not an equally free election of good and evil*, and can only be said to have free will, because he does evil voluntarily, and not by constraint;" and this he ironically calls "egregious liberty indeed! if man be not compelled to serve sin, but yet is such a willing slave that his will is held in bondage by the fettors of sin." These quotations, I think, show satisfactorily that the early Calvinists believed man to have lost his power to choose good by apostasy, and can only regain it by grace. It is true, they generally believed that whenever this grace was imparted to an extent to restore the mind the power of choosing good, it was regenerating grace. And herein they differ from the Arminians, who believe that grace may and does restore the power to choose good before regeneration. This, however, does not affect the point now under examination, but involves a collateral question, which will be examined in its proper place. One thought more, and I pass to the arguments on the main questions in the articles quoted above. These articles are taken from the 9th and 10th of the articles of the Church of England. Our 8th is indeed identically the same as the 10th of the Church of England; and the latter part of that article, commencing, "Wherefore, &c," is taken substantially from St. Austin himself. Thus much for the Calvinistic authority of the doctrine we defend. To which, if it were necessary, we might add quotations from Beza, Dr. Owen, a decided Calvinist, and many of the ancient fathers. Nay, the Remonstrants declared, in the presence of the synod of Dort, that this was "the judgment of all antiquity."

Let us now notice some arguments in favour of this doctrine.

1. The doctrine above stated, and now to be defended, must be true, as is believed, since only this view of man's condition will accord with the Scripture account of depravity. If the Scriptures teach that man is constitutionally depraved, that a blight and a torpor have come over his moral nature, comparable to sleep, to disease, and to death, how can it be otherwise than that this should affect his power to choose good? Had man any too much moral power in the first instance to constitute him an accountable moral agent? And if he had not, has he enough now that his mind has become darkened, his judgment perverted, and his moral powers corrupted and weakened? Or will it be denied that the moral energies of his nature have been impaired by sin? If not, how has he been affected? Let any one spend a thought on this question, and decide, if he can, what definite vicious effect can be produced on man's moral nature which will not necessarily imply a weakening and an embarrassment of his original power to a right choice. Should it be said that his power is somewhat weakened, but he has enough left to constitute him free to choose good, this would imply that before the loss he had more than enough! Besides, such an idea would rest on the principle that man's moral nature was not *wholly* vitiated. It is said, I know, that all the embarrassment which man has to a right choice is a disinclination to moral good. But if this disinclination to good be derived and constitutional, it exists in the mind previous to any act of choice, and is therefore the very thing we mean—it is this very thraldom of the mind which utterly incapacitates it to choose good. If it be asked whether disinclination can ever be so strong as to destroy the freedom of the will to act in one particular direction? I answer, most unhesitatingly, Yes; and if that disinclination is either created or derived, and not the result of an antecedent choice, the possessor is not morally obligated to act in opposition to it, unless he receive foreign aid to help his infirmities, and to strengthen him for a contrary choice.

It follows then, I think, that we must either give up constitutional depravity, or discard the notion that we can make a right choice without Divine aid. And here, if I mistake not, we shall find the precise point on which modern Calvinism has verged over into the New Divinity theory of depravity. Perceiving that to acknowledge any depravity of man's moral constitution would either imply the necessity of supernatural aid in order to a right choice, or else free man from responsibility, Dr. Taylor and his associates have resolved all depravity into *choice* or *voluntary preference*. They deny that there is any thing in the nature of man, antecedently to his act of willing, that possesses a moral character. Their idea is perfectly consistent with the notion of natural ability; and that the advocates of the New Divinity have embraced this idea is evidently a proof that they think closely and are seeking after consistency, let it lead them where it will. The only wonder is, that all who cleave to the dogma of natural ability do not follow them. The doctrine of natural ability, if it is any thing more than a name, appears evidently to be a part of the old Pelagian system, and should never be separated from its counterpart—the doctrine of self conversion and the natural perfectability of the human character. But this clearly implies that there is no serious derangement or radical viciousness of the moral man. Here, then, is another instance in which Calvinists in general revolt at the legitimate results of their own system.

But while the New Divinity advocates have fearlessly removed an important objection to their doctrine, they have, by this very act, as it is believed, however little they may have designed it, set themselves in fearful array against the Scripture doctrine of depravity and salvation by grace, and have opened a wide door for the introduction of numerous and dangerous heresies. It is true, they will not own that they have gone very far from the old system. They think the doctrine of natural depravity is asserted when they say, "nature is *such* that he will sin, and only sin, in all the appropriate circumstances of his being." (See Dr. Taylor's Sermon.) But what this "nature" is, we are at a loss to determine; as also what the "*such*" is that is predicated of this nature; nor has Dr. T. told us how he knows that all men will sin and only sin, when in fact they have natural power to avoid it; or in what other than "the appropriate circumstances of their being" those are who become regenerate. In fact, while this theory claims to be orthodox, and thus to assimilate itself with the old theory, it has only exchanged one inconsistency for a half score. Its advocates, to be consistent, must come out plain and open Pelagians, and then meet the Scripture doctrine of depravity and salvation by grace as they can, or they must go back to their old ground, and endure the manifest inconsistency they are now endeavouring to avoid; or, what seems to me better than either, come on to the Arminian ground, which shuns all these difficulties, while it maintains constitutional depravity and salvation by grace from the foundation to the top stone, including of course a gracious ability to choose life and gain heaven.

2. Another argument in favour of the *necessity* of Divine grace, in order to a right choice, is the fact, that God actually gives grace to those who finally perish, as well as to those who are saved. Of this fact the Scriptures afford decisive proof. They speak in general terms. Jesus Christ "is the true light that lighteth every man that cometh into the world." "The grace of God that bringeth salvation hath appeared unto all men." They speak in special terms of the unregenerate—that they *grieve*, *resist*, and *quench* the *Spirit* of *grace*, which certainly they could not do if they had it not. But if they have the operations of the Spirit, what are these operations? What is the Spirit doing to the inner man? Will it be said he is bringing motives to bear upon the mind? But what motives other than those found in the Gospel? These the sinner has without the Spirit. If these motives can convert sinners, any of us can convert our neighbours. "But," it is said, "the Spirit makes the heart *feel* these motives." Aye, truly he does, and that not by operating upon the motives, but upon the *heart*, and this is the very work we contend for. It is thus that the Spirit graciously arouses and quickens the dead soul, and brings it to *feel*, and excites it to *act*, in the great work of salvation.

Since, then, it must be granted that unregenerate sinners, and those who are finally lost, have the operations of this Spirit of grace, let me seriously inquire, For what purpose is this grace given? On the Calvinistic ground it cannot be that they may have a chance for salvation, and thus be without excuse; for this is secured without grace. Since they have natural ability to come to Christ, the abuse of that ability is sufficient to secure their just condemnation. So say the Calvinists; and on this ground they maintain that the reprobates are justly condemned. For what purpose, then, is this grace given? If we may establish a general principle by an induction of particulars; if we may judge of the design of the God of providence or grace, by noticing, in any given case, the uniform results, then we can easily determine this point. *God gives grace to the reprobates that their condemnation may be the more aggravated.* The argument stands thus: God gives grace to the reprobates for some important purpose. He does not give it that salvation may be possible to them, for they are able to be saved without it; he does not give it to make salvation certain, for this it does not effect; nevertheless he gives them grace, the invariable effect of which is to increase their condemnation. The only consistent inference; therefore is, that he gives grace to the reprobates that they may have a more aggravated condemnation. Here, then, we trace the Calvinistic theory to one of these *logical consequences* charged upon it in the sermon, and which has been so strenuously denied by the reviewers—a consequence which, revolting as it is, must nevertheless be charged upon it still, unless its advocates can show why grace is given to the reprobates when they have all necessary ability to repent and believe without it.

3. On the ground of this doctrine, also, there would be some difficulty in accounting for the necessity of giving grace, in all cases, even to the elect. Why may not some of these repent without grace? Nay, why may not some of the reprobates, in the plenitude of their natural ability, repent and be converted, in despite of the decree of reprobation? Did God foresee that they would not, and on that foresight predicate his decree of reprobation? But that would be a *conditional* reprobation, and would therefore imply its counterpart—a conditional election. This no class of Calvinists will admit. How happens it, then, that some of these reprobates do not get converted, since they not only have natural powers enough to make a right choice but have some grace beside? Is it because God has fixed the barrier in something else, by which this ability, grace, and all are rendered nugatory? But this would render their condemnation unjust, Calvinists themselves being judges. They tell us that the only just ground of condemnation is, that *the sinner will not come to Christ*. Here, then, is the most extraordinary thing that angels or men ever knew; for almost six thousand years there has been upon our earth a succession of generations of sinners, and its the present generation of them there are eight hundred millions. All of these, throughout all their generations, have had no other obstruction to salvation but what exists in their own will, and each and all have had by nature all needful ability in the will to a right choice, and have had a measure of grace super-added, and yet not a reprobate among them all has ever made a right choice; and not one of the elect ever did or ever will make such a choice until God, by an omnipotent act, "makes his elect willing in the day of his power!!" This is a miracle to which all the other miracles in the world are as nothing—a miracle which Omnipotence alone can accomplish by a Divine constitution and an all-controlling energy. Thus this doctrine destroys itself. It assumes positions, with respect to free will, that cannot be maintained, only on the supposition of an *efficient* superior agency to direct the action of that *free will*, in a course of sinful volition, in hundreds of millions of cases, without a single variation, save where that variation is the result of the same superior Power acting in the opposite direction.

4. That the sinner receives aid by Divine grace to enable him to repent; and that he could not repent, without this, appears evident from the Scriptural representation of the ground of man's responsibility. "If I had not come," says the Saviour, "ye had not had sin." "This is the condemnation, that light has come into the world, and men loved darkness rather than light." "He that believeth not is condemned already, *because* he hath not believed in the only begotten Son of God." "*Because* I have called, and ye have refused, &c, I also will laugh at your calamity." These and many other passages seem to imply that the sinner is rejected on the ground of his neglecting offered grace. But if this is the ground of his condemnation, it is not for the abuse of natural power. I see no way for a plausible attempt even to get rid of this argument, unless it should be attempted to raise a question respecting the nature of this grace. It may be said that "these passages only relate to gracious provisions, such as the atonement, the Scriptures of truth, &c, and have no reference whatever to a gracious influence upon the mind. The mind had sufficient strength to believe, repent, &c, but something must be presented to believe in; and some provision must be made to make repentance available." In reply I would say, First, Even this shows that man could not have been saved from sin without grace, and hence on this ground this theory would be involved in the very difficulty which it attempts to throw upon our view of the subject, viz., that grace is necessary to make men guilty, because none can be guilty in a case where their course is unavoidable. But, leaving this for another place, I would say farther, in reply to the above, that the Scriptures do not represent this grace as confined to *external provisions*, but on the contrary speak of it as operating upon and influencing the mind, and that, too, in the very

way for which we contend. Look at a few Scriptural expressions, promiscuously selected, and see how clearly they sustain our position. In the first place, to give the argument full force, let us notice the Scripture account of man's natural condition. He is "in darkness," "asleep," "dead," "without strength," "sick," "deaf," "blind," "lame," "bound," "helpless;" and all this in consequence of sin. Indeed, this is the very definition of his sinful character and condition. If such language does not describe *utter inability* of the sinner to serve God, then no language can do it. Now let us see what grace does. Its very design is to "awake the sleeper;" to unstop deaf ears, and "open blind eyes;" to "lighten every man;" to "strengthen with might by the Spirit in the inner man." "Christ strengthens" the sinner, that he may "do all things." It is on the ground that "God worketh in him to will and to do," that man is exhorted to "work out his salvation with fear and trembling." "Thou strengthenedst me with strength *in my soul*." But leaving farther quotations of this kind, let the reader fix his attention on the stress which the Scriptures lay upon the striving of the Spirit. All the efficacy of the word is ascribed to the Spirit; and hence the apostle declares that he "preached the Gospel, with the Holy Ghost sent down from heaven;" that it "came, not in word, but in *power*." Indeed, "the letter (of the word) killeth, but the Spirit giveth life." Hence the frequent cautions not to "grieve" or "quench the Spirit." Now what, I ask, can all these scriptures mean? Is there any plausibility in the idea, that by such expressions nothing is meant but the general provisions of grace in the Gospel economy? That no direct, gracious influence of the Spirit upon the heart is intended? In fact, the new idea of conversion by motives and moral suasion seems to be a device to meet this very difficulty. The old Calvinists charge the advocates of the New Divinity with holding that all the Spirit does in operating upon the heart, is not by operating upon it directly, but indirectly *through the truth*: which has given rise to the saying, "If I were as eloquent as the Holy Ghost, I could convert souls as well as he." And if they do hold this, it is no wonder, for indeed it is the legitimate consequence of the doctrine of natural ability. They doubtless arrive at it thus:— According to the Scriptures, man's responsibility turns on his rejecting or improving the grace of God. That grace cannot be an internal gracious influence upon man's moral nature, because that would conflict with the notion of responsibility, on the ground of natural power. These scriptures therefore can mean nothing more than that a gracious atonement is provided, and a record of Divine truth made, and now, in the use of his natural power, the sinner is required to judge of and embrace this truth, which if he does, he in this sense improves the grace of God, and is converted; but if he does it not, he grieves the Spirit, and is condemned. Thus in the one case, if he is converted, it is in the use of his natural power, "choosing in the view of motives;" and in the other case, if he is not converted, it is in the use of his natural power, refusing in view of motives. Is not this correct reasoning? And ought not the New-Haven divines to be commended for carrying out the system to its legitimate results? And ought not all to follow them in this, who hold to natural ability? And yet no wonder that they hesitate here, for cold and spiritless indeed must be that system of religious experience that resolves the conversion of the soul into a mere natural operation of choosing, through the influence of moral suasion.

Leaving this system, therefore, to labour under its fatal embarrassments, it may be seen, I think, that the system here vindicated corresponds with the Scriptures and is consistent with itself; for it makes man's responsibility turn upon grace improved or misimproved, and it makes that grace an internal quickening influence, and a strengthening energy upon the heart; and these different features of the theory, when placed together, all seem at once to be compatible with each other.

5. Express passages of Scripture teach the doctrine here maintained.

I need not now repeat the passages already referred to, in which the state of the depraved heart is described, and which show, if any human language can show it, that man is naturally "without strength." But my object is to call the attention of the reader to some very direct and express passages, to show that it is grace, and grace alone, that enables the soul to do the will of God. "I can do all things," saith the apostle, "through Christ who strengtheneth me." Query: would not the apostle have thought it presumption to have said, I can do all things without strength from Christ? Has he ever intimated such a sentiment in all his writings? Does he not rather say, "We are not sufficient of ourselves *to think any thing as of ourselves*, but our *sufficiency is of God?*" This is the apostle's general language, and it is in perfect accordance with the declaration of his Master, "Without me ye can do nothing." "As the branch *cannot* bear fruit of itself, except it abide in the vine, *no more can ye*, except ye abide in me." "No man *can come* to me, except the Father draw him." "Likewise the Spirit Helpeth our infirmities; for we know not what to pray for as we ought." "My grace is sufficient for thee; for my strength is made perfect in weakness." "The God of all grace—stablish, strengthen, settle you." "For this cause I bow my knees to the Father, &c, that he would grant you, according to the riches of his glory, to be strengthened with *might*, by his *Spirit*, in the *inner* man," "according to the power that worketh *in us*." It is useless to quote farther. If these passages do not show that our strength to do good is of grace, then it appears to me the Holy Spirit must fail of an *ability* to communicate that idea through human language. Will it be said that some of these passages refer to the regenerate, and therefore are not in point to meet the case of the unregenerate? I would ask, in reply, whether regenerating grace takes away our natural ability? Certainly if the regenerate can neither think nor do any thing acceptable without grace, much more do the unregenerate need this grace to enable them to make a right choice. And yet in the face of these most explicit scriptures, we are repeatedly told that man has natural power to make himself a new heart!

To the foregoing considerations, I might add, if any farther proof of our doctrine were necessary, and if this paper had not been extended so far already, the universal experience of all Christians. This appears, from their language, to be the experience of Bible saints, under both the Jewish and Christian dispensations. And what Christian now living, but feels now, and felt when he first embraced the Saviour, that the strength to do this was from God—directly from God, through grace. Hear his prayers—he pleads his weakness —he asks *for strength*. And what does he mean by that prayer? Does he ask for some external accommodation and aid? No; he wants strength, *by the Spirit, in the inner man*. And this is the prayer of all Christians, whether they advocate this notion of natural ability or not. The sayings and writings also of these very advocates of natural ability, so powerful is this feeling of dependence, are often in perfect coincidence, with the doctrine we defend. A most striking instance of this is found in Dr. Wood's pamphlet (page 97) in opposition to Dr. Taylor, as follows:—"The common theory (of Calvinistic orthodoxy) leads us to entertain low thoughts of ourselves, especially in a moral view; and to feel that we are not of ourselves *sufficient for any thing spiritually good*, and that, for whatever holiness we now possess, or may hereafter attain, we are dependent on Divine grace." What stronger gracious ability do Arminians hold to, than this? "Not of ourselves sufficient for any thing spiritually good." And is this the common theory of Calvinism? Then Calvinism here, as in other points, is divided against itself. Indeed one would be induced to think, were it not for the context, either that Dr. Wood differed from his brothers generally, on this point, or was off his guard at this moment. But he tells us, in this very paragraph, that he "does not differ at all from the generality of ministers, in New-England, respecting the natural powers and faculties of man, as a moral and accountable being." But he fears the "unqualified language" which Dr. T. "employs respecting the natural state, the free will, and the power of man." On reading this last passage, I confess I am at a loss to know what to say or believe of this Calvinistic opinion of natural power. Dr. Taylor's "unqualified language" respecting "the power of man," I take to be a frank statement of Dr. Wood's opinion, and that of other Calvinists. Dr. T. says man has natural power *sufficient* to make a right choice. Does not Dr. Wood say this? He says he does not differ from "the generality;" and it is notorious that this is the doctrine of the generality of those ministers. Dr. Tyler, of Portland, one of Dr. Wood's coadjutors in opposing Dr. Taylor, says, in a sermon[5] on free salvation, "There is no reprobation taught in the Scriptures, which destroys human liberty, or which impairs the sinner's *natural power*. Every man is a free moral agent. Life and death are set before him, and he is *capable* of choosing between them." What language can be more "unqualified" than this? It teaches us that man has *natural power*, which renders him *capable* to make a right choice. It is true, Dr. Taylor, and "those who believe with him," carry out this doctrine into its legitimate and practical bearings. On the ground of this power, they exhort sinners "to make themselves new hearts." One of them, as reported to me by a preacher, went so far as to say, in a public address, that sinners ought to be ashamed to ask the aid of the Holy Spirit to convert them, since they had power to convert themselves. And what objection can any, who hold to natural power to choose life, urge against this? If, as Dr. Tyler teaches, in his "Examination of Dr. Taylor's Theological Views," a right choice implies regeneration; and if every man is *naturally capable* of a right choice, as taught by this same Dr. Tyler, and the "generality" of his brethren, then it follows conclusively, and I see not how any sophistry can cover up the inference, these sinners have natural power to convert themselves. Instead therefore of hypocritically pleading their own weakness, before a *throne of grace*, and asking for mercy and grace to help them in their time of need, they ought to be crimsoned with shame, for their folly and hypocrisy, turn away from their impertinent suit, throw themselves upon the *resources of nature*, and regenerate their own hearts. If however these gentlemen believe it impossible for sinners to do this, then, taking their whole theory together, this power is no power, and community, up to this hour, has been deluded by unmeaning words—words which only serve to conceal the deformity of a theological system, which, when thoroughly examined, is found after all, to teach that the poor reprobate has no adequate power by nature, and receives no available aid from grace to choose salvation, and must therefore, from the imperious necessity of his nature and condition, go down to interminable death.

NUMBER XI.

SAME SUBJECT CONTINUED.

It is not pretended that there are no difficulties in our view of the subject. What important theory is there in philosophy, politics, morals, or religion, against which some apparently plausible objection may not be urged? But the inquiry in each case should be, Are those objections fatal to the system? Or are the difficulties in the proposed system greater than in some other view of the subject? For reasonable men will refuse to be driven into the vortex of skepticism merely because there are some difficulties and obscurities in all subjects of faith, which the limitations to human vision will not permit us to penetrate. To form an enlightened comparative view in the case before us, it will be important that we glance at the different theories on the subject of depravity and the ground of responsibility.

1. One form in which this subject has been held is, "That the sin of Adam introduced into his nature such a radical impotence and depravity that it is impossible for his descendants to make any voluntary efforts toward piety and virtue, or in any respect to correct and improve their moral and religious character, and that faith and all the Christian graces are communicated by the sole and irresistible operation of the Spirit of God, without any endeavour or concurrence on the part of man." This of course makes the elect entirely passive in their conversion; and consigns the reprobate to destruction for

the sin of Adam, which, it is maintained, is imputed to him by virtue of a federal relation; or at best gives him over to unavoidable personal and eternal condemnation for possessing a nature which he had no agency in bringing upon himself, and from which he has no power to extricate himself. The difficulties of this system are so numerous and so palpable, whether it be tried by the standard of Scripture, of reason, or of common sense, that I need not here allude to them. Suffice it to say that they have pressed so heavily upon the Calvinists themselves as to baffle all their ingenuity and invention at defence, and have driven them finally into all those changes and modifications so frequently alluded to in this controversy. I will here say in advance that, in my opinion, this, after all, is the strongest position Calvinism can assume. The moment its advocates depart from this, they must either, to be consistent with themselves, verge over into the other extreme of Pelagianism, or strike off into the "golden mean" of Arminianism. This may be more clearly seen in the sequel.

2. Pelagianism is another, and an opposite theory. It has a variety of shades, called Pelagian, Semi-pelagian, &c. Its varieties, however, relate to some minor modifications of the relation of the human family to Adam, touching natural evil, the death of the body, and greater exposure to temptation. But there is a uniformity in the essential part of the theory, which is, that human nature is free from sin or guilt until it becomes guilty by *intelligent, voluntary exercise*. The objections to this theory are, among others, as follows. It is in direct opposition to the Scripture doctrine of native depravity—a doctrine which has been often and ably treated of and defended by Calvinistic and, Arminian divines—a doctrine which is embodied in a palpable form in every man's own experience —a doctrine which not only flashes upon the mind of the student in every page of the history of man, but also upon the mind of the unlettered nurse in the earliest emotions of the infant that struggles in her arms.

Another objection to this theory is, that it gives to infants, previous to intelligent voluntary exercise, no moral character. Hence, should they die at this age, as multitudes doubtless do, they would not be fit subjects either for the rewards of heaven or the pains of hell. At the Judgment, as they will not be subjects of praise or blame, they will neither be on the right hand nor the left, and of course will neither be sentenced to "everlasting punishment," nor welcomed "into life eternal." If, however, they by any means go into a state of punishment, their sufferings will be unjust; or if they are admitted into heaven, it will not be a salvation by grace, nor will it be preceded by regeneration, nor will their song be, "Unto Him that hath loved us," &c. This is not only contrary to the whole Gospel system, but also is in direct opposition to many scriptures, especially Rom. v, 18: "Therefore, as by the offence of one, judgment came upon all men to condemnation; so, by the righteousness of one, the free gift came upon all men unto justification of life." It also leaves infants involved in the natural evils of diseases, pains; and death, not only without any assignable cause, but also in direct opposition to the cause assigned by the apostle—"And so death passed upon all men, for that all have sinned."

A third objection to this theory is, that it destroys the Scripture doctrine of regeneration. The Scripture account of this matter is, in substance, that there is a radical change of our moral nature by the efficient operations of the Holy Ghost. But as this doctrine makes sin consist exclusively in exercise, so holiness must consist wholly in exercise. The whole work, therefore, of regeneration is a mere change of volition; and this volition is not the result of a preceding change of moral constitution, but it is, like any other volition, produced by the native power of the mind, under the exciting influence of motives. The Holy Spirit, therefore, may well be dispensed with in this work. The supernatural character of the change must be given up, and the whole work is resolvable into a natural process. It is here worthy of remark that this is not mere speculation. Such has, in fact, been the final result of this theory, I believe, in every case where it has long been defended. And hence, in close connection with this, the supernatural efficacy of the atonement, and of course the Divine character of the Redeemer, are found to be notions not at all essential to the system, and somewhat discordant with the philosophy of its other parts, and are therefore soon brought into discredit. And this, too, as may be seen by the history of the Church, has been the practical result wherever Pelagianism or Semi-pelagianism has been cherished. It has degenerated into Socinianism. It may be said, then, in one word, that this doctrine of Pelagianism does, in its teachings, tendencies, and practical results, supplant and overthrow all the essential principles of the Gospel system.

3. A third and intermediate theory on the subject of depravity and human responsibility is the one presented and advocated in the preceding number. This system is presented, in part, in the very language in which the Ultra-Calvinists present theirs. Arminians, as well as "Calvinists, say that the sin of Adam introduced into his nature such a radical impotence and depravity that it is impossible for his descendants [who, it is believed, are propagated in the moral likeness of their fallen ancestor] to make any voluntary efforts [unassisted by grace] toward piety and virtue, or in any respect to correct and improve their moral and religious character." Thus far we go together; but this is a point of divergency, from which we take very different directions. Instead of going on to say "that the Christian graces are communicated by the irresistible operation of the Spirit of God, without any endeavour or concurrence on the part of man," we say that "the saving grace of God hath appeared unto all Men;" and that this grace so enlightens, strengthens, and aids the human mind, that it is thereby enabled to make that choice which is the turning point, conditionally, of the soul's salvation; and that it is by this same gracious aid that the man, when he has this good will, is enabled "to work out his salvation" unto the end. It is in this latter part of the statement that we are at issue with the Calvinists; but we are at issue on both parts with the Pelagians of every grade, including, of course, the advocates of the New Divinity in our country.

To the foregoing statement of our doctrine it is proper to add that we believe that the merits of the atonement are so available for and in behalf of the whole human family, that the guilt of depravity is not imputed to the subject of it until, by intelligent volition, he makes the guilt his own by resisting and rejecting the grace of the Gospel; and that being thus by grace in a justified state, the dying infant is entitled to all the promised blessings of the new covenant, and will, of course, have wrought in him all that meetness necessary to qualify him for the gracious rewards of the saints in glory. Thus, according to this system, the dying infant, as well as the dying adult believer, is sanctified by the blood of the covenant, and saved by grace.

These are the three systems which are presented to the inquirer after truth as the alternatives, and perhaps I may say the only alternatives of choice, in reference to this subject. It is true, the doctrine of *natural ability* has been proposed as another alternative, holding an intermediate place between the doctrines of native impotency as first stated and of Pelagianism. And it may therefore appear to some, that I ought, in my enumeration, to have given this as a separate and distinct theory. My reason, however, for not doing this is, that there cannot, in my opinion, be such a resting place between the doctrines of derived constitutional depravity and Pelagianism. Natural ability that is any thing more than a name—that is, in fact, an *ability*, destroys the idea of constitutional depravity; and depravity that is any thing more than a name—that is, in fact, *constitutional depravity*, destroys the idea of natural ability. A striking proof of this is found in the fact that a great portion of those divines in the Calvinistic Churches who have been most decided in preaching up natural ability, have gone over and embraced the New Divinity, which, as we have seen, abjures the doctrine of constitutional depravity. The New-Haven divines are certainly gentlemen of talents and of close thought; and they have been following up this doctrine for a number of years, and it has landed them upon the logical conclusion that *there is no such depravity*. But we need not trust to the conclusions of the New Divinity advocates, to show that the notions of natural ability and natural freedom from guilt and sin necessarily and reciprocally imply each other. Why have Calvinists left their old ground of natural impotency, and resorted to the dogma of a natural ability? It is for the avowed reason that there can be no guilt without an ability to avoid it. But since the sin of his nature is unavoidable to the new-born infant, of course he can have no guilt, and by consequence *no sin*, until he is capable of an intelligent moral choice. Again: this same theory tells us that where there is no natural ability there is no moral character. But as the infant cannot be reasonably supposed to have ability to put forth an intelligent holy volition, he can have no moral character, and of course no sin.

The only way to avoid this conclusion in connection with the assumed premises is, to maintain that "the infant, from his birth, is a voluntary agent; and thus, in fact, to a certain extent, sinful." And would you believe, reader, that any reasonable man would resort to such an idea for the sake of helping out a theory? *And yet it is even so.* A paper lately published under the sanction of the New Divinity, purporting to be an inquiry into "what is the real difference between the New-Haven divines and those who differ from them," says, "The ground has of late been taken (if we understand the discussions on this subject) that mankind are literally *at birth* voluntary and accountable agents, and actual sinners against God; that the new-born infant is a responsible subject of God's moral government, and actually sins with a knowledge of his duty, and in the same sense with the adult sinner violates moral obligation, does wrong, ought to be penitent, and to change its moral character." And as a proof that this is the ground now assumed, the same writer gives us a quotation from Rev. Mr. Harvey, who has been one of the most active in this state in opposition to the New-Haven divines, in which he says, "A moral being, for aught we know, may commence his existence in an *active, voluntary* state of the will; he may be a voluntary agent from his birth, and thus, in fact, to a certain extent sinful, and that without supposing that *depravity is seated in any thing but the will.*" This same writer also states that Dr. Spring, in a treatise on "native depravity," a work which I have not at hand, has advanced and defended the sentiment of "*actual* sin from birth." And has it indeed come to this at last, that this natural ability, for which Calvinists have so strenuously contended, is nothing more than the power the new-born infant has to commit actual sin on the one hand, or "make himself a new heart" on the other! Alas for Calvinism! To what miserable shifts—yes, I must call them *miserable* shifts—is this system driven! On this subject I will not express myself in accordance with my feelings. The respect I have for the intelligent, learned, and pious gentlemen who have advanced this idea, restrains me in this matter. Such a result, in the advocacy of a favourite theory, is however in strict accordance with the known obliquity of the greatest and purest minds. But while we respect the authors of such a theory, and while we feel the necessity of taking heed to ourselves, lest we also fall by the same example of prejudice, we cannot suffer our common sense to be imposed upon by such gross absurdities. In this, however, we see that, as before, in trying to maintain their *ability*, they gave up their *depravity*: so here, in trying to establish their *depravity*, they destroy their *ability*. Nay, what is still worse for this theory, this very attempt to prove that infants are "*actual* sinners from their birth," is an indirect denial of the doctrine of derived depravity. Why do these gentlemen wish to establish this point? Why, forsooth, in order to show that men are *guilty* from their birth, which is an acknowledgment, of course, that they cannot prove them guilty only by proving that they have intelligent moral exercise. Consequently it is a concession that this exercise is the occasion and origin of their guilt. This is not the first time that Calvinism, in trying to save itself, has gone over and joined the ranks of its opposers. Can the reader see the difference between this doctrine of actual sin from the birth, viewed in connection with its origin and bearings, and the New Divinity, which makes sin consist exclusively in moral exercise? Let these old-side Calvinists, then, sheath the sword of controversy which they have drawn against their brethren, and join in with them to defend, if possible, the Pelagian doctrine which, it would seem, after all, they hold in common stock. Has the Rev. Mr. Harvey been so active in getting up an opposition theological school in Connecticut to teach that the infant "commences his existence in an *active voluntary* state of the will, and is thus (*on this account*) to a certain extent sinful?" This is clearly a work of supererogation—a useless expenditure of money and of talents. The New-Haven Theological School is capable—alas! too capable of carrying on this work, especially if Mr. Harvey and his friends will cease their opposition, and unite in their assistance. Does Mr. Harvey fear that the New-Haven divines will not begin their "*moral exercise*" early enough to make it *natural depravity?* They have given assurances that they will not be particular on that point. Only allow that there is no sin previous to the first intelligent act of choice—previous to the corresponding power to make themselves new hearts, and they will be satisfied. They have said already that "this capableness of sinning, if it is not at the exact moment of birth, [and they do not affirm that it is not,] commences so early in their existence, that it is proper, for all the great purposes of instruction, to speak of it as existing from the beginning of their days." Hence we see nothing between these gentlemen on this point worth contending about. It will, however, be important that all who hold to conversion by motives and mere moral suasion should not put the commencement of these "moral exercises" so far back that the subject cannot understand Gospel truth; otherwise they may yet get into another difficulty as serious as the one they are trying to avoid. But to the subject. It has been very distinctly shown, I think, from the reasoning of the Calvinists themselves, and from the nature of the case, that there can be no such intermediate theory as they contend for, between the native impotency of old Calvinism and Pelagianism. But as this is an important point, I will illustrate it farther by an examination of the *seat* of this Calvinistic depravity. It is seen, by the quotation above from Mr. Harvey, that he considers "depravity as seated in nothing but the will." And this is avowedly the sentiment of at least all those Calvinists who believe in natural ability. It is on this ground that they reiterate incessantly, "You can if you will;" "There is no difficulty except what is found in a perverse will." It is on this ground, also, that they tell us "a right choice is conversion." They do not say a right choice is a *condition* or a fruit of the new birth; but *it is itself the new birth.* But to understand this subject clearly, it is important to know what they mean by the will. It appears to me they use this term with great indefiniteness, if not latitude of meaning. If they mean by this what I understand to be the legitimate meaning of the term "the mental power or susceptibility of putting forth volitions;" then to say that all depravity is seated in the will, is to be guilty of the gross absurdity of teaching that the affections have not a moral character. If by the will, however, they mean, as they frequently seem to mean, the affections themselves going out in desire after some proposed good, then indeed they establish the New-Haven theory, that all sin consists in moral exercise. Thus by placing all depravity in the will, whether by this is meant the power of willing, or the exercise of the affections, they, in the one case, exclude sin from the affections altogether, and in the other affirm the doctrine of Pelagianism. But if by the will they mean something different from either of the above definitions, then I frankly confess I know not what they mean. Should they however, change their ground, and place the seat of this depravity in the constitution of man's moral nature, as it exists anterior to any act of volition, then and in that case they throw the subject back on the old ground of natural impotency; for to talk of a natural power to change the moral constitution, as it existed prior to choice, and which constitution must, by the law of its nature, exercise a controlling influence over the mind, is the same as to talk of a natural power to alter one's own nature, or to unmake and remake himself. In this case we must have supernatural aid, or we must remain as we are.

We shall not be fully prepared to judge correctly on this subject until we have examined one more preliminary question, viz. What is the precise meaning that we are to attach to the terms, *natural* and *moral ability*, as used by the Calvinists? To ascertain this, I have examined such authors as I have had access to, with care; and I have been particular to consult *recent* authors, that I might not be accused of charging old and exploded doctrines upon our opposers; and *various* authors, that I might ascertain any varieties that appertain to the different Calvinistic schools. In particular, the author of "Views in Theology;" Dr. Griffin, in a late work on "Divine Efficiency;" Rev. Tyler Thatcher, of the Hopkinsian school; and a doctrinal tract, entitled, "Man a Free Agent without the Aid of Divine Grace," written, it is presumed, by one of the divines of the New-Haven school have been consulted. There is among them all a remarkable uniformity on this point. If I understand them, the substance of what they say is, "Natural power consists in the possession of understanding, conscience, and will; and moral power is the *exercise* of these faculties." Mr. Thatcher says this in so many words.—The tract alluded to gives this definition of natural power. Dr. Griffin says "their [sinners'] faculties constitute a natural ability, that is, a full power to love and serve God, if their hearts are well disposed." It certainly must appear, at the first glance, very singular to every mind not embarrassed by theory, that either the *possession* of faculties, or the *exercise* of faculties, should be called *power*. The idea of *power* is supposed, by the best philosophical writers, to be undefinable, from the fact that it is a simple idea; but here, strange to tell, we have it analyzed in two different forms. Faculties are power—the exercise of faculties is power. Now, although we cannot define power, every one doubtless has a clear conception of it; and I humbly conceive that the common sense of every man will decide that neither of the above definitions embraces the true idea of power. The *exercise* of faculties *implies* power, it is granted; but every one must see that it is not power itself. And although the *faculties* of the mind are sometimes called the *powers* of the mind by a kind of borrowed use of the term power, just as the limbs or muscles are called the *powers* of the body, yet it requires very little discrimination to see that as we may possess these powers of the body entire, and yet they be defective from some cause, as to some of their appropriate functions, so we may possess these powers or faculties of mind entire, and yet they may be defective in that moral strength necessary to a holy choice. Hence the possession of these faculties does not even *imply* power adequate to a holy choice; much less are they *power itself*. I marvel therefore at these definitions of moral and natural power, and am thereby confirmed in the opinion advanced in my former number, viz. "That the whole of this distinction (of natural and moral ability) and the reasoning from it, proceed on the ground of a most unphilosophical analysis of mind, and an unwarranted definition of terms." This may seem a strong statement from so humble an individual as myself, in view of the many able minds that have adopted the opinions here opposed. But neither their opinion nor mine will weigh much, in this controversy, except as sustained by reasonable arguments; and by such arguments the present writer expects to stand or fall. Look then, reader, to both sides of this subject. Dr. Griffin himself seems to be at a loss how to explain himself on this subject. When he wishes to oppose the New-Haven divines, and guard against their error, he says, "If you mean by power, an ability that works without Divine efficiency, I hope I shall be the last to believe that." "And every body knows that the mass of the New-England divines, from the beginning, have acknowledged no such doctrine."

And why is *Divine efficiency* necessary?—Because man has no ability that will "work," without it. Thus the moment he sets up a guard against Pelagianism, he throws himself back either upon our doctrine, or upon the old Calvinistic doctrine of "native impotency."

There is no standing place any where else. The New-Haven divines are right, if natural ability is right; and the time cannot be far distant when the love of consistency will drive all, who hold to natural ability, either on to the New Divinity ground, or back to old Calvinism. From this remark the reader will see how much depends, if my views are correct, upon the proper adjustment of this question. It is in fact the turning point, which is to give a character to the theology of the Churches. Let us not then be in haste to pass over it. Hear Dr. Griffin farther. "Now if you ask me what is that power, which is never exerted without Divine efficiency? I can only say, that, in the account of the Divine mind, it is the proper basis of obligation, and therefore by the decision of common sense, must be called a power." The doctor had a little before told us, that this power was faculties—he is not satisfied with this; and what well instructed mind, like the doctor's, could be? It is something that forms the "basis of obligation," he knows not what it is. He merely infers there is such a power, because men are held responsible. But this inference will flow quite as naturally, by taking the Arminian ground of gracious ability, and save the other difficulties beside. At any rate, it will save the absurdity of holding to an ability, that will not "work," without being strengthened by Divine aid, and yet that this same ability is sufficient for all purposes of obligation without that aid.

We shall find equal difficulty, if we take up and examine this definition of *moral* power. It is "the exercise of natural power." But these same writers tell us that, while we have this natural power sufficient without Divine grace to form a basis of obligation, "we are entirely dependent upon God's grace for moral power"—in other words, according to the definition of moral power, we are dependent upon grace for the *exercise* of our natural power—and since natural power means the faculties of the understanding, will, and conscience—the statement is simply and evidently this: we are dependent upon Divine grace for the exercise of our understanding, conscience, and will, in making a holy choice. Why? Because the understanding, conscience, and will are so depraved by nature, that it is not in their nature to "work" in this exercise, without this Divine grace. Is not this holding the gracious ability after all? Is it singular then that Dr. Griffin should say, in another place —"They (sinners) are bound to go forth to their work at once, *but they are not bound to go* alone: it is their privilege and duty to cast themselves *instantly* on the Holy Ghost, and not to take a single step in their own *strength?*" Or is it any wonder that the Christian Spectator should say, that "this statement of Dr. Griffin brings him directly on the ground of evangelical Arminianism?" And is this the ability that "the mass of the New-England divines have held to from the beginning?" Not exactly. They only slide over on this ground occasionally, when they are pressed hard with Pelagianism on the one hand, and the old doctrine of passivity on the other. For the truth is, as before remarked, they have not a single point to balance themselves upon between these two, only as they light upon our ground.

There is still another difficulty in this moral power, as it is called. It implies the absurdity, that power to obey God is obedience itself. For a right exercise of our natural powers is obedience. But the right exercise of our natural power is moral power—therefore

Our moral power to obey God is obedience!! And this will give us a clue to the proper understanding of that oft-repeated Calvinistic saying—"You have power to obey God, if your heart is rightly disposed," or in short hand—"You can if you will." Now the verb *will* here evidently means the right *exercise* of the natural faculties—that is, as shown above, it means obedience. Hence the whole and proper meaning of this notable saying is—"You have power to obey God, *if you obey him*." "You *can* if you *do*." This is a sort of logic which, when scanned down to its naked character, one would get as little credit in refuting, as its abettors are entitled to for its invention and use. And yet this is the logic which, in its borrowed and fictitious costume has led thousands in our land to suppose that Calvinism, as it is now modified, is the same, or nearly the same with Methodism.

There is still another striking solecism, necessarily connected with this definition of power. It supposes it to have no actual existence, until the necessity for it ceases. For in the order of cause and effect, natural power effects the act of obedience; and this effect of natural power, producing obedience, gives existence to moral power. Thus we have power to obey, super-added to the power that has actually obeyed! If, however, Calvinists say this is treating the subject unfairly, because their very definition shows that they do not mean by it any thing which *enables* man to obey—I answer, that my reasoning went upon the ground, that it was what they call it—*power;* and if they do not mean power, that is only acknowledging the position I started upon, that this Calvinistic power is no power at all. And here I ask, in the name of candour, What is the use of calling things by wrong names? What confusion and error may not be introduced by applying common and well defined terms in such a manner, that, when the things to which they are applied, are defined, it is seen that the terms thus applied are worse than useless; they directly mislead the mind! It is the direct way to bring Christian theology and Christian ministers into distrust and reproach.

One thought more, with respect to this moral power, and I will pass on. The doctrine of Calvinism is, if I understand it, that God controls the natural power of men, by means of their moral power. This some of them expressly affirm. And to show that I am not mistaken with respect to the others, let the reader carefully attend to the following considerations. What is it secures the fulfilment of the Divine decrees, in respect to the elect and the reprobate? Why do not some of the reprobates, in the use of natural ability, repent and get to heaven? Because they have not the moral power. Why do not some of the elect, in the use of the same ability, fall into sin and finally perish? Because God makes and keeps them willing in the day of his power—that is, he irresistibly imparts to them this moral power. Thus, by means of this, which he keeps in his own hands he executes his decrees. For God, of set purpose, so constituted this natural power, that it does not "work" without Divine efficiency. By moral power; therefore, natural power is controlled. Now, to say nothing here of the absurdity of efficiently and irresistibly controlling one power by another, and yet calling that other the essence of free agency, and the basis of obligation—look at the absurdity in another point of view. Since moral power is the exercise of natural power, the former must be the *effect* of the latter. And since, according to Calvinism, natural power is controlled by moral power, it follows conclusively; that the effect controls its cause!! And since the cause must act, before the effect is produced, it follows that the effect, before it has an existence, acts upon its cause to produce its own existence!!! This is certainly a nullification of both cause and effect: Such are some of the difficulties of these definitions of power—definitions as contrary to the common understandings of men, and the common laws of language, as they are to sound philosophy—definitions which, if they were always understood, when the terms were used; would make the propositions in which these terms are found, sound very differently to the common ear. I trust therefore it has been made to appear, that "this distinction of natural and moral ability, and the reasonings upon it, are founded on a most unphilosophical analysis of mind and an unwarranted definition of terms," and that, after all the efforts of the Calvinists to find out another alternative, they will be under the necessity, if they would be consistent, either of going back to the old Calvinistic ground, of remediless impotency, or of advancing on to the Pelagian ground of the New Divinity; or they must accept of the Arminian theory of gracious ability. And that the reader may be prepared to make his selection, I will here remind him of the arguments adduced in favour of the latter doctrine, in the last number, while I next proceed to answer more specifically the objections that have been urged against it, which however for an obvious reason must be withheld until the next number.

NUMBER XII.
OBJECTIONS TO GRACIOUS ABILITY ANSWERED.

In consulting different authors to find the strongest objections that have been urged against our doctrine of ability by grace, I have fixed upon the doctrinal tract, already alluded to, entitled, "Man a Free Agent without the Aid of Divine Grace," as concentrating in a small compass, and in a clear and able manner, the sum total of these objections. I may not follow the precise order of this writer, and possibly shall pass over some of his remarks as of minor importance, but the substance of his reasoning shall receive such notice as I shall be able to give it.

1. The first objection is, in substance, this: that without being a free agent man cannot be *man;* that free agency in fact enters into the very definition of an intelligent, morally responsible being; and therefore he must be such by nature.

This objection gains all its plausibility from the writer's definition of free agency. "It consists," he says, "in the possession of *understanding, conscience,* and *will.*" Now we grant that the being who possesses these is an intelligent voluntary agent. But these faculties, as we have seen, may be disordered, so that, for all holy purposes, they may be defective. The understanding may be darkened, the conscience may be seared, the power to choose good may be weakened either positively or relatively. *Liberty* is a distinct faculty of the soul; and as such is as subject to derangement as any other mental susceptibility. It has, we say, suffered materially by the fall; so that man has not his original aptitude or facility to good. And whether we consider this as a weakness appertaining directly to the faculty of the will itself, or whether we consider it a relative weakness, (which is probably the more philosophical,) resulting from the loss of a moral equilibrium in the mind, by reason of the uncontrolled sway of the passions, in either case the primary cause and the practical result are the same. Sin has perverted the soul, and given it an unholy declination from righteousness to an extent which none but God can rectify. With this view of the subject, the writer may call man a free agent if he pleases; but he is only free to unrighteousness, and not to holiness.

Our objector was aware that his argument might be disposed of in this way; and hence in a note he says, "Some writers speak of man, in his natural state, as *free only* to evil. But in what does such freedom differ from mere instinct? With no power to do otherwise, how is he who murders a fellow creature more criminal than the tiger, or even a falling rock that destroys him?" The fallacy of this argument consists chiefly in a misrepresentation of our theory. Instead of holding that man "has no power to do otherwise," we believe, as much as this author, that man has ample power at his command to do otherwise; but that this power is of grace, and not of nature. Any farther supposed difficulties growing out of this view of the subject will be explained, I trust satisfactorily, as we advance.[6]

2. "Every man is conscious that he possesses the faculties which constitute free agency."—Here again we must keep in view the writer's definition. We shall find no difficulty in granting that every man is conscious that he possesses the faculties of understanding, conscience, and will; but that these, unaided by grace, constitute man free to a holy choice, is denied; and this is the very question in debate. To affirm it therefore in argument is begging the question.

It however, the author means to say, as his reasoning on this point seems to imply, that man is conscious of being a free agent, in the responsible sense of the term, this is also granted; but then this does not touch the question whether this power is of grace or of nature. But, says the writer, "When man, under the influence of grace, does choose the good, he is not conscious of any new faculty or power to choose, but only he uses that power in a different manner. The power or faculty which chooses evil and which chooses good, is the same power differently used." Whoever disputed this? —understanding by power a faculty of the soul, as this author evidently does. We all acknowledge that the soul gets no new faculties by grace; but we believe that the mind, in the exercise of its natural faculties, is assisted by grace to make a right choice. But, says the writer, in this connection, "Power to choose between two objects is power to choose either." If the writer means to say that power to choose either the one or the other of two objects *is* power to choose either—this is an identical proposition: it is only saying, *If a thing is, it is*. But if he means to say, when two objects are presented to the mind, and the mind finds itself possessed of a power to attach itself voluntarily to one, that therefore it has the *same power* to attach itself to the other, this is denied; and as no proof is given or pretended by the objector, nothing but a denial is necessary. On this point the founder of the Calvinistic school was undoubtedly correct —philosophically and theologically correct—when he said, "Man has not an equally free election of good and evil."

But that I may meet this objection founded on consciousness, full in the face, I am prepared to assert, and I think prove, that man, so far from being conscious that he has by nature adequate power to serve God, is conscious of the very reverse of this. What truly awakened sinner has not a deep conviction of his utter helplessness? How many experiences of intelligent and pious Calvinists could I quote on this point? As a specimen take that of the Rev. David Brainerd, who stands high in the Church, not only among Calvinists, but among all Christians who know him. I quote a passage from his experience quoted by Dr. Griffin: "I saw that it was utterly impossible for me to do any thing toward helping or delivering myself. I had the greatest certainty that my state was for ever miserable for all that I could do, and wondered that I had never been sensible of it before."—This passage is very strong; too unqualified, perhaps, but it is the natural language of a weak sinner, convinced, as all must be before they *can become strong*, of their utter helplessness without grace. How fully does such a one prove the truth of Scripture, that "the *natural* man receiveth not the things of the Spirit of God, for they are foolishness unto him, neither *can* he know them, for they are spiritually discerned;" that "no man knoweth the Father, but the Son, and he to whom the Son shall reveal him." Hence the necessity that "the Spirit should take of the things of Jesus Christ, and show them unto them." Indeed, but for this darkness and weakness of the understanding, the penitent sinner would not feel the necessity of the agency of the Spirit: nor would it in fact be necessary. It is on this ground that the doctrine of natural ability has led to the idea of conversion by *moral suasion*. Thus it is evident that a man may be conscious of having an understanding, but at the same time be as *fully* conscious that that understanding is too dark and weak for holy purposes, unaided by grace. The same is also true of conscience. Experience teaches us that it often becomes languid or dead, and needs quickening. Hence the Christian often prays—

"Quick as the apple of an eye,

O God! my conscience make;

Awake my soul when sin is nigh,

And keep it still awake."

Hence also we pray God to alarm the conscience of sinners. So also we learn from Scripture and experience that the conscience needs purging "from dead works," for the very object that we may be able "to serve God with filial fear;" we learn also that we may have "defiled consciences," "weak consciences," "seared consciences," &c. And here let it be noticed, that whether we understand these passages as applying to the regenerate or unregenerate, to derived depravity or contracted depravity, the argument against the objector will in every case apply with resistless force, viz. it shows that this faculty of the soul may become so disordered as to have its original healthy action impaired, and that in this case nothing can give it its original sensibility and strength but the God who made it. If sin does disorder the conscience, it disordered Adam's: and if he begat children in his own moral likeness, then his posterity had a similar conscience. And therefore it is necessary that, as by the offence of the first Adam sin abounded, so by the obedience of the second, grace may abound in a way directly to meet the evil.

Let us next examine the will. Are we not conscious that this also is weak? How repeatedly does the awakened sinner resolve and fail! until he becomes deeply impressed that he is "without strength!" He tries to keep the law, but cannot; for he finds that "the carnal mind is not subject to the law of God, neither indeed *can be*." Hear his complaint! and that we may be sure of taking a genuine case, let us select a Bible experience from Rom. vii; "I am carnal, sold under sin." (How much liberty to serve God has a bond slave to sin?) "That which I do I allow not; for what I would do that I do not, but what I hate that do I." "To will is present with me, but how to perform that which is good, I find not," &c. (See through the chapter.) Hear him finally exclaim, in self despair, "Who shall deliver me from the body of this death?" Why, Saul of Tarsus! are you not conscious that you have understanding, conscience, and will? Why make such an exclamation? Who shall deliver you? *Deliver yourself.* No! such philosophy and such theology were not known to this writer, neither as a penitent sinner, nor as an inspired apostle. "I thank God, through Jesus Christ my Lord."—"The law of the spirit of life, in Christ Jesus, hath made me free from the law [the controlling power] of sin and death."

Should any one say that the apostle was not describing his *conversion* here, but his experience as a Christian believer, I reply: If any thing, *that* would make the passage so much the stronger for my present purpose; for "if these things are done in the green tree, what shall be done in the dry?" If a saint—one who has been washed and renewed—finds nevertheless that his will is so weak as to need the continued grace of God to enable him to do the things that he would, much more is this true of the unrenewed sinner. If this account of the apostle's experience means any thing, *it is as express a contradiction of the doctrine, that we have natural strength to serve God, as could be put into words.* And I am bold to say that this is the experience of all Christians. And it presents an argument against the doctrine of natural ability which no metaphysical reasoning can overthrow—not indeed an argument to prove that we have not understanding, conscience, and will; but to show that, having these in a disordered and debilitated state, grace is indispensable to aid them, in order to an efficient holy choice. How often soever the judgment may be brought to a preference of the Divine law, it will as often be carried away by the strength of the unholy passions until it is delivered by the grace of our Lord Jesus Christ. *We are conscious therefore that we have not natural power to keep the Divine law.*

3. But it is objected again, "that the Scriptures require us to use our natural faculties in the service of God;" and hence the inference is, that these faculties are adequate to this service.

It is certainly no objection to our doctrine, that the Scriptures, dealing with man as he is, require him to use his natural powers to serve God. With what other powers should he serve him? I again repeat that the question is not, whether we have *mental faculties*, nor whether man may or can serve God with these faculties, but simply whether the command to obey is given independently of the considerations of grace. We say it is not; and in proof refer to the Scriptures, which give a promise corresponding with every command, and assurances of gracious aid suited to every duty—all of which most explicitly imply, not only man's need, but also the ground on which the command is predicated. And with this idea agrees the alleged condemnation, so often presented in the Scriptures: "This is the condemnation, that light has come into the world, and men have loved darkness." "He that believeth not is condemned already." "But they grieved his Holy Spirit, therefore he is turned to be their enemy." "How shall we escape, if we neglect so great salvation." These, and many other passages, show that the turning point of guilt and condemnation is not so much the abuse of natural powers, as the neglect and abuse of grace bestowed.

This point may be illustrated by Christ's healing the withered hand. He commanded the man to stretch it forth. What was the ground of that command, and what was implied in it? The ground of it was, that aid would be given him to do it; otherwise the command to stretch forth a palsied limb would have been unreasonable. And yet it was understood that the man was to have no new muscles, or nerves, or bones, to accomplish this with; but he was to use those he had, assisted, as they would be, by the gracious power of God. So man, it is true, is commanded to use his natural powers in obeying God; but not without Divine aid, the promise of which is always either expressed or implied in the command.

4. "The Scriptures ascribe no other inability to man to obey God, but that which consists in or results from the perversion of those faculties which constitute him a moral agent."

It is true, the Scriptures blame man for his inability—for inability they certainly ascribe to him, and why? Because where sin abounded grace has much more abounded. That sinners are perverse and unprepared for holy obedience up to this hour is undoubtedly their own fault, for grace has been beforehand with them. It met them at the very threshold of their moral agency, with every thing necessary to meet their case. It has dug about the fruitless fig tree. It has laid the foundation to say justly, "What more could I have done for my vineyard?" If the sinner has rejected all this, and has increased his depravity by actual transgression, then indeed is he justly chargeable for all his embarrassments and moral weakness, for he has voluntarily assumed to himself the responsibility of his native depravity, and he has added to this the accumulated guilt of his repeated sins.

5. It is farther objected, with a good deal of confidence, that Arminians, after all, make man's natural power the ground and measure of his guilt, since "no part of his free agency arises from furnished grace, but it consists simply inability to use or abuse that grace, and of course in an ability distinct from, and not produced by the grace."

Let us see, however, if there is not some sophistry covered up here. Arminians do not mean that man's ability to use grace is independent of, and separate from the grace itself. They say that man's powers are directly assisted by grace, so that through this assistance they have ability or strength *in those powers* which before they had not, to make a right choice. To talk of ability to use gracious ability, in any other sense, would be absurd. It would be like talking of *strength* to use *strength*—of *being able to be able*. This absurdity, however, appears to me justly chargeable upon the natural ability theory, taken in connection with the Scripture account of this matter. The Scriptures instruct us to look to God for strength; that he gives us "power to become the children of God;" that he "strengthens with might in the inner man, that we may be *able*," &c. This theory, however, tells us that we have an ability back of this; an ability on which our responsibility turns, and by means of which we can become partakers of the grace of the Gospel. This is certainly to represent the Divine Being as taking measures to make *ability able*, and adding power to make *adequate strength sufficiently strong*.—Such is the work of supererogation which this theory charges upon the Gospel, for which its advocates alone are answerable; but let them not, without better ground, attempt to involve us in such an absurdity. But the strongest objections, in the opinion of those who differ from us, are yet to come. They are of a doctrinal, rather than of a philosophical character, and are therefore more tangible, and will, for this reason, perhaps, be more interesting to the generality of readers. Let us have patience, then, to follow them out.

6. *Doctrinal Objections.*—On the ground of gracious ability it is objected that, 1. "As the consequence of Adam's fall, Adam himself and all his posterity became incapable of committing another sin." 2. "Every sinful action performed in this world, since the fall of Adam, has been the effect of supernatural grace." 3. "Man needed the grace of God, not because he was wicked, but because he was weak." 4. "The moral difference between one man and another is not to be ascribed to God." 5. "The posterity of Adam needed no Saviour to atone for actual sin." 6. "This opinion is inconsistent with the doctrine of grace." 7. "There can be no guilt in the present rebellion of the infernal regions." 8. "Is not this grace a greater calamity to our race than the fall of Adam?"

I have thrown these objections together, and presented them in connection to the reader, for the reason that they all rest mainly on one or two erroneous assumptions, to correct which will be substantially to answer them all.

One erroneous assumption of this writer is, that "there is no free agency to do wrong, which is not adequate to do right." This writer seems to think this a self-evident proposition, which needs no proof; for although he has used it in argument a number of times, he has left it unsustained by any thing but his naked assertion. This proposition has already been denied, and an unqualified denial is all that in fairness can be claimed by an antagonist to meet an unqualified assertion. Our object, however, is truth, and not victory. Let me request you then, reader, to look at this proposition. Can you see any self-evident proof of this assertion? If the Creator should give existence to an intelligent being, and infuse into his created nature the elements of unrighteousness, and give to his faculties an irresistible bias to sin, and all this without providing a remedy, or a way for escape, then indeed all our notions of justice would decide that such a being ought not to be held responsible. But this is not the case with any of the sinful beings of God's moral government.—Not of the fallen angels, for they had original power to stand, but abused it and fell—not of fallen man, for in the first place his is not a created depravity; but, in the case of Adam, it was contracted by voluntary transgression when he had power to stand; and in the case of his posterity, it is derived and propagated in the ordinary course of generation: and in the second place, a remedy is provided which meets the exigencies of man's moral condition, at the very commencement of his being. This it does by graciously preventing the imputation of guilt until man is capable of an intelligent survey of his moral condition; for "as by the offence of one, judgment came upon all men unto condemnation: even so, by the righteousness of one, the free gift came upon all men unto justification of life." And when man becomes capable of moral action, this same gracious remedy is suited to remove his native depravity, and to justify him from the guilt of actual transgression; for "if we confess our sins, he is faithful and just to forgive us our sins, and cleanse us from all unrighteousness." It does not appear, then, either from the obvious character of the proposition itself; or from the condition of sinful beings, that "the same free agency which enables a man to do wrong, will enable him also to do right." Hence it is not true that Adam, by the fall, lost his power to sin, or that there is now no sin in the infernal regions. It is true, the writer tries to sustain this idea farther, by asserting that "*that* ceases to be a moral wrong which is unavoidable; for no being can be held responsible for doing what is unavoidable." This is little better, however, than a reiteration of the former assumption. If the character and conduct of a being are not *now*, and never *have been* avoidable, then indeed he ought not to have guilt imputed to him. But to say that there is "no moral wrong" in the case, is to say that characters and actions are not wrong in themselves, even where it would not be just to impute guilt. And this is an idea which is implied also in another part of this writer's reasoning; for he tells us that, according to the doctrine of gracious ability "every sinful action performed in this world, since the fall of Adam, has been the effect of supernatural grace;" and that "man needed the grace of God, not because he was wicked, but because he was weak," &c. This reasoning, or rather these propositions, are predicated on the assumption, that there is no *moral wrong* where there is no *existing* ability to do right: in other words, that dispositions and acts of intelligent beings are not *in themselves* holy or unholy, but are so only in reference to the *existing* power of the being who is the subject of these dispositions and acts.

But is this correct? Sin may certainly exist where it would not be just to impute it to the sinner. For the apostle tells us that "until the law sin was in the world;" and yet he adds, "Sin is not imputed (he does not say sin does not exist,) where there is no law." The fact there are certain dispositions and acts that are *in their nature* opposite to holiness, whatever may be the power of the subject *at the time* he possesses this character or performs these acts. Sin is sin, and holiness is holiness, under all circumstances. They have a positive, and not merely a relative existence. And although they have not existence abstract from an agent possessing understanding, conscience, and will, still they may have an existence abstractly from the power of being or doing otherwise at the time. If not, then the new-born infant has no moral character, or he has power to become holy with his first breath. Whether the subject of this unavoidable sin shall be responsible for it, is a question to be decided by circumstances. If a being has had power, and lost it by his own avoidable act, then indeed he is responsible for his impotency—his very weakness becomes his crime, and every act of omission or commission resulting from his moral impotency, is justly imputed to him, the assertion of our objector to the contrary notwithstanding. Hence it is incorrect to say there is now "no guilt in the rebellion of the infernal regions." It is of little consequence whether, in this case, you assume that all the guilt is in the first act, by which the ability to do good was lost, or in each successive act of sin, which was the unavoidable consequence of the first. In either case, the acts that follow are the measure of the guilt; and hence, according to the nature of the mind, the consciousness of guilt will be constantly felt, as the acts occur. For all practical purposes, therefore, the sense of guilt, and the Divine administration of justice will be the same in either view of the subject. The writer supposes the case of "a servant's cutting off his hands to avoid his daily task," and says, "this he is to blame, and ought to be punished;" but thinks he ought not to be punished for his subsequent deficiencies. But I ask, How much is he to blame, and to what extent should he be punished? His guilt and punishment are to be measured, certainly, by the amount of wrong he has done his master—that is, by every act of omission consequent upon this act, which rendered these omissions unavoidable. Therefore he is justly punishable for every act of omission; and you may refer this whole punishment to the first act exclusively, or to all the acts separately: it amounts to the same thing in the practical administration of government and of justice. Indeed, to say that each succeeding act is to be brought up and taken into the estimate, in order to fix the quantum of punishment, is to acknowledge that these succeeding acts are sins; else why should they be brought into the account at all, in estimating guilt and punishment? Take another case. The drunkard destroys or suspends the right use of his reason, and then murders. Is he to be held innocent of the murder because he was drunk? or was the whole guilt of the murder to be referred to the act of getting intoxicated? If you say the former, then no man is to be punished for any crime committed in a fit of intoxication; and one has only to get intoxicated in order to be innocent. If you say the latter, then, as getting drunk is the same in one case as another, *every* inebriate is guilty of murder, and whatever other crimes drunkeness *may* occasion, or has occasioned. Is either of these suppositions correct? Shall we not rather say that the inebriate's guilt is to be measured by the aggregate of crimes flowing from the voluntary act of drowning his reason? And so in the case before us. Instead then of saying, that on our principles "there is no guilt in the present rebellion of the infernal regions," I would say that their present rebellion is the fruits and measure of their guilt. Thus we see, that a being who has had power and lost it, is guilty of his present acts.

And by examination we shall find that by how much we enhance the estimated guilt of the first act, it is by borrowing so much from the acts of iniquity which follow. And will you then turn round and say, the acts which follow have no guilt? Why have they no guilt? Evidently because you have taken the amount of that guilt and attached it to the first act. And does this make these acts in themselves innocent? The idea is preposterous. As well may you say that the filthy streams of a polluted fountain are not impure in themselves, because but for the fountain they would not be impure; as to say that the current of unholy volitions which unavoidably flows from a perverted heart is not unholy and criminal.

Another clearly erroneous assumption of this writer is, that if it would be unjust for the Divine Being to leave his plan *unfinished*, after it is begun, the *whole* plan must be predicated on justice, and not on grace. It is true, he has not said this, in so many words, but his reasoning implies it. For he says this scheme of gracious ability "annihilates the whole doctrine of grace." Because God, if he held man accountable, was bound to give him this ability, as a matter of justice; hence it is not an ability by grace, but an ability by justice. The whole of this reasoning, and much more, goes upon the principle, that the *completion* of a plan of grace, after it is begun, cannot be claimed on the scale of justice, without making the whole a plan of justice. But is this true? Is not a father, after he has been instrumental of bringing a son into the world, bound *in justice* to provide for and educate him? And yet does not the son owe a debt of gratitude to that father, when he has done all this? If a physician should cut off the limb of a poor man, to save his life, is he not bound *in justice*, after he has commenced the operation, to take up the arteries and save the man from dying, by the operation. And if he should not do it, would he not be called a wanton and cruel wretch? And yet in both these cases the persons may be unworthy. The son may show much obliquity of moral principle, and yet the father should bear with him, and discipline him. The man on whom the physician operated may be poor and perverse. Here then are cases in which *justice demands that un merited favour begun should be continued*, or else what was favour in the commencement, and what would be favour in the whole, would nevertheless by its incompleteness, be most manifest injustice. Such is the state of the question in respect to the Divine administration. The whole race of man had become obnoxious to the Divine displeasure, in their representative and federal head, by reason of *his* sin. This is expressly stated: "By the offence of one, judgment came upon all men to condemnation." "In Adam all die." In this situation we may suppose that the strict justice of the law required punishment in the very character in which the offence was committed. Adam personally and consciously sinned; and so, according to justice, he must suffer. The prospective generations of men, existing seminally in him, as they had not consciously and personally sinned, could, in justice, only experience the effects of the curse in the same character in which they sinned, viz. passively and seminally, unless provision could be made, by which, in their personal existence, they might free themselves from the effects of sin. Now God, in the plenitude of his wisdom and grace, saw fit to make provision for a new probation for man, on the basis of a covenant of grace, the different parts of which are all to be viewed together, in order to judge of their character. In this covenant Adam had a *new trial;* and when the promise was made to him he stood in the same relation to his posterity as he did when he sinned, and the curse was out against him. If, by the latter, the prospective generations of men were justly cut off from possible existence; by the former this existence was mercifully secured to them. If by the corruption of the race, through sin, the possibility of salvation was cut off, on all known principles of administrative justice;

by the provisions of grace the possibility of salvation was secured to the whole race; and this possibility implies every necessary provision to render grace available and efficient, in accordance with moral responsibility. If "God, who spared not his own Son, but freely gave him up for us all," had not "with him also freely given us all things" necessary for our salvation, would not the Divine procedure have been characterized both by folly and injustice? If his plan of grace had only gone so far as to have given us a conscious being, without giving us the means of making that existence happy, would it not have been wanton cruelty? And yet, taking the whole together, who does not see that it is a most stupendous system of grace, from the foundation to the top-stone? Let us not then be guilty of such manifest folly, as to take a part of the Divine administration, and make up a judgment upon that, as viewed independently of the rest, and then transfer this abstract character to the whole. As in chemical combinations, though one of the ingredients taken alone might be deleterious, yet the compound may be nutritious or salutary, so in the new covenant, if we separate legal exactions and penalties from gracious provisions, the operations of the former may be unjust and cruel, yet the whole, united as God hath combined them, may be an administration of unparalleled grace. It is in this heavenly combination that "mercy and truth are met together, righteousness and peace have kissed each other." Now, therefore, "if we confess our sins, he is faithful and *just* to forgive us our sins," for on this ground he can be "*just* and the justifier of them that believe." Although justice is thus involved in the system, and to leave out part of the system would be manifest injustice, yet the whole is the "blessed Gospel;" "the Gospel of the grace of God." It is objected, I know, that the idea that, but for the provisions of the Gospel, man would not have propagated his species, is fanciful and unauthorized by Scripture. The Scriptures, I grant, do not strike off into speculations about what God might have done, or would have done, if he had not done as he has. This is foreign from their design; and I am perfectly willing to let the whole stand as the Scriptures present it. But when our opponents set the example of raising an objection to what we think the true system, by passing judgment on a part, viewed abstractly, we must meet them. On their own ground, then, I would say, the idea that man would have been allowed to propagate his species, without any provisions of grace, is altogether fanciful and unauthorized by Scripture. Will it be said, that it seems more reasonable, and in accordance with the course of nature, to suppose that he would? I answer, It seems to me more reasonable, and in accordance with the course of justice, to suppose that he would not. Whoever maintains that the personal existence of Adam's posterity was not implied and included in the provisions of grace, in the new covenant, must take into his theory one of the following appendages;—he must either believe that the whole race could justly be consigned to personal and unavoidable wo, for the sin of Adam, or that all could be justly condemned for the sin of their own nature, entailed upon them without their agency, and therefore equally unavoidable; or he must believe that each would have a personal trial on the ground of the covenant of works, as Adam had. If there is another alternative, it must be some system of probation which God has never intimated, and man, in all his inventions has never devised. Whoever is prepared to adopt either of the two former propositions is prepared to go all lengths in the doctrine of predestination and reprobation charged upon Calvinism in the sermon that gave rise to this controversy, and, of course, will find his system subject to all the objections there urged against it. If any one chooses to adopt the third alternative, and consider all the posterity of Adam as standing or falling solely on the ground of the covenant of works, such a one need not be answered in a discussion purporting to be a "*Calvinistic* controversy." He is a Socinian, and must be answered in another place. All that need be done here, is to show the embarrassments of *Calvinism proper*, the utter futility of all its changes to relieve itself from these embarrassments, unless it plunge into Pelagianism and Socinianism, or rest itself upon the Arminian foundation of gracious ability. It is on this latter ground we choose to rest, because here, and here alone, we find the doctrines of natural depravity, human ability and responsibility, and salvation by grace, blending in beautiful harmony.

Having noticed some of the erroneous assumptions on which the doctrinal objections to our theory are based, the objections themselves, I think, may all be disposed of in a summary way. We see, on our plan, that, 1. Adam did not render himself incapable of sinning, by the fall, but rather rendered himself and his posterity incapable of any other moral exercise but what was sinful; and it was on this account that a gracious ability is necessary, in order to a second probation. 2. Sin, since the fall, has not been the result of supernatural grace, but the natural fruit of the fall; and supernatural grace is all that has counteracted sin. 3. "Man needed the grace of God," *both* "because he was wicked," *and* "because he was weak."—4. "The moral difference between one man and another is —to be ascribed to God." How any one could think a contrary opinion chargeable upon us, is to me surprising. It is more properly Calvinism that is chargeable with this sentiment. Calvinism says, Regeneration is a right choice. It says, also, that power to sin implies power to be holy; and of course we become holy by the same power as that by which we sin. And it farther says, that the power is of nature and not of grace. Now let the reader put all these together, and see if it does not follow most conclusively, that "the moral difference between one man and another is not to be ascribed to God." But, on the contrary, *we* say the sinful nature of man is changed in regeneration by the power of the Holy Ghost. 5. "The posterity of Adam" *did* "need a Saviour to atone for actual sin." For actual sin is the result, not of gracious power, as this author supposes, but of a sinful nature voluntarily retained and indulged. If our opponents charge us with the sentiment, that grace is the cause of the actual sin of Adam's posterity, because we hold that grace was the cause of their personal existence, we grant that, in that sense, grace was a cause without which the posterity of Adam would not have sinned. But if this makes God the author of sin, by the same rule we could prove that God is the author of sin, because he created moral agents—and if there is any difficulty here, it presses on them as heavily as on us. But in any other sense, grace is not the cause of sin. 6. "This opinion is," as we have seen, perfectly "with the doctrine of grace." 7. "There is" *constant* "guilt in the present rebellion of the infernal regions." 8. "This grace is a greater" *blessing* "to our race than the fall of Adam" was a "calamity;" for "where sin abounded, grace did much more abound."

Thus I have endeavoured to *explain*, *prove*, and *defend* the doctrine of gracious ability, a doctrine always maintained in the orthodox Church, until the refinements of Calvinism made it necessary to call it in question; and a doctrine on which, viewed in its different bearings, the orthodox Arminian system must stand or fall. I have been the more minute and extended in my remarks from this consideration; and also from the consideration that while this doctrine has of late been most violently assailed by all classes of Calvinists, very little has been published in its defence. If the reader has had patience to follow the subject through, he is now perhaps prepared to judge whether our holy volitions are the result of a gracious ability or of natural power.

Should I find time to pursue this subject farther, it would be in place now to examine the doctrine of regeneration; in which examination the nature of inherent depravity, and of that choice which is conditional to the new birth, would be more fully noticed. "This will I do if God permit."

NUMBER XIII.

REGENERATION.

An important error in any one cardinal doctrine of the Gospel will make a glaring deformity in the entire system. Hence when one of these doctrines is marred or perverted, a corresponding change must be made in most or all of the others to keep up the appearance of consistency.

These remarks apply with special emphasis to the doctrine of regeneration. As this is a focal point, in which many other leading doctrines centre, this doctrine must of necessity give a character to the whole Gospel plan. This might be inferred *a priori* from the knowledge of the relation of *this* to the other parts of the Christian system, and it is practically illustrated in the history of the Church. There are those who believe, that by the various terms used in Scripture to express the change commonly called regeneration or the new birth, nothing is intended but some outward ceremony, or some change of opinion in matters of speculative belief or the like. Some say it is baptism, or a public profession of faith; others that it is a mere speculative renunciation of heathen idolatry, and an acknowledgment of the Christian faith; others that it is merely a reformed life; and a few maintain that it is the change that we shall undergo by death, or by the resurrection of the body. These persons, and all in fact who make the new birth something short of a radical change of heart, are obliged, for consistency's sake, to accommodate the other doctrines to their views of regeneration. Hence they very generally deny constitutional or derived depravity, the inflexibility and rigorous exactions of the Divine law, the destructive character of sin, the atonement, the supernatural agency of the Spirit upon the human heart, justification by faith, and the like. Thus a radical error on one point actually leads to *another gospel*—if gospel it may be called.

It does not come within the scope of my present design to enter into a refutation of the foregoing errors. But from the disastrous results of these errors we may infer the importance of guarding carefully and of understanding clearly the Scripture doctrine of the new birth. Even where the error is not so radical, as in the instances above alluded to, the evil may be considerable, and in some cases fatal.

The Arminians and Calvinists agree in this doctrine, in so far as that they both make it a radical change of moral nature, by the supernatural agency of the Holy Ghost. But they differ in respect to the *order* in which the several parts of the change take place—in respect to the manner and degree of the agency of the Holy Spirit, and also in respect to the part which human agency has in the accomplishment of this change. And in some, if not all of these points, Calvinists differ as much from each other as they do from us.

It is my present purpose to point out some of the more prominent Calvinistic modes of stating and explaining this doctrine, with the difficulties attending them: after which I shall endeavour to present and defend what we believe to be the Scripture doctrine of regeneration.

First Theory.—The notion that the mind is entirely passive in this change, that is, that nothing is done by the subject of it, which is preparative or conditional, or in any way co-operative in its accomplishment, has been a prevailing sentiment in the various modifications of the old Calvinistic school. It is not indeed pretended that the mind is inactive, either before or at the time this renovation is effected by the Holy Spirit. On the contrary, it is said that the sinner is resisting with all the power of the mind, and with all the obstinacy of the most inveterate enmity, up to the very moment, and in the very act of conversion. So that the sinner is regenerated, not only *without* his *co-operation*, but also in *spite* of his *utmost resistance*. Hence it is maintained, that, but for the *irresistible* influence of the Holy Ghost upon the heart, no sinner would be converted.

1. One of the leading objections to this view of conversion is, that it is inseparably connected with the doctrine of particular and unconditional election. The two reciprocally imply each other, and must therefore, stand or fall together. But this doctrine of particular and unconditional election has been sufficiently refuted, it is hoped, in the sermon that gave rise to this controversy; if so, then the doctrine of passivity and irresistible grace is not true.

2. Another very serious difficulty which this theory of conversion has to contend with is, that the Scriptures, in numerous passages, declare that the Spirit of God may be *resisted, grieved, quenched,* and utterly disregarded; and that the grace of God may be abused, or received in vain. The passages to establish these propositions are so frequent that I need not stop to point them out. But if this be so, then the grace of God and the Spirit of grace are not irresistible.

3. It may be yet farther objected to this doctrine of the mind's passivity in conversion, that it is a virtual denial of all gracious influence upon the heart before regeneration. It has been shown in previous numbers that man was not able to comply with the conditions of salvation without grace—and that the gracious influences of the Divine Spirit are given to every sinner previous to regeneration. But there would be no necessity for this, and no consistency in it, if there are no conditions and no co-operation on the part of the sinner in the process of the new birth. Hence the advocates of this doctrine very consistently maintain that the first act of grace upon the heart of the sinner is that which regenerates him. Since then this theory conflicts with the Bible doctrine of a gracious influence anterior to conversion, it cannot be admitted.

4. This theory of regeneration removes all conditions on the part of the sinner to the removal of the power and guilt of sin. It teaches that if the sinner should do any thing acceptable to God, *as a condition* to his conversion, it would imply he did not need converting; that such an idea, in fact, would be inconsistent with the doctrine of depravity, and irreconcilable with the idea of salvation *by grace*. And this is the ground on which the old Calvinists have so repeatedly charged us with the denial of the doctrines of grace, and with holding that we may be justified by our works.

There is something very singular in these notions respecting the necessity of *unconditional* regeneration, in order that it may be by grace. These same Calvinists tell us that the sinner *can* repent, and ought to repent, and that the Scriptures require it at his hand. What! is the sinner able and obliged to do that which would destroy the whole economy of grace! which would blot out the Gospel and nullify the atonement itself? Ought he to do that which would prove him a practical Pelagian and an operative workmonger? Is he indeed, according to Calvinists themselves, required in Scripture to do that which would prove Calvinism false, and a conditional regeneration true? So it would seem. Put together these two dogmas of Calvinism. 1. *The sinner is able, and ought to repent.* 2. *The idea that the sinner does any thing toward his regeneration destroys the doctrine of depravity and of salvation by grace.* I say put these two together, and you have almost all the contradictions of Calvinism converged to a focus—and what is most fatal to the system, you have the authority of Calvinism itself to prove that every intelligent probationer on the earth not only has the ability, but is authoritatively required to give practical demonstration that the system is false!! What is this but to say, "You *can,* and you *cannot;*"—if you *do* not, you will be justly condemned—if you *do,* you will ruin the Gospel system, and yourself with it? Where such glaring paradoxes appear, there must be something materially wrong in, at least, some parts of the system.

5. But the inconsistency of this theory is not its only, and certainly not its most injurious characteristic. In the same proportion as men are made to believe that there are no conditions on their part to their regeneration, they will be likely to fall into one of the two extremes of carelessness or despair, either of which, persisted in, would be ruinous. I cannot doubt but that, in this way, tens of thousands have been ruined. We should infer that such would be the result of the doctrine, from only understanding its character; and I am fully satisfied that, in my own personal acquaintance, I have met with hundreds who have been lulled in the cradle of Antinomianism on the one hand, or paralyzed with despair on the other, by this same doctrine of passive, unconditional conversion. Calvinists, it is true, tell us this is the abuse of the doctrine; but it appears to me to be the

legitimate fruit. What else could we expect? A man might as well attempt to dethrone the Mediator, as to do any thing toward his own conversion. Teach this, and carelessness ensues, Antinomian feelings will follow—or if you arouse the mind by the curse of the law, and by the fearful doom that awaits the unregenerate, what can he do? Nothing! Hell rises from beneath to meet him, but he can do *nothing*. He looks until he is excited to phrensy, from which he very probably passes over to raving madness, or settles down into a state of gloomy despair.

6. Another very decisive objection to this doctrine is, the frequent, and I may say uniform language of Scripture. The Scriptures require us to *seek—ask—knock—come to Christ—look unto God—repent—believe—open the door* of the heart—*receive Christ*, &c. No one can fail to notice how these instructions are sprinkled over the whole volume of revelation. And what is specially in point here, all these are spoken of and urged upon us as conditions of blessings that shall follow—even the blessings of salvation, of regeneration—and as conditions, too, without which we cannot expect these blessings. Take one passage of many—"As many as received him, to them gave he power to become the sons of God, even to them that believe on his name." If any one doubts whether "becoming the sons of God," as expressed in this text, means regeneration, the next verse will settle it—"Which were born not of blood, nor of the will of the flesh, nor of the will of man, but of God," John i, 12, 13. The latter verse I may have occasion to remark upon hereafter; it is quoted here to show that the new birth is undoubtedly the subject here spoken of. And we are here expressly taught, in language that will bear no other interpretation, that *receiving* Christ and *believing* on his name are the conditions of regeneration. If there were no other passage in the Bible to direct our minds on this subject, this plain unequivocal text ought to be decisive. But the truth is, this is the uniform language of Scripture. And are there any passages against these, any that say we cannot come, cannot believe, seek, &c? or any that say, this work of personal regeneration is performed independent of conditions? I know of none which will not fairly admit of a different construction. We are often met with this passage—"It is not of him that willeth, nor of him that runneth, but of God that showeth mercy." See Rom. ix, 16. But whoever interpreteth this of personal and individual regeneration can hardly have examined the passage carefully and candidly. But we are told again, it is God that renews the heart; and if it is his work, it is not the work of the sinner. I grant this; this is the very sentiment I mean to maintain; but then there may be conditions—*there are conditions*—or else we should not hear the psalmist *praying* for this, in language that has been preserved for the edification of all subsequent generations, "Create in me a clean heart, O God, and renew a right spirit within me." This is a practical comment on Christ's conditional salvation, "Ask and ye shall receive."

Since then this doctrine of passive and unconditional regeneration implies unconditional election—since it is in opposition to those scriptures which teach that the Spirit and grace of God may be resisted and received in vain—since it is a virtual denial of all gracious influences upon the heart before regeneration—since it leads the abettors of the theory into gross contradictions, by their endeavours to reconcile the can and the *cannot* of their system —since its practical tendency is to make sinners careless, or drive them to despair—and finally, since it contradicts that numerous class of scriptures, some of which are very unequivocal, that predicate the blessings of regeneration and justification upon certain preparatory and conditional acts of the sinner—*therefore* we conclude that this theory cannot be true.

Second Theory.—To avoid these difficulties, to make the sinner feel his responsibility, and to bring him into action, a new theory of regeneration is proposed. This constitutes a leading characteristic of the New Divinity. It is the theory of *self-conversion*. Its advocates maintain that there is no more mystery or supernatural agency in the process of the change, called the new birth, than there is in any other leading purpose or decision of the mind. It is true, they do not wholly exclude the Holy Spirit from this work, but his agency is mediate and indirect. He acts in some undefinable way, through the truth as an instrument. The truth acts upon the mind, in the way of *moral suasion,* and the sinner, in the view and by the influence of truth, resolves to give himself up to God and to his service—and *this is regeneration.* The preparation is of God—but the actual change is man's own work. The God of providence reveals the truth and arranges the means for its promulgation, the Spirit of grace applies it to the understanding, the sinner looks at it, reflects upon it, and at length is persuaded to set about the work, and regenerates himself!

That we may be the better prepared to meet this hypothesis, it should be noticed that it is inseparable from the notion that all sin consists in voluntary exercise, or in other words, in a series of sinful volitions. Regeneration is a change from sin to holiness —and hence a regenerate state is the opposite of a sinful state. If then a regenerate state is nothing more than a series of holy volitions, an unregenerate state, which is its opposite, is nothing more than a series of unholy volitions. Thus it appears that this doctrine of regeneration by the act of the will must stand or fall with the notion that all sin consists in voluntary exercise. Any argument, therefore, brought against this latter theory will bear with equal weight against this new idea of regeneration. Bearing this in mind, we are prepared to object to this doctrine,

1. That it is inconsistent with the doctrine of constitutional depravity. This is granted by the supporters of the theory, and hence constitutional depravity is no part of their system. All the arguments therefore that have been adduced in favour of derived, inherent depravity, or that can be urged in favour of this doctrine, will stand directly opposed to this view of regeneration. The arguments in favour of our views of depravity need not be repeated; and the reader is referred to a previous number in which this point has been discussed.

2. Another objection to this theory of regeneration is, that it makes *entire* sanctification take place at the time of regeneration. Conversion, holiness, are nothing more than a decision of the will; and since the will can never be *more than decided,* of course the decision at regeneration is the *perfection of holiness.* On this ground, therefore, though Christians are exhorted to "cleanse themselves from all filthiness of flesh and spirit, *perfecting holiness* in the fear of the Lord;" though the saints are commanded to "grow in grace," to "confess their sins," that they may be "cleansed from *all unrighteousness,*" though some of the Corinthian Christians were "carnal and walked as men," and for that reason were, after years of experience, only *babes* in Christ —still, if we embrace this sentiment, we must call the convert, at his first spiritual breath, as holy as he ever *can be* in any of the subsequent stages of his experience! Surely the apostles taught not this! And yet so strongly are men impelled forward by their systems, this doctrine of perfect holiness at conversion is the very sentiment that many of the advocates of the New Divinity are now propagating—a clear proof that it necessarily follows from their theory of conversion. This of itself, it strikes me, ought to destroy the doctrine.

3. Another bearing of this hypothesis, and one which I think must prove fatal to it, is, that the Scriptures represent this change to be chiefly in the affections, whereas this doctrine makes it exclusively in the will. That the Scriptures place the change in the affections chiefly, I suppose will not be denied. If it should be, without stopping here to quote specific passages, or use many arguments, one consideration alone will be sufficient to set the question at rest.—True evangelical holiness consists in love to God and man; and sin is loving the creature rather than the Creator. The apostle brings into view both the regenerate and the unregenerate state in this passage—"Set your affection on things above, and not on things on the earth." Numerous are the passages which teach that love to God is the essence of the Christian character. The affections, therefore, are

the seat of this change. But we are told by this new theory the change is in the will. It is only to resolve to serve God, and we are converted.—Either this theory, therefore, or the Bible account of this matter must be wrong.

To avoid this difficulty, it may be said, that a change of the will implies a change of the affections. But this is changing the position—which is, that a decision of the will is regeneration. If however this new position be insisted upon, it can be reconciled with the phraseology used only by making a change of the affections a mere *subordinate* part of regeneration, whereas the Scriptures make the change consist essentially in this. But there is still a more serious difficulty in this idea, that the change of the will implies a change in the affections. It necessarily implies that the affections are at all times under the control of the will. But this is as unphilosophical as it is unscriptural. It is even directly contrary to the observation and knowledge of men who have paid only common and casual attention to mental phenomena. The will is oftener enthralled by the affections, than the affections by the will. Even in common and worldly matters let a man try by an effort of the will to beget love where it does not exist, or to transfer the affections from one object to another, and how will he succeed? Will love and hatred go or come at his bidding? You might as well attempt, by an act of the will, to make sweet bitter, or bitter sweet to the physical taste. How much less can a man, by an act of the will, make all things new, and transfer the heart from the grossness of creature love to the purity of supreme love to God. The Apostle Paul has taught us his failure in this matter. When he "would do good, evil was present with him." "For," says he, "the good that I would do, I do not; but the evil which I would not, that I do." And this is the fact in most cases of genuine awakening. Resolutions are formed, but the current of the unsanctified affections sweeps them away. Over the untowardness of the unregenerate heart the will has, in fact, but a feeble influence; and this is the reason why the man, struggling with the corruptions of his heart, is driven to despair, and exclaims, "O! wretched man that I am, who shall deliver me from the body of this death?"

We shall see hereafter how the action of the will is indispensable in regeneration; but not in this *direct* way to change and control the affections, by the power of its own decisions. When I find my will capable of doing this, I must have an essentially different intellectual character from the one I now have.

Since the Scriptures make the new birth a change of affections, and this theory makes it a change of volitions; and especially since the affections cannot be transferred from *earth* to *heaven* by a *mere act of the will*, therefore the doctrine which teaches and implies these views must be false.

4. This idea of the character of sin and of the new birth makes man sinless, at particular times, even *without* regeneration. I do not mean by this that he is not obnoxious to punishment for past unholy volitions. But if sin consists only in voluntary exercise, whenever the mind does not act; or whenever its action is not under the control of the will, there is nothing of sin personally appertaining to the man.—When the action of the will is suspended by an all-absorbing emotion of wonder or surprise—in sound sleep when the mental states, if there are any, are not under the control of the will—in cases of suspended animation, by drowning, fainting, or otherwise—in short, whenever the mind is necessarily wholly engrossed, as is often the case, by some scientific investigation, or matter of worldly business, not of a moral character, then, and in every such case, whatever may be the guilt for past transgressions, there is no personal unholiness. And by the same reasoning we may show that the regenerate pass a great portion of their time without any personal holiness!

5. According to the theory we are opposing, regeneration, strictly speaking, means nothing. The work of grace, by which a sinner is made meet for heaven, embraces two essential points, *pardon* and *renewal*. The former is not a positive change of character,

but a relative change, from a state of condemnation to a state of acquittal. But as regeneration, if it have any appropriate meaning, cannot mean a mere change of relation, any construction or system that forces such a meaning upon it does, in fact, do it away. Hence, being *born again, being renewed, being created anew, being sanctified, being translated from darkness to light, being raised from the dead*, and numerous other scripture expressions, are figurative forms of speech, so foreign from the idea they are used to express, that they are worse than unmeaning—they lead to error. But if these expressions mean any thing more than pardon, what is that meaning? This doctrine makes the principal change take place in the *neighbourhood* of the will; not in the will itself, meaning by that, the mental power by which we put forth volitions. This *faculty* of the mind is sound, and needs no change—all the other mental susceptibilities are sound, the essence of the mind and the susceptibilities of the mind are perfectly free from any moral perversion. It is the mental *action* that is bad.—What is there then in the man that is to be changed? Do you say his volitions? But these he changes every hour. Do you say, he must leave off wrong volitions, and have right ones? This too he often does. "But he must do it with right motives," you say, "this acting from *right motives* is the regenerate state." Indeed! Suppose then that he has resolved to serve God, from right motives, what if he should afterward resolve, from false shame or fear, to neglect a duty, is he now unregenerate? This is changing from regenerate to unregenerate, from *entire* holiness to *entire* unholiness with a breath. Truly such a regeneration is *nothing*. But you say, after he has once submitted, he now has a "governing purpose" to serve God, and this constitutes him regenerate; aye, a *governing* purpose that *does not govern* him. Let it be understood, you cannot divide a volition; it has an entire character in itself; and if it be unholy, no preceding holy volition can sanctify it. Hence every change of volition from wrong to right, and from right to wrong, is a change of state, so that regeneracy and unregeneracy play in and out of the human bosom in the alternation of every criminal thought or every pious aspiration. Is this the Bible doctrine of the new birth? And yet this is all you can make of it, if you resolve it into the mere action of the will.

6. This doctrine of self-conversion, by an act of the will, is directly contrary to Scripture. It would be tedious to me and my readers to quote all those passages that attribute this work directly to the Holy Spirit, and that speak of it as a work which *God himself* accomplishes for, and in us. There is one passage which is much in point, however, and is sufficient of itself to settle this question. "But as many as received him, to them gave he power to become the sons of God, even to them that believe on his name. Who were born, not of blood, nor of the will of the flesh, nor of the will of man, but of God," John i, 12, 13. This is a two-edged sword—it cuts off, as we have remarked before, passive and unconditional regeneration on the one hand; and also, as we may now see, self conversion by an act of the will, on the other. I know not how words can be put together, in so small a compass, better to answer the true objects of destroying these two opposite theories of regeneration, and asserting the true theory. Here is, first—the *receiving of Christ*, the *believing on his name*—this is the condition. Second, Christ gives the "power," viz. strength and privilege, to become the sons of God. This is the regeneration. Third—This becoming "the sons of God," or being "born," is not in a *physical way*, by flesh and blood, nor yet by *human will*, but of or by God. Can any thing be clearer or more decisive?

Indeed the very terms, *regeneration, born, birth*, &c, imply of themselves another and an efficient agent; and then to connect these with the Divine agency, as the Scriptures have done some half dozen times in the phrase, "born of God," and several other times in the phrase, "of the Spirit:" to have this called being "begotten again," and the like, is enough, one would think, if words have any meaning, to show that man does not change his own heart. The same may be said of the terms *resurrection, translation, creation, renewal*, and various other terms the Scriptures use to express this change. Jesus Christ claimed that he had "power to lay down his life, and *to take it again;*" but this is the only instance of self-resurrection power that we read of; and even this was by his Divine nature; for he was "quickened by the Spirit," and raised "by the power of God." But these theorists teach that man has power to lay down his life, and then, after he is "dead in trespasses and sins," he has power to take his life again. Truly this is giving man a power that approaches very near to one of the Divine attributes. To Christ alone does it belong "to quicken whom he will." To change the heart of the sinner is one of the Divine prerogatives, and he that attempts to convert himself; and trusts to this, will find in the end that he is *carnal* still. For "whatsoever is born of the flesh is flesh, but whatsoever is born of the Spirit is spirit."

Let me not here be misunderstood. I shall endeavour to show, in its proper place, the conditional agency of man in this work. I have only time to add, in this number, that I consider those scriptures which press duties upon the sinner as applying to this conditional agency. And even those strong expressions which sometimes occur in the Bible, requiring the sinner to "make himself a new heart"—"to cleanse his hands and purify his heart," &c, will find an easy solution and a pertinent application in this view of the subject. For if there are certain pending conditions, without which the work will not be accomplished, then there would be a propriety, while pressing this duty, to use expressions showing that this work was conditionally, though not *efficiently*, resting upon the agency of the sinner.

In my next I shall endeavour to show that there is no intermediate *Calvinistic* ground between the two theories examined in this number. If that attempt prove successful, and if in this it has been found that the two theories examined are encumbered with too many embarrassments to be admitted, then we shall be the better prepared to listen to the teachings of the Scriptures on this important and leading doctrine of the Christian faith.

NUMBER XIV.

REGENERATION, CONTINUED.

An inconsistency in any received theory is constantly driving its supporters to some modification of their system. This is a redeeming principle in the human mind, and greatly encourages the hope that truth will finally triumph.

It has already been noticed that the doctrine of entire passivity, in regeneration, is so pressed with difficulties that it has sought relief in the opposite notion of self-conversion. But this latter hypothesis is, in turn, encumbered, if possible, with still greater embarrassments. The presumption therefore is, that the truth lies between them; and it will doubtless be found, by a fair and thorough investigation, that this is the fact. But here the question arises, Can *Calvinists* consistently occupy any such middle ground? In other words, retaining the other peculiarities of Calvinism, can our Calvinistic brethren assume any position between these two extremes which will avoid the difficulties of both? A brief examination, it is hoped, will decide this question.

Third Theory.—Dr. Tyler is a highly respectable clergyman of the Calvinistic faith, and is now at the head of the theological school in East Windsor, Conn., which was got up with the avowed purpose of counteracting the New-Haven theology. We should not therefore suspect him of leaning too much toward the New Divinity. He tells us that the only depravity is to be unwilling to serve God—that there is "no other obstacle in the way of the sinner's salvation except what lies in his own will"—that "to be born again is simply to be made willing to do what God requires." What is this but the New Divinity? The will is here made, most explicitly, the sole seat of depravity; and regeneration is an act of the will. But every act of the will is the sinner's *own act*, and therefore the agent, by that act of the will which constitutes regeneration, converts himself. —Perhaps Dr. Tyler will say, the sinner in this case does not convert himself, because he is "*made willing*." God makes him willing "in the day of his power." It is remarkable what a favourite phrase this is with the Calvinists. It is borrowed from the third verse of the hundred and tenth Psalm, "Thy people shall be willing in the day of thy power." Now although the word "made" is not in the text; although there is not the *slightest* evidence that the text speaks of regeneration at all, but on the contrary, it is most evidently intended to describe the character and conduct of God's people, viz. the regenerate; and although every scholar, at least, among the Calvinists, knows this as well as he knows his right hand from the left, yet we hear it repeated by the learned and the ignorant, at all times and places—"God's people are made willing in the day of his power." It is not only a gross perversion of a Scripture phrase, but its repetition, in this perverted sense, renders it wearisome and sickening. But, waiving this, it becomes us to ask whether there is any more rational or Scriptural ground for the idea itself than there is for this use of the text. What is meant by making the soul willing? I confess I cannot understand it. Is it meant that God *forces* the soul to be willing? This is a contradiction in terms. To say that God acts directly on the will, and thus changes its determination by superior force, is to destroy its freedom—is to produce a volition without motive or reason—which would, at any rate, be an anomalous action of the will. And what is still more fatal to the theory, it implies *no act* of the sinner whatever, but an irresistible act of the Divine power, which therefore necessarily throws the theory back upon the doctrine of passive conversion. There is no avoiding this conclusion, I think, on the ground that God changes the action of the will, by an exertion of power upon the will itself. If, to avoid this, it should be said that the will is not changed by a direct act of power, but influenced to a holy determination indirectly, through the medium of motives, presented by the Holy Spirit—then and in that case we should be thrown forward on to the self-conversion system. The sinner's voluntary act, by which he regenerated himself, would be as truly and entirely *his own* as any other act of the will; therefore he would be self-regenerated. This also would be regeneration, not by the Holy Spirit, but *by the truth;* which is another feature of the New Divinity. This also would make all depravity consist in the will, or rather in its *acts;* which has been shown in the preceding number to be unscriptural as well as unphilosophical. This objection is valid, whether the depravity is supposed to be in the *power* of willing, or in the *acts* of the will. But since, in Dr. Tyler's view, to will in one direction is depravity, and to will in another direction is regeneration, and since all that motives *can* do is, not to change the will itself, but only prompt it to new voluntary states, it follows conclusively that Dr. T. makes all holiness and all unholiness consist in volitions; and therefore the *moral-exercise* system is true; which is another feature of the New Divinity. Truly I may repeat, we do not need another theological seminary in Connecticut to teach this doctrine.

Finally, according to this theory of Dr. T., he and all those who reason like him, are chargeable, I think, with a palpable paralogism they reason in a circle. They say, in the express language of Dr. Tyler, "All men may be saved if they will"—"No man is hindered from coming to Christ who is willing to come"—that is, since to will and to be willing is to be regenerated, this language gravely teaches us, "All men may be saved, if they *are regenerated*"—"No man is hindered from coming to Christ (to be regenerated) who *is regenerated!*" And indeed this view of regeneration not only makes learned divines talk nonsense, but the Scriptures also. The invitation, "Whosoever will, let him come," &c, must mean, "Whosoever *is regenerate*, let him come," and so of other passages. Thus this theory of Dr. Tyler, and of the many who hold with him, is so closely hemmed in on both sides, that it must throw itself for support, either upon the doctrine of passivity, or self-conversion; at the same time that in other respects it involves itself in inconsistent and anti-scriptural dogmas.

But that we may leave no position unexamined, let us take another view of the subject. Suppose, instead of saying regeneration is simply a change of the will, it should be argued that a change of the will implies a change of the affections, and this therefore is included in regeneration. Then I would ask, whether this change of the affections is in the order of cause and effect, or in the order of time, *prior* or *subsequent* to the act of the will. If this change is prior to any action of the will in the case, then the sinner has no voluntary co-operation in the work; and this brings us up once more upon the doctrine of passive regeneration. The heart is changed before the subject of the change acts. If the action of the will precedes the change of the heart, then this change will be effected in one of two ways. Either this anterior volition does itself change the heart; or it is a mere preparatory condition, on *occasion of which* God changes the heart. In the former case the man himself would change his own heart, and this is self-conversion; and in the latter alternative we have a conditional regeneration wrought by the Holy Ghost, and this is the very doctrine for which *we contend*, in opposition to Calvinism. If it should be said, this change of the will and this change of the heart take place independent of each other, that would not help the matter, since in this view the change of *heart* would be passive and unconditional. Thus whichever way this system turns, its difficulties press upon it still, and it finds no relief. Indeed there can, as I conceive, be no intermediate Calvinistic theory of regeneration, and there *can be* but two other alternatives—either God must renew the heart, independent of all co-operation on the part of the subject of this change—and this is the old doctrine of unconditional Divine efficiency—or the first acceptable act of the will must be regeneration; and this is the new doctrine of *self-conversion*. Let the reader, let any one reflect closely on this subject, and I cannot doubt but he will say with me, *There is no third alternative*. The nature of the case will admit of none. The former theory may not contradict many of those scriptures that speak of *Divine efficiency* in the work of grace upon the heart, but it is utterly incompatible with those that urge the sinner to duty.—The latter theory corresponds well with the urgent injunctions to duty, so abundant in the Scriptures, but is wholly irreconcilable with those that speak of Divine efficiency. The true theory must answer to both; and must also correspond with all the other parts of the Christian system. Is there such a theory? Every honest inquirer after truth will embrace it doubtless, if it can be presented—for truth, wherever, and whenever, and by whomsoever discovered, is infinitely to be preferred to error, however long and fondly it may have been cherished. Such a theory I will now try to present—and although I may fail in making it very explicit, and in bringing forward all its defences, yet if the general outlines can be seen and be defended, it will, I trust, commend itself to the favourable notice of the reader.

Scripture Doctrine of Regeneration.—I approach this subject by laying down the two following fundamental principles:—

1. The work of regeneration is performed by the direct and efficient operations of the Holy Spirit upon the heart.

2. The Holy Spirit exerts this regenerating power only on conditions, to be first complied with by the subject of the change.

The first principle I deem it unnecessary to defend farther than it has been defended in the foregoing remarks. It is not objected to by any orthodox Christians that I know of, only so far as the new views of self-conversion, and of conversion by moral suasion, may be thought an exception. And this we have reason to hope will be an exception of limited extent and short duration. The sentiment conflicts so directly with such a numerous class of scriptures, and with the most approved principles of mental philosophy; and has, at the same time, such a direct tendency to annihilate all the essential features of regeneration, it cannot long find encouragement in a spiritual Church. It may however make many converts for a time, for men are fond of taking the work of salvation into their own hands; but if it should, between such converts and the true Church there will ultimately be a separation as wide as that which now separates orthodoxy and Socinianism.

The other fundamental principle seems to follow, almost of necessity, from the scriptures that so abundantly point out the sinner's duty and agency, in connection with his conversion. The principle, however, is strenuously opposed by all classes of Calvinists. The opposite of this is in fact the essential characteristic of Calvinism, if any *one* notion can be so called; for however much the Calvinistic system may be modified, in other respects, this is clung to as the elementary germ which constitutes the identity of the system. Even the New Divinity, which makes so much of human agency, does not allow it a *conditional action*—it allows of no intermediate volition between the mental states of worldly love and Divine love, as the occasion on which the transfer is made, or the conditional hinge on which the important revolution is accomplished. On the contrary, it considers the volition itself as the transfer—the volition constitutes the *entire change*. Thus warily does Calvinism, in all its changes, avoid conditional regeneration. Hence if I were called upon to give a general definition of Calvinism, that should include all the species that claim the name, I would say, *Calvinists are those who believe in unconditional regeneration*. For the moment this point is given up by any one, all parties agree that he is not a Calvinist.

But why is conditional regeneration so offensive? Is it because the Scriptures directly oppose it? This is hardly pretended. It is supposed, however, by the Calvinists, that to acknowledge this doctrine would require the renunciation of certain other doctrines which are taught in the Scriptures. This lays the foundation for the objections that have been made against this doctrine. It is objected that *a depraved sinner cannot perform an acceptable condition until he is regenerated*—that *God cannot consistently accept of any act short of that which constitutes regeneration*—that *the idea of a conditional regeneration implies salvation by works, in part at least, and not wholly by grace*.

I have mentioned these objections in this connection, not so much to attempt, at this moment, a direct refutation of them, as to advert to what I conceive to be the ground of the difficulty in the minds of those making the objections. It appears to me that the difference between us results principally from a difference of our views in respect to the constitution and the constitutional action of the mind itself. The philosophical part of our theology will be modified very much by our views of the philosophy of mind. Let it be granted then:—

1. That the mind is possessed of a moral susceptibility, generally called *conscience*, which lays the foundation of the notions of right and wrong, and by which we feel the emotions of approval or disapproval for our past conduct, and the feelings of obligation with respect to the present and the future; and that even in an unregenerate state this susceptibility often operates in accordance with its original design, and therefore agreeably with the Divine will.

2. That the understanding or intellect, which is a general division of the mind, containing in itself several distinct susceptibilities or powers, may, in an unregenerate state of the mind, be so enlightened and informed on the subjects of Divine truth as to perceive the right and the wrong; and as to perceive also, to some extent at least, the way of salvation pointed out in the Gospel.

3. That the affections and propensities (sometimes called the heart) are the principal seat of depravity—and these are often arrayed in direct hostility to the convictions of the judgment and the feelings of moral obligation.

4. That the will, or that mental power by which we put forth volitions, and make decisions, while it is more or less, directly or indirectly, influenced by the judgment, the conscience, and the affections, is in fact designed to give direction and unity to the whole mental action; and it always accomplishes this, where there is a proper harmony in the mental powers. But by sin this harmony has been disturbed, and the unholy affections have gained an undue ascendancy, so that, in the unregenerate, in all questions of preference between God and the world, in spite of the judgment, of conscience, and of the will, the world is loved and God is hated.

5. That in those cases where we cannot control our affections by a direct volition, we may, nevertheless, under the promptings of conscience, and in the light of the judgment, resolve against sin —but these resolutions, however firmly and repeatedly made, will be carried away and overruled by the strength of the carnal mind. This shows us our own weakness, drives us to self-despair, until, under the enlightening influences of grace, and the drawings of the Spirit, the soul is led to prayer and to an abdication of itself into the hands of Divine mercy, through Christ; and *then*, and on *these conditions*, the Holy Spirit changes the character and current of the unholy affections—and *this is regeneration*.

In laying down the preceding postulates I have endeavoured to express myself with as much brevity, and with as little metaphysical technicality as possible; for the reason that they are designed to be understood by all. Bating the deficiencies that may on this account be noticed by the philosophical reader, I think it may be assumed that these, so far as the powers and operations of the mind are concerned, embrace the basis and general outlines of what we call *conditional regeneration*. I am not aware that they are in opposition to an one principle of Scripture theology, or mental philosophy. And if this process is found consonant with reason and Scripture, in its general features, it will be easy to show that its relative bearings are such as most happily harmonize all the doctrinal phenomena of the Gospel system.

We plant ourselves then upon these general positions, and as ability will permit, or truth may seem to justify, shall endeavour to defend them against such objections as may be anticipated, or are known to have been made against any of the principles here assumed.

1. It may be objected perhaps that this is making too broad a distinction between the different mental powers, giving to each such a distinctive action and operation as to infringe upon the doctrine of the mind's unity and simplicity. It is believed, however, the more this point is reflected upon by an attentive observance of our own minds, or the minds of others, the more satisfied shall we be that the principles here assumed are correct. That there are these distinct properties of mind no one doubts. It is in accordance with universal language, to speak of the intellect, of the conscience, of the will, and of the affections, as distinct properties of the mind. The properties of mind are as clearly marked by our consciousness, as the properties of matter by our senses. And although, in consequence of the invisibility of mind, there is doubtless a more perfect unity in each individual mental property, than in each distinct quality of matter, still each of the mental qualities has its appropriate and distinctive character. Calvinists themselves acknowledge this. They allow we have a moral sense which tests good or evil, even in an unregenerate state; they allow the intellect may perceive and approve of truth, even when the heart rejects it; they allow that to perceive and to judge, to feel moral obligation and to will, are distinct operations of the mind; and that our perceptions and our conscience may be right, when our affections are wrong. So far then we are agreed, and so far they make distinctions in the mind, as wide as any that have been claimed in the principles above laid down. Theologians, I grant, have, in many instances, confounded in their reasonings the will and the affections. And this has also sometimes been done by writers on the philosophy of the mind. But it is most evident, I think, they have done this without good

reason. Mr. Locke says, "I find the will often confounded with several of the affections, especially desire, and one put for the other." This he thinks is an error, of which "any one who turns his thoughts inward upon what passes in his own mind" will be convinced. Rev. Professor Upham, of Bowdoin College, Maine, himself a Calvinist, as is generally supposed, in a late excellent treatise on the will, asserts, and clearly proves, I think, that *the state of the mind, which we term volition, is entirely distinct from that which we term desire.*" Nay, he proves that desires and volitions are often in direct opposition. Hence as love implies desire, our volitions may often conflict with our love. And this is precisely the state the awakened sinner is in when he "would do good, but evil is present with him."

2. It may be said, and has sometimes been said, that this view of the subject involves a contradiction; that it is the same as to say, the man wills against his preference, or in other words, he wills what he does not choose. I cannot answer this objection better than by an argument in Professor Upham's work, already alluded to, in which he says, of a similar objection on this very subject, "It will be found on examination to resolve itself into a verbal fallacy, and naturally vanishes as soon as that fallacy is detected." "It is undoubtedly true that the common usage of language authorizes us to apply the terms choice and choosing indiscriminately to either the desire or volition; but it does not follow, and is not true, that we apply them to these different parts of our nature in precisely the same sense." "When the word choice implies desire at all, it has reference to a number of desirable objects brought before the mind at once, and implies and expresses the ascendant or predominant desire." "At other times we use the terms choice and choosing in application to the will—when it is applied to that power, it expresses the mere act of the will, and nothing more, with the exception, as in the other case, that more than one object of volition was present, in view of the mind, before the putting forth of the voluntary act. It is in fact the circumstance that two or more objects are present, which suggests the use of the word choice or choosing, in either case." "But the acts are entirely different in their nature, although under certain circumstances the same name is applied to them." Hence he adds, "The contradiction is not a real, but merely a verbal one. If we ever choose against choosing, it will be found merely that choice which is volition, placed against that choice which is desire." And this is nothing more than to say that volitions and desires may conflict with each other, which we know to be the fact in numerous instances.

If in reply to the foregoing, and in farther defence of the objection, it should be urged, that there could be not only no motive for the volition in this case, but that it would in fact be put forth against all motive, since the feelings of the heart would be of a directly opposite character, I reply, that it is not true that there would be no motive for the action of the will, in opposition to the sinful affections. It is seen already that the judgment in the awakened sinner is against continuing in sin, and the rebukes of the conscience for the past, and its admonitions for the future, are powerful motives in opposition to the unholy affections. The feelings of compunction and of moral obligation gain great accessions of strength, moreover, from the terrors of the Divine law, which alarm the fears, and from the promises of the Gospel, which encourage the hopes of the awakened sinner. And it is especially and emphatically true that under the existing influence of these fears and hopes, the voice of conscience is most effectual in prompting the sinner to "flee from the wrath to come," and "lay hold on the hope set before him." Can it be said then that there is no motive for a volition, or a mental effort that shall conflict with the unsanctified affections?

3. Again it is said, for every inch of this ground is disputed, that the action of the mind under such motives is purely selfish, and cannot therefore perform conditions acceptable to God. To this it may be replied, that to be influenced by motives of self preservation

and personal salvation is not criminal; nay, it is commendable. In proof of this but one argument is necessary. God moves upon our fears and hopes, for the *express purpose* of inducing us to forsake sin, and serve him; and he applies these motives to man in his unregenerate state. This is so obvious a fact, it is presumed none will deny it. But is it wrong for us to be prompted to action by those considerations which God himself urges upon us? If he attempts to excite our fears and hopes to prompt us to a course of self preservation, can it be wrong for us to be influenced by this means, and in this direction? I should hardly know how to hold an argument with a man that should assert this —and yet this sentiment is implied in the objection now under examination. Beside, these acts conditional to regeneration are not wholly, perhaps not chiefly, from motives of personal interest. Our moral feelings have a great part in this work. And it is principally by arousing an accusing conscience that fear and hope aid in the performance of the conditions of regeneration. But whatever proportion there may be of the ingredients of personal fear and hope in the feelings that enter into this conditional action of the mind, it is certain that the fear of the consequences of sin, and the hope to escape them, are not themselves criminal, much less then are they capable of rendering a complex state of the mind, of which they are but a part, unacceptable to God. Indeed this objection to a mental act, merely because it is prompted by self love, has always been to me a matter of wonder. Selfishness is a term which we generally use in a bad sense, and we mean by it that form of self love that leads us to seek our own gratification at the expense and the injury of others, or in opposition to the will of God. But that self love which leads us to seek our own highest interests, and especially our eternal interests, without injury to others, and in accordance with the Divine will, is never thought criminal, I believe, except where one has a particular system to support by such a notion. But that system is itself of a doubtful character which requires such an argument to sustain it.

4. Another objection which has been made to one of the principles above laid down is, that "it is the province of the will to control the affections, and not the affections the will; and that the will always possesses the power to do this, even in an unregenerate state." If so, then man has power, at any time, by an act of the will, to love God. Let him try—let that unholy sinner try. Can he succeed? You say perhaps, for so the Calvinists have said, "He can if he will;" that is, he can will to love God if he does will to love God! This is no great discovery surely, and it is certainly no proper answer to the question. I ask it again, Can he, by a direct act of the will, love God? Do you say, by varying the form of the answer, "He can if he chooses?" If you mean by choice the act of the will, this is the same answer over again, the folly of which is so apparent. But if you mean by choice the desires of his heart, then your answer amounts to this: If the desires of the heart are in favour of loving God, he can, by an act of the will, love him. But if the desires of the heart are in favour of loving God, the love is already begotten, and there is no need of the act of the will to produce it. In that case your proposition would be, the sinner can love God by an act of the will, *if he loves him!* the absurdity of which is too evident to require comment. It is thus that the coils of error run into each other in endless circles.

But, perhaps, to help the argument, if possible, it may be urged that the will can decide in favour of a closer examination, and by voluntary attention may get such strong perceptions of truth as will give it the voluntary power over the heart. To this I would reply, in the first place, this is giving up the argument, it is acknowledging that certain preparatory acts of the will are necessary before the mind can love God—but *this is conditional regeneration.* And it may be farther maintained, in opposition to this sentiment that the mere perception of truth, even when united with conscience, and personal fear and hope, is not sufficient to give the will power over the unrenewed affections. In proof of this, Scripture might be adduced; but reserving the Scripture argument for the present, we may quote good Calvinistic authority in proof that the will may be enthralled by the affections. Professor Upham says, "Whenever there is a want of harmony in the mind, there is always a greater or less degree of enthralment." And then he proceeds to show how the mind may be enslaved by the *propensities, appetites, affections,* and *passions.* He illustrates; for example, the progress of this enthralment in the case of an appetite for strong drink; which, "like a strong man armed, violently seizes the will, binds it hand and foot, and hurls it into the dust." Again he says, "There are not unfrequently cases where the propensities and passions have become so intense, after years of repetition, as to control, or in other words, enthral the voluntary power almost entirely." (Treatise on the Will.) Dr. Griffin, also an able Calvinistic writer, says, in decided terms, "The judgment of the intellect and the decisions of the will are both controlled by the heart."

The idea of the enthralment of the will, however, may be objected to on another ground, viz. that if admitted it would destroy accountability, since none are accountable for what they cannot avoid. But I have not said they cannot avoid it; neither have I said we are not voluntary either in keeping or discarding the unholy heart. I assert directly the contrary. Every probationer decides whether he will be holy or happy. But his decisions to be holy are effectual only when he seeks that from God which he cannot do for himself. Then, and then only, will God give him the victory over the old man, with the deceitful lusts of the heart. *But this is conditional regeneration.*

Having said thus much in defence of the philosophy of the principles laid down, the way is prepared to show that they accord with Scripture, and to defend them with the doctrine which we build upon them from the supposed Scripture objections which have been urged against them. But this will furnish matter for another number.

NUMBER XV.

REGENERATION, CONTINUED.

In proposing and vindicating, in the preceding number, those views of the philosophy of mind which are supposed to throw light upon the process of regeneration, it was not intended to be intimated that a knowledge of this theory is necessary in order to experience the new birth. In the practical purposes of life men do not ordinarily stop to analyze their mental states before they *judge, feel,* and *act.* They have the *practical* use of their mental faculties, and that suffices. In this way the most ignorant and the most unphilosophical may be saved. Why, then, it may be asked, is it necessary to enter into this analysis at all? To this it may be replied, that whenever we can trace the adaptation of the provisions of grace and the reason of the Divine requirements to the known facts and laws of the human mind, it will strengthen our confidence in the economy of grace, increase our admiration of the wisdom and goodness of God, and sharpen our weapons of defence against the cavils and assaults of an opposing skepticism. But especially is this philosophical examination necessary whenever a superficial or an erroneous philosophy would force upon us an erroneous theology. The metaphysical mist with which some theories have veiled the doctrine of regeneration, and the delusive and distorted views that have resulted from this obscuration, may be removed and corrected by the radiance of a pure philosophy. But as human philosophy is, at best, more likely to err on these subjects than revelation, the former should always be corrected or confirmed by the latter. How is it in the case under examination? How do the assumed opinions correspond with revelation?

Let us glance again at our positions. The principal points assumed are—that there is often a conflict between the feelings of moral obligation on the one hand, enlightened as they are by reason and by grace, sanctioned as they are by fear and hope, and the unholy affections on the other; that under the promptings of the moral feelings the will frequently puts forth its strength to resist and subdue the unholy affections, but in every such case the effort fails when unaided by the sanctifying grace of God—and that victory is finally gained by a conditional act of the will, through which, or on occasion of which, God subdues the passions and changes the heart. These views have been vindicated, as being in accordance with the philosophy of mind. The question now is, Are they sustained by Scripture? I answer, *Yes, most clearly.*

If the Apostle Paul had attempted, by a set argument, to illustrate and affirm these views, he could not have done it better or more explicitly than he has done in the latter part of the 7th, and the first part of the 8th chapters of the Epistle to the Romans. "I see," says the apostle, "another law in my members, warring against the law of my mind, and bringing me into captivity to the law of sin, which is in my members." *The law of sin in his members* was undoubtedly the carnal mind, the unholy affections. These *warred* against the *law of his mind*, his enlightened judgment, his feelings of moral obligation; and in this warfare the former were victorious, and carried captive the will; so that "the good that he would, he did not, and the evil that he would not, that he did." "To will was present with him," but "how to perform, he knew not." See the entire passage, for it beautifully illustrates our whole theory. Here is the conflict, the struggle between conscience and sin; here is pointed out the seat of sin, viz. the "flesh" or carnal mind, which is but another name for the unsanctified affections and appetites; here is the will struggling to turn the contest on the side of duty, but struggling in vain; every effort results in defeat—*it is taken captive, and overcome.*—Despair finally settles down upon the mind, as far as personal strength is concerned, and the anxious soul looks abroad for help, and cries out, "Who shall deliver me from the body of this death!" Then it is that deliverance comes! Jesus Christ, the Saviour of sinners, sets him free!

Professor Stuart, of Andover, himself a Calvinist, has shown most conclusively, what Arminians have long contended for, that this portion of revelation refers specifically to the work of regeneration. But whether this be granted by every Calvinist or not, no man can deny but that the grand philosophical principles heretofore contended for, are here fully illustrated—the same *division* of the mind—the same *conflict*—the same *thraldom* of the *will*, and the same *deliverance*, through *faith* in Jesus Christ our Lord.

The same principles, in part at least, are recognized in Gal. v, 17, "For the flesh lusteth against the Spirit, and the Spirit against the flesh; and these are contrary the one to the other, so that ye *cannot* do the things that ye *would.*" In short, all those passages where the difficulty of subduing the carnal mind, of keeping the body under, of crucifying the old man, all those passages that speak of a *warfare*, an *internal conflict*, and the like, recognize the principles here contended for. These principles, so frequently adverted to in the Scriptures, are proved to be in exact conformity with experience. Who that has passed through this change, but remembers this conflict, this war in the members? Who but recollects how his best resolutions were broken as often as made; and how, after various and vigorous efforts, his heart seemed to himself to grow worse and worse? He found secret treason lurking in his bosom even when he was trying to repent of his past disloyalty.

"The more he strove against its power,

He felt the guilt and sin the more."

Every additional effort sunk him apparently but the lower in "the horrible pit and miry clay," until "the Lord heard his *cry*," until "the Lord brought him up, and set his feet upon a rock, and established his goings, and put a new song in his mouth."

That the Scriptures speak of a conditional action of the mind, preparatory to the work of regeneration, appears from express passages, as well as from the general tenor of that numerous class of scriptures which enjoin duty upon the sinner, and predicate justification and salvation upon those duties. John i, 12, has already been quoted and commented upon, in which the new birth is suspended upon *receiving* Christ, or *believing* on his name. The many cases of healing the body, by Christ, are evident illustrations of the healing of the soul. In fact, we have good reasons for supposing that, in most of these cases at least, the soul and body were healed at the same time; and this was always on the condition of *asking* and *believing*. John iii, 14, 13, "As Moses lifted up the serpent in the wilderness, even so must the Son of man be lifted up; that whosoever believeth in him should not perish, but have everlasting life." Here our Saviour shows the analogy between the cure of the Israelites by looking at the brazen serpent, and of sinners by looking to Christ. But how were the Israelites healed? By the conditional act of *looking* at the brazen serpent. So looking at Christ is the condition of healing the soul. Take away this condition and the whole analogy is destroyed. Let this condition be understood, and the text will accord with others, equally expressive of conditions. "Look unto me and be ye saved, all the ends of the earth." "Seek first the kingdom of God and his righteousness." "Seek the Lord while he may be found." God hath determined that all nations "should seek the Lord, if haply they might feel after him, and find him, though he be not far from every one of us." Will any one pretend to say that this looking and seeking implies regeneration? This is mere assumption; where is the proof? who would ever infer this idea from the Scriptures themselves? What! is the sinner regenerated before the malady of his soul, the poisonous bite of sin, is healed? Has he found the Lord before he has sought him? And must he seek after he has found him? The *kingdom of God* is religion in the soul—it is "righteousness, peace, and joy in the Holy Ghost;" and when we are regenerated, we have it in possession, and have therefore no need to seek it. But we are commanded to *seek* the kingdom of God; this, therefore, must be a work preparatory to, and conditional of regeneration. "Come unto me all ye that labour and are heavy laden, and I will give you rest." "Take my yoke upon you," &c. To be *restless*, and not to have on the yoke of Christ, is to be unregenerate; but such are to *come* and *take* the yoke, and then, and on that condition, they will find rest to their souls. "The Spirit and the bride say, Come, &c, and whosoever will, let him come and take of the water of life freely." To take of the water of life is to be regenerate; but to this end we must *come*, and must first *will* in order to *come*. "Behold, I stand at the door and knock; if any man hear my voice and open the door, I will come in and sup with him, and he with me." Before Christ is *in* the soul, there is no regeneration; but before he will *come* in, he knocks, and the sinner must first *hear*, and then *open the door*, and on this condition Christ comes in and imparts his grace.

But it is useless to proceed farther in quoting particular texts. They might be extended indefinitely, with a force and pertinency that cannot be evaded: all going to establish the fact that the work of grace on the heart is conditional.

Will any one pretend to deny, that the unregenerate sinner is called upon to *seek, ask, repent, believe,* &c? And what do such scriptures mean? The acts of the mind here enjoined must *constitute* regeneration, or they must follow regeneration as an effect of that work, or they must precede it as a necessary and required condition. To say that these acts are the very definition of regeneration itself—are only synonymous terms to express this renewal of the heart, is to make regeneration consist in *exercises* merely—is in fact to make it the sinner's appropriate and exclusive work; unless it can be shown that this commanding the sinner to ask, &c, is nothing more nor less than a promise that God will ask, seek, repent, and believe for him! But this will hardly be pretended; and the idea that these acts do themselves *constitute* the new birth, has already been seen to be defective and indefensible.

To suppose that these acts follow regeneration, as an effect or fruit of the change itself, is to deny them that position and relation in which they are actually placed by the word of

God. It makes one seek, after he has found; ask, after he has received; repent and believe, after he is possessed of that salvation, to obtain which these duties are enjoined. The phraseology to suit this theory, should evidently be of an entirely different character. When the sinner asks what he shall do to be saved, the answer should be —"*Nothing* until God renews the heart; and then as a fruit of this you will of course *seek, ask, believe,*" &c. If, indeed, the sinner is to do nothing until God renews him, why is it necessary that he should first be awakened? Why is the command addressed to him at all? Why does not the Holy Spirit immediately renew the heart, while the transgressor is stupid in his wickedness, instead of calling after him to *awake, flee,* and *escape* for his life? Do you say you can give no other reason than that it pleases God to take this course with the sinner, and to call up his attention to the subject before he renews him? I answer, then it pleases God that there should be certain preparatory acts of the mind in order to regeneration: and this is in fact admitting the principle for which we contend, and this more especially if it be acknowledged, as it evidently must be, that these preparatory mental states or acts are, to any extent, voluntary. Thus, not only is the absurdity of making these acts the *result* of regeneration most apparent; but in tracing out the consistent meaning and practical bearing of those scriptures that are addressed to the unconverted, we find them establishing the third alternative, that these acts of the mind are *preparatory* to regeneration, and are the prescribed conditions on which God will accomplish the work. Thus the Scripture argument is found to confirm the philosophical view of the subject, and both are strengthened by Christian experience. The doctrine of conditional regeneration, therefore, is confirmed by a threefold argument, no part of which, it is believed, can be easily overthrown. Against it, however, there are several strong objections urged, which have already been mentioned, and which we are now prepared to hear and examine.

1. It has been objected, that to admit human agency and co-operation in this change, is to deny salvation by *grace*. But how does this appear? Suppose the very conditions are by a gracious appointment —suppose the operations of a gracious system are in this way better adapted to a moral government—suppose this conditional action of the mind to be itself the result of a gracious influence, enlightening the understanding, and quickening and arousing the moral sense—finally, suppose these conditions not to be *efficient*, much less *meritorious* causes, by which the mind either changes itself, or renders itself more morally deserving of the Divine favour—I say suppose all this, and then show if you can, how such conditions can detract at all from the grace of this salvation.

2. It has been objected, that "since man never is what he ought to be until he is renewed and made holy, therefore any act short of that which either constitutes or implies regeneration cannot be acceptable to God—God cannot consistently approve of any step that falls short of man's duty. It is his duty to be holy, and therefore any thing short of this is sin, and consequently cannot be accepted as a condition." We should be careful to discriminate between things closely related, and yet actually distinct from each other. It is one thing to be pleased with the character of the mind as a whole, in view of its relations to the Divine law and its necessary qualifications for heaven, and another thing to be pleased with a particular mental state, or conditional volition, in reference to its adaptation to a proposed end, or a specific object. For instance: the Calvinists think that an awakened and an anxiously inquiring sinner is in a more suitable state of mind to receive the blessing of regeneration, than one perfectly stupid and thoughtless. If they do not, why do they try to bring sinners to thoughtfulness? Why do they try to awaken them to a sense of their danger, and make them tremble under the view of the Divine displeasure? Or why do they call their attention to Gospel provisions and a crucified Saviour? Is not this a preparatory process? And have they the Divine warrant for such a course? Is this the method which the Divine Being takes to save his rebellious subjects?

Then, doubtless, this method is well pleasing to him: and in reference to this specific end he has in view, he is pleased with each successive step in the process. He is pleased when the shiner pays attention to the word; he is pleased when he is awakened, and when he begins to tremble and inquire, "What shall I do to be saved?" This is just as he would have it, and just as he designed; although the entire character of the sinner is not acceptable to him until he is made holy. The very principle, then, objected to by the Calvinists is recognized by their own theory and practice. Now if we say God is pleased to accept of the sinner's prayer, and faith, and sorrow for sin, as a condition of what he will do for him, what propriety is there in replying, God cannot accept of any thing short of a holy heart? We know he cannot approve of a heart until it is holy; but he can approve of certain feelings and volitions as suited, according to the Divine appointment, to be the condition on which he will make the heart holy. Do you ask on what ground he accepts of this? I answer, on the ground of the merits of Christ; the ground on which the whole process rests. God does not accept of the prayer, repentance, and faith of the *regenerate*, because they are regenerate, and by reason of their holiness; but their acceptance is wholly and continually through Christ. Through the same medium and merits the prayer of the inquiring sinner is heard and answered.

If your servant had left you unjustly, and deserted the service he was obligated to perform, and you should finally tell him, if he would return and resume his duties you would forgive the past, and accept of him for the future, would it be inconsistent to say, you were pleased when he began to listen to the proposal, and pleased when he took the first and every succeeding step, as being suitable and necessary to the end proposed, although, in view of *his* duty and *your* claim, you would not be pleased with him, as your acceptable servant, until he was actually and faithfully employed in your service?

Let it not be inferred from the above that I advocate a gradual conversion. I do not. I believe when God renews the heart he does it at once; but the preparatory steps are nevertheless indispensable to the accomplishment of this work. And God is well pleased with the first step of attention on the part of the sinner, and with every succeeding step of prayer, anxious inquiry, feeling of moral obligation, purpose to forsake sin, looking after and attempting to believe in Christ, not because these are *all* that he requires, but because they are the necessary preparatives for what is to follow.

3. The foregoing remarks will prepare the way to meet a similar objection to the last, and one to some extent the same in substance. It is this: "Are these conditional acts of the mind holy or unholy exercises? If holy, then the work of regeneration is accomplished already, and therefore these cannot be the *conditions* of that change. If unholy, then they can be no other than offensive to a holy God, and therefore cannot be conditions well pleasing to him." In addition to what has been already said, having a bearing upon this question, it may be stated that the terms holy and unholy may be equivocal, as used in this connection; and thus the supposed dilemma would be more in words than in fact, more in appearance than in reality. This dilemma is urged in the argument under the idea that there can be but the two kinds of exercises, holy and unholy. And this may be true enough, only let us understand what is meant. If by holy exercises are meant those in which the entire feeling is on the side of God, I readily answer, *No*, the mind before regeneration has no such exercises. If by holiness is meant, that the judgment and conscience are on the side of truth, I answer, *Yes*, this is the state of the mind when it is truly awakened by the Holy Spirit and by Divine truth. It is entirely immaterial to me, therefore, whether the objector call the exercise holy or unholy, provided he draw no special inferences from the use of a general term that the positions here assumed do not authorize. Sure I am that the objector cannot say there is nothing in the exercises of the unregenerate, awakened sinner, such as God would have for the end proposed, until he is prepared to say that a fear of the consequences of sin, an enlightened judgment, the

remorse of conscience for the past, the feelings of obligation for the future, and the hope of victory over sin through Christ, all combining to induce the sinner to flee for refuge, and lay hold upon the hope set before him, are all wrong, and not as God would have them? But when a man is prepared to say this, it is difficult to see how he could be reasoned with farther, for he would seem to have given up reason and Scripture. And yet who does not know that these are the exercises of the soul awakened to a sense of sin and its consequences, even while as yet his unholy affections hang upon him like a *body of death*:—Yea, who does not know that it is this body of death, from which he cannot escape, and this abhorrence of sin and its consequences, that rein him up, and incline him to a surrender of his soul into the hands of Christ, from whom, as a consequence, he receives *power* to become a son of God. "But what is the motive?" it is asked, "is not this unholy?" And pray what does this inquiry mean? If by motive is meant the moving cause *out* of the mind; *that* cannot be unholy, for it is the Holy Spirit, and the holy word of God, that are thus urging the sinner to Christ. If by motive is meant the judgments and feelings of the mind, that prompt to these voluntary efforts to avoid sin and its consequences, these are the enlightened understanding and the feelings of obligation, already alluded to, which, I repeat, the objector is welcome to call holy or unholy as he pleases; all I claim is, they are what God approves of, and are the necessary conditions of his subsequent work of renewing the heart.

But perhaps it may be asked here, Is not the sinner, in the performance of these conditions, *partly* converted? I answer, This again depends entirely upon what you mean by conversion. If by conversion you understand the whole of the preparatory work of awakening and seeking, as well as the *change* of the *heart*—then of course you would say he is *partly* converted. If you mean by conversion only a change of views and a consequent change of purpose, by which the sinner determines to seek, that he may find the pearl of great price—the blessing of a new heart and of forgiveness, then you would say he is *wholly* converted. But if you mean, by conversion, the change of heart itself, the washing of regeneration, and the renewing of the Holy Ghost, then not only is not the work done, but it is not begun. The way of the Lord is prepared and the renewal will follow.

Thus the objections that have been thought so formidable against the doctrine of conditional regeneration are found, on a closer inspection, to be more in appearance than in reality. They receive their influence, as objections, rather from their indefiniteness and the ambiguity of terms, than from any intrinsic force.

There is, however, one form more in which an objection may be urged in a general way against the ideas of the new birth here advanced. And as I wish fearlessly and candidly to state and meet, if possible, every difficulty, it will be necessary to touch upon this. It may be urged that "the only exercises that can be claimed as conditions of regeneration on Bible grounds are *repentance* and *faith;* for 'repentance toward God and faith in our Lord Jesus Christ' are laid at the foundation of all Gospel requirements. Whenever the awakened sinner came to the apostles to know what he should do to be saved, they always met him with, 'Believe on the Lord Jesus Christ, and thou shalt be saved.' Whenever the apostles went out to preach the Gospel, they preached 'every where that men should repent.'" "But," continues the objector, "if repentance and faith are the only duties or exercises which can be claimed as conditions, it is evident there are no such conditions; for repentance and faith, so far from being conditions of regeneration, are either the new birth itself, or are Christian graces, implying the new birth."

The premises, in the above objection, will not be denied. Repentance and faith are supposed to be the Gospel conditions of regeneration. But it is denied that these are necessarily regeneration itself, or that they imply regeneration in any other sense, than as antecedents to it. There are, it is acknowledged, a repentance and a faith that are Christian graces, and imply the new birth. This is the faith that "is the substance of things hoped for." It is that principle of spiritual life which the Christian has in his soul when he can say, "The life that I now live I live by faith in the Son of God." This is that repentance, also, which keeps the soul continually at the foot of the cross, and leads it constantly to feel,

"Every moment, Lord, I need

The merit of thy death."

But because repentance and faith are the necessary characteristics of the Christian, and because they are the more perfect as the Christian character ripens, it does not therefore follow that there are no repentance and faith conditional to the new birth. The very fact that repentance and faith were urged by Christ and his apostles, as the initiatory step to salvation, proves the opposite of this. They do not say, Repent and believe the Gospel, and this is salvation, but, "Repent and believe, and ye shall (on this condition) be saved." And surely it is unnecessary to prove here that salvation in the New Testament generally means a meetness for heaven or holiness. Our blessed Saviour was called Jesus, because he *saved* his people *from their sins*.

Beside, it may well be argued, that faith and repentance are acts of the mind, and cannot therefore be considered as the new birth itself, unless the mind converts itself, especially since they are *enjoined duties*, and must therefore be *voluntary* acts. It is no where said that God repents and believes for us; but it is expressly and repeatedly taught, that God *renews* us.—Repentance and faith, then, are our work, but regeneration is his. I know it is said in one place, Acts v, 31, that Christ was exalted "to *give repentance* to Israel." But the *act* itself of repentance cannot be said to be *given*. This would be an absurdity. How can any one give me a mental *act?* Hence Dr. Doddridge, although a Calvinist, very candidly and very justly remarks, on this passage, that "to *give repentance* signifies to *give place*, or *room* for repentance," to sustain which interpretation he quotes Josephus and others who use the phrase in this sense. If then repentance and faith are enjoined upon us, as *our duties*, and if they are every where spoken of as prerequisites in the work of salvation, and as preparatory steps and conditions to the process of holiness, how can it be otherwise than that these are antecedent, in the order of nature, to regeneration?

It may farther be argued, in support of this view of faith and repentance, that no sin can be forgiven until repented of—repentance therefore must precede remission of sins. This I suppose Calvinists allow, but they say that, in the order of nature, the heart is renewed before sin is forgiven—and that repentance, therefore, which is either the new birth itself, or the immediate fruit of it, is a condition of justification, but not of regeneration. If this be correct, then the soul is made holy before it is forgiven. But St. Paul informs us, Romans iv, 5, that God through faith "justifieth the *ungodly*." If then there be any antecedence in the order of the two parts of the work of grace, we must suppose that justification has the precedence, and that regeneration follows, and hence repentance and faith precede regeneration. Indeed I cannot see why repentance is not as necessary to remove the sin of the heart as to forgive the sin of the life. If God will not forgive sin without repentance, will he renew the heart without it? Has he any where promised this? If not, but if, on the contrary, he every where seems to have suspended the working out of our salvation *in us*, upon our repentance, then may we safely conclude—nay, then we must necessarily believe that we repent in order to be renewed. The same may be said of faith. Faith in fact seems to be the exclusive channel through which every gracious effect is produced upon the mind. The sinner cannot be awakened without faith, for it precedes every judgment in favour of truth, and every motion of moral feeling, and of course every favourable concurrence of the will. The sinner never could throw himself upon the Divine mercy, never would embrace Christ as his Saviour, until he believed. Hence the

Scriptures lay such great stress upon faith, and make it the grand, and indeed the only *immediate* condition of the work of grace upon the heart. Repentance is a condition only remotely, *in order* to justifying faith; agreeable to the teaching of Christ, "And ye, when ye had heard, afterward *repented* not that ye *might believe* on him." But faith is necessary *immediately*, as that mental state directly antecedent to the giving up of the soul into the hands of Divine mercy. And shall we still be told that faith is not the condition of regeneration? The order of the work seems to be—1. A degree of faith in order to repentance. 2. Repentance, in order to such an increase of faith as will lead the soul to throw itself upon Christ.—3. The giving up of the soul to Christ as the only ground of hope. 4. The change of heart by the efficient operation of the Holy Spirit.—Now on whichever of these four stages of the process, except the first, the objector lays his finger and says, *That* is not a condition of regeneration, for it is regeneration itself, it will be seen that *that* very part is conditional. If, for instance, he fix on the second stage, and contend that that is regeneration, which I call repentance *in order* to regenerating faith; even *that* would be *conditional* regeneration, for it is preceded by faith—and so of all that follow. And surely no one will pretend that what I call the first stage, the faith which precedes awakening and remorse of conscience, and the exciting alternations of fear and hope in the anxious and inquiring sinner, is regeneration. And if this first degree of faith is not the change, then it is utterly inconsistent to talk of unconditional regeneration, for this faith stands at the head of all that follows—it is a mental act necessarily preparatory to the whole work. And as we shall presently see, it is an act that depends upon the agency of the will. Hence we are brought again to our conclusion, that the change called the new birth is effected by the Holy Spirit, on the ground of certain conditional acts of him who is the subject of the change.

"But the very *nature* of repentance and of faith, the very *definition* of the two mental states expressed by these terms," it is said, "proves that a person, to possess them, must be regenerate; or at any rate, that these states cannot be conditions of regeneration, to be performed by the sinner." Let us attend for a moment to this objection in detail.

What is repentance? "It is," say some Calvinistic writers, "a *change of mind*. The original means this, and so it should have been rendered; and if it had been so rendered, it would have set this controversy at rest." But what if we should grant (what I do not believe) that the original word means this, and this only, still it would not follow that the change of mind called the new birth is meant by this term. A change of judgment is a change of mind—a change of purpose is a change of mind—any change of the general current of feeling, such as that from carelessness and stupidity in to a state of anxiety and earnest inquiry, what shall I do to be saved? is a change of mind.—And such a change of mind indispensably precedes regeneration. No person ever, from being a careless, hardened sinner, becomes an anxious and earnest inquirer after salvation, without an important change in his judgment, moral feeling, and volitions. Hence this definition does not at all help the objector, unless he can prove that the Scriptures always mean by this term that change which they elsewhere call the new birth. Indeed, since we have already shown that repentance is our work, and the renewing of the heart exclusively God's work, it follows incontrovertibly, that the change of mind called repentance is not the new birth.

If repentance meant that change of mind called the new birth, then the regenerate would be *often born again*, and that, too, without backsliding; for those who are growing the fastest in grace repent the most constantly and the most deeply.

Again: it is objected, that "faith is not a voluntary state of mind, and therefore cannot be considered a condition, performed by the sinner, in order to regeneration." To believe is doubtless, in many instances, perfectly involuntary. There are numerous cases in which a man is obliged to believe, both against his will and against his desires. There are other cases, again, in which the will is not only much concerned in believing, but in which its action is indispensable in order to believe. And the faith of the Gospel is pre-eminently an instance of this kind. "Faith," saith the word, "cometh by hearing." But hearing implies attention; and every deliberate act of attention implies an act of the will. A man can no more leap, by one transition, from a state of entire carelessness into the faith that justifies the soul, than he can make a world. But he can take the steps that lead to this result. To believe to the saving of the soul requires *consideration, self examination*, a *knowledge* of the object of faith, or the truth to be believed, *earnest looking*, and *prayerful seeking*. But is there no act of the will in all these? It is said that "the Spirit takes of the things of Jesus Christ, and shows them unto us." And it is doubtless true, that the soul cannot get such a view of Christ as encourages him to throw himself unreservedly upon the mercy of the Saviour, until the Spirit makes, to the mind's eye, this special exhibition of the "things of Christ." But when does he do this? Does he come to the sinner when he is careless and inattentive, and show him the *things of Christ?* No! it is only to the inquiring and self-despairing sinner, who is earnestly groaning out the sentiment in the bitterness of his heart, "Who shall deliver me from the body of this death?" And is there no voluntary action in all this?

But it will perhaps be wearisome to the reader to pursue these objections farther. I should not have gone so fully into this part of the subject, but for the fact, that this sentiment of unconditional regeneration is considered the strong hold of Calvinism. This point moreover appears to have been but slightly handled by most of the anti-Calvinistic writers; and therefore I have felt it the more necessary to attempt an answer to all the most important arguments that are adduced in opposition to our view of this doctrine. I am far from thinking I have done the subject justice, and may have cause perhaps hereafter to acknowledge that some of my minor positions are untenable, and that some of my expressions need modifying or explaining, although I have used what care and circumspection my time and circumstances would permit in reference not only to the doctrine itself, but also in reference to the forms of expression. And as it respects the leading doctrines here inculcated, I repose upon them with entire confidence. However the theory clashes with that of many great and good men, it is believed to be the only theory that will consistently explain the practice and preaching of these very men. It is, in my view, the only theory that will satisfactorily and consistently explain those great and leading principles by which evangelical Christians expect to convert the world to Christ. And, if this be true, the sooner the Christian Church is established on this foundation, the better. We have already seen that a mixture of error in the essential doctrines leads to various mutations from extreme to extreme of dangerous heresy. How long before the Church shall be *rooted and grounded in the truth!* May He who said, Let light be; and light was, hasten that glorious day!

THE END.

Footnotes

[1] Many objections have been made, by the reviewers, to my manner of stating the doctrine of predestination. It is objected, that the great body of Calvinists believe, no more than the Arminians, that God "efficiently controls and actuates the human will." On a careful, and I hope, candid revision of the subject, however, I cannot satisfy myself that the objection is valid. I am quite sure God must control the will, or he cannot, as Calvinists teach, secure the proposed end, by the prescribed means. It is readily granted that Calvinists deny *such a control* as destroys the freedom of the will. But it is the object of the sermon and of the following controversy to show that Calvinistic predestination is, on any ground of consistency, utterly irreconcilable with mental freedom. How far this has been done, of course, each will judge for himself.

[2] It seems, to the author of the sermon, but little better than trifling, to object, as some have, to this argument on foreknowledge, that "God must predetermine his works before

Lightning Source UK Ltd.
Milton Keynes UK
UKOW06f1921121015

260391UK00009B/155/P